Medal for Malaya

David Tipton
Medal for Malaya

Shoestring Press

All rights reserved. No part of this work covered by the copyright hereon may be reproduced or used in any form by any means – graphic, electronic, or mechanical, including copying, recording, taping, or information storage and retrieval systems – without written permission of the publisher.

Typeset and printed by Q3 Print Project Management Ltd,
Loughborough, Leicestershire.
(01509 213456)

Published by Shoestring Press
19 Devonshire Avenue, Beeston, Nottingham, NG9 1BS
(0115) 925 1827
www.shoestringpress.co.uk

First published 2002
© Copyright: David Tipton
ISBN: 1 899549 75 7

east midlands
arts
making creative
opportunities

Shoestring Press gratefully acknowledges financial assistance from East Midlands Arts

Acknowledgements

Earlier versions of some parts, or chapters, of this novel were first published in *Argo*, *Sheaf* and *Global Tapestry*. Two articles, "You Always Remember the First Time" (*Quartet Anthology*, 1974) and "From Catterick to Kuala Lipis" (*London Magazine*, Vol. 25. No. 12) formed the basis for other sections of the novel.

To Alan G. Hill

Chapter 1

Three months after he'd left grammar school Steve Revill was summoned for a medical. He went into the city and spent most of the day at an Army Recruitment Centre. While he was there he was asked if he had a preference for any particular regiment.

"If you want to travel," his barber had told him a few days before, "join the Royal Signals. They're attached to the infantry and go everywhere." The comment flashed into his head when he was asked the question.

"Royal Signals," he said with the confidence of a young man who believed he'd had a privileged education.

Another couple of months passed before his papers arrived. He was to report to the Royal Signals 7th Training Regiment at Catterick Camp. A railway ticket and travel instructions were provided. So it was that on a cold January morning a few days after Christmas and New Year his mother saw him off at Castle Bromwich station.

Leaning from the window, waving, the train pulling slowly out of the station, he felt suddenly apprehensive. From his seat he could see to his right the Saxon tumulus above the village and the square red-towered church while to his left was the bluish-grey rectangle of Fort Dunlop. This view, these places, had been familiar landmarks for eighteen years. He'd taken them for granted. And as the train gathered speed, he felt a sudden nostalgia for the place, the home, he was leaving.

His mind racing, memories assailed him. He thought of the walks he'd taken round the old village; confident hours in the sixth-form library reading history and poetry; long afternoons at the school grounds playing rugby and cricket; faces of girls he'd been out with

David Tipton

and his room in his parents' semi-detached house on the Coleshill Road. With unexpected nostalgia he recalled the last four months when he'd been working as a labourer – waiting for tarmac to arrive, then hard muscle-building work shovelling, barrowing and raking until it was laid. A temporary job, but safely in the environs of the city, Birmingham, where up until now he'd spent his life.

But the moment of panic passed and he began to feel a certain excitement – of the unknown – as the train pushed further north. He was fit from the labouring, he told himself; had been something of an athlete at school and had good A-Level passes therefore had nothing to fear from the Army.

At Derby where he had to change more young men boarded the northbound train. They too were travelling to Catterick. It stopped at Sheffield which from the train looked almost surreal: a city of furnaces, chimneys, slag heaps, of mining and steel. This was the furthest north Steve had ever been. And it felt like a foreign country.

The train trundled remorselessly on. At Darlington he had to change again for the last lap of the journey to Catterick. Milling about the platform were hundreds of young men looking worried, glum. The station was swirling with steam from various trains that appeared to have terminated there. Some military police, tall aggressive-looking characters, herded them into a special troop-train. It was late in the afternoon, almost dark, when they arrived and were taken in a stream of lorries to 7TR as it was known.

Catterick seemed a dismal place, reddish-brick buildings in the centre and miles of barracks in every direction. 7TR lines looked old and bleak. Each hut was of wood and concrete with an open stove at the far end. After being checked in – a slow and laborious process, they had a meal in the canteen and were told to go to bed early. Steve couldn't sleep. Several of the young lads in his barrack-room appeared to be weeping. Muffled sobs broke the silence. Others couldn't sleep either. He could see the red glow of their cigarettes in the darkness.

At five-thirty in the morning the lights went on suddenly and several NCOs, looking incredibly smart and efficient, were barking at them to get dressed. Outside they marched in mufti across to the canteen for breakfast. It was bitterly cold and still dark, the sky studded with

Medal for Malaya

stars. Steve couldn't eat the greasy food dumped on his plate. He drank a mug of sweet odd-tasting tea and smoked a cigarette. Outside they washed their plates and cutlery in huge vats of boiling water, skeins and globules of fat gleaming on its surface. Ablutions occupied the next half-hour.

At seven-thirty, still in their civvies, they were lined up on parade. In the twelve hours Steve had been in camp he'd spoken to no one. Most of the morning was spent getting kitted out with their battle-dress, trousers, shirts, a jumper, great coat, woollen vests and underpants, grey socks, cap-badge, garters, beret, belt and boots. Just under medium height, Steve was lucky; his uniform fitted relatively well. Some tall thin blokes looked decidedly gangly and awkward in ill-fitting khaki.

Afterwards they were documented for their Part I paybooks.

"Religion?" the corporal asked him.

"I haven't got one," Steve said.

"I've got to enter one in your paybook. I can't leave it blank."

"Put me down as an atheist."

"That's not a religion. You've got to be C of E or RC or something."

"What about existentialist?"

"What?"

"Existentialist."

"Never heard of it. Sorry."

"Put me down as a Buddhist then."

"That's like the Baptists, isn't it?" And he wrote the word *Budist* in Steve's paybook. Steve felt it was a minor triumph.

After documentation they were shorn of their hair at the camp barber's. Steve, who made a comment about the gross nature of the haircuts, received a particularly severe one. Back in the barrack-room, looking bullet-headed, they were shown how to make up their bed-packs and lay out their surplus kit in the lockers. And that evening, in laconic terms, the NCOs explained about blanco-ing belts and gaiters and bulling boots. Such tasks were to occupy their evenings for the following month. Steve was astonished to discover that they were expected to heat spoons and burn away the little dimples on the

3

leather of their boots until they were smooth, then polish them up with black lead and spittle until they shone like the black ball on a snooker table.

The next day their training began. Up at five-thirty, they were kept constantly on the go: ablutions, across to the canteen in moonlight or mist, back to the barracks to clean them – including brasso-ing the verdigris-stained outlets of the urinals; then parades, drill, PE, weapon-training, manoeuvres, route marches until evening; after supper, cleaning equipment until lights out at ten.

Every other evening there were fatigues; every four days guard-duty, patrolling the perimeter with truncheons. The only respite was during the brief NAAFI breaks for cups of hot Bovril and pasties. Their only solace was the Woodbines and Weights that encouraged by the NCOs they were all beginning to smoke.

The routine might have been more bearable had it not been for the NCOs. Everything the soldiers did was accompanied by their sarcasms and invective. The language they employed was a species of assault Steve had never experienced before. It was not just a stream of four-letter words but a language of hatred and contempt – for women and for sex, he felt. They were taught by NCOs to repress any gesture that might be interpreted as "feminine" – holding a cigarette in a girlish manner; standing with a hand on the hip or a hip thrust forward. Consciously, the soldiers tried to look more military in posture, more masculine, ready for combat. Like the others Steve cultivated a more brutal language too. Inevitably they were all undergoing a metamorphosis to suit the system. In the four weeks at 7TR such pre-conceived notions as belief in justice and democracy took a battering. Freedom, he realised, was relative and in the Army it seemed to be practically non-existent.

During the last week of basic training they were invited to select a trade. Steve put down cipher-operator as his first choice and despatch-rider as second. A few weeks later he was told that once he had completed his training he'd be posted to 2TR as a clerk.

Like many of them at 7TR he never expected to get through the month at all, but by the time their passing-out parade arrived, he felt like a soldier. He was smartly turned-out and, in the end, good at drill although, like the others, he'd been accused of marching *like a pregnant duck* or *a girl who'd been fucked rigid*; for doing manoeuvres as if *enjoying a wet dream* and using his 303 Enfield rifle on the range *like a virgin holding a hot prick.*

In fact he attained his crossed-rifles, second-class, came top in map-reading and along with the rest in his platoon actually felt pride and exhilaration at the passing-out parade when they were complimented by the CO on their turn-out and drill. It was as if they had been through a species of initiation. Afterwards they were granted forty-eight hour leave-passes and felt tremendous gratitude at being released into the world again. Coming home by train, Steve absorbed the scenery like someone suffering from sensory deprivation, but simultaneously felt a pride in the smartness of his uniform.

Back in Catterick, he reported to 2TR. The routine there was somewhat more relaxed. They studied Queen's Regulations, office procedure, army acronyms and spent hours typing to music. Clerical work had replaced infantry training. The NCOs were less brutal and soldiers were free to go into the town-centre at night. Steve made friends with a draughtsman from Bromsgrove, Jim Melville, who regarded the Army as a joke and took nothing seriously. On paydays they could afford a pint or two in the NAAFI, but much of their time was spent listening to pop-music in the barrack-room and writing letters. In three months he would have finished the course and be able to get a posting overseas; his one worry was that he might fail the typing test.

One morning he had a report for Quarter Guard duty. This was considered important. Steve had to get bulled-up and with four others was inspected by the duty officer at 8 AM. The evening before he'd pressed his uniform and great-coat, blancoed his webbing and buffed up his boots until they gleamed. To his surprise he was chosen as the best turned-out and made stick-man. This meant he'd be employed running messages while the others took turns to march between sentry boxes outside the guard-room.

Off-duty, in the late afternoon, they watched the MPs bring in a prisoner. A deserter, they were told, who was shouting and struggling.

Once inside the cells, the MPs apparently worked him over. The guard could hear muffled blows and grunts. Appalled, they listened as the beating continued, spasmodically, for what seemed ages. Later they were able to chat to the prisoner whose face looked red and swollen. He'd been doing his National Service for seven years already and still had twelve months to serve as time spent in detention didn't count. On this occasion he'd been absent-without-leave for several months. He was likely to get three months in Colchester and would still have a year to serve upon his release.

"Why do you keep going AWOL," Steve asked. "If you hadn't, you'd have finished five years ago."

"I hate the Army."

"But if you do go absent, why don't you get the hell out of the country?"

"I miss my family and me mates at home."

"But it's stupid, getting caught and sent to Colchester."

"It's hell there," he said. "They can put you on bread-and-water for three days at a stretch. Sometimes blokes die there in mysterious circumstances."

"You've got to just stick it out. Twelve months and you'll be a free man."

Steve felt a surge of impotent anger at the sheer injustice of the system. He was determined to get out of Catterick as soon as he could. *Fly the ocean in a silver plane, see the jungle when it's wet with rain. See the pyramids along the Nile and watch the sunrise on a tropic isle.* So went the song. So thought Steve.

A few nights later Jim and Steve went to the NAAFI in the centre of Catterick and got talking to a dark-haired little Geordie in the WRACS. At closing time Steve escorted her back to her lines. The road was dark and bordered with pine trees. He'd had enough beer to make him reckless. At some point he kissed her and she responded. The contact was like an oasis in the aridity of Catterick. There was a moon shining between the trees. Steve's hands moved over the girl's body in its smooth khaki serge. She felt warm and soft. At once he was half-in love with her. He loved her short black hair, brown eyes and tip-tilted nose. They lay down on the grass verge in the shadow of the pines, kissing, his hand up her skirt. Suddenly a torch beam shone in their faces. The scrambled to their feet, automatically adjusting their dress. A couple of regimental police-women approached.

"You're out-of-bounds," one of them shouted at Steve. "The WRAC lines are off-limits to men."

"I didn't know."

"Well, we could arrest you."

"I'm sorry," he said. "I was just escorting my friend home."

"Sergeant to you."

"Sorry Sergeant."

"Just get going – and think yourself lucky. Right?" She turned to the girl. "We're escorting you back, it's gone ten."

"She's done nothing," Steve said.

"Get moving, soldier."

"I'll be all right, Steve," the girl said. "Don't worry, I'll see you in town."

She went up the hill with the police-women. Steve got back to 2TR without further mishap. In the barrack-room Jim was still awake."

"Did you screw her?"

"No," Steve said and then explained what had happened. "But I did get to touch her."

"Where?"

"Well, you know."

"Oh God! Let me have a sniff of your fingers ... God!" he moaned. "That's beautiful."

Steve didn't wash his hands until the following morning. It was some small solace. But, as for Geordie, he never saw her again, nor found out what had happened.

Some days later Steve was on perimeter guard. He had a nasty sore throat and the glands in his neck were swollen. He should have reported sick, but didn't because he had a thirty-six hour leave pass once he'd completed the duty. He managed to get through it but in his feverish state it became a surreal experience for the weather was cold with a biting wind from the east. At midday on the Saturday, he caught the train south. When he arrived home he had a high temperature and couldn't eat. He went straight to bed and fell into a delirious sleep. On Sunday night he was in no condition to return to Catterick. The doctor diagnosed acute tonsillitis and gave him a medical certificate to post to his unit. On the Monday he forwarded it to 2TR, but must already have been posted AWOL for the MPs called on the Wednesday. They were a bit overawed by his parents' semi-detached, middle-class house. Steve was able to convince them that he was actually sick-on-leave and, a little disappointed, they left.

After two weeks he returned to his regiment. The moment he reached the barrack-room he was told that his in-take was about to pass out and had already been given their postings. As he had missed two weeks' training, Steve had been put back an in-take, but he was shocked to discover that he'd also been put down for a home posting – the choice of the majority. At once he hurried across to the CSM's office to query it.

"Glad to see you back, Signalman," the CSM said. "As you know we've put you back a couple of weeks."

"Yes Sir, but I see I'm down for a home-posting."

"Don't you want it?"

"No Sir."

"Where would you like to be posted then?"

"I want to volunteer for Korea, Sir," Steve said. The Korean war was in its closing stages. Moreover conscripts were not usually sent there unless they volunteered. The CSM had been in Korea; he had the two medal ribbons to prove it.

"Are you crazy?" he said laughing. "It's rough out there, I can tell you."

"I want to go, Sir."

"But why Korea?"

"Well, to be honest, to get as far away from Catterick Camp as I can." The CSM laughed again. Steve didn't tell him that he had this Hemingway-inspired desire to experience combat, believing it would prove useful to an aspiring writer.

"All right lad," the CSM said. "I'll put you down for a FARELF posting. I'll even try and get you to Korea, if that's what you want. We

Medal for Malaya

had hoped you'd stay at Catterick to play rugby for 2TR. I've heard you're a useful fly-half."

"I'd prefer to go to the Far East, Sir."

Over the next two weeks Steve passed all the clerical tests, even the typing. Apprehensively he waited for his posting. When it came he was down for the Far East Land Forces; the CSM had been as good as his word. Before having to report to the Royal Signals Transit Camp in Newton Abbot, he was granted three weeks embarkation leave.

It was May, the weather beautiful and he spent three relaxing weeks at home. Unlike when he'd been sick-on-leave, there was no Catterick to return to, but the south-west and then a troopship to the Far East.

When finally he left by train from Birmingham he knew that he wouldn't be back again for eighteen months, but that didn't worry him. It was a long enough journey, but by late afternoon the train was trundling along the coast, the Channel bluish-grey in the sunlight, sandstone cliffs bright red against the vegetation. Once in camp he reported to the guard-room, then went to the canteen for some supper. There he met Jim Melville again and Jock Robinson, a short ginger-headed man from Glasgow who had also been with them at 2TR.

Their only duties at the Transit Camp were to clean their own barrack-rooms and occasionally do fatigues in the cookhouse. They were given an array of jabs to protect them from tropical diseases and Steve was issued with a jungle-green, light-weight uniform, skyblue light-weight pajamas and green puttees. The rest of the time they were free to come and go as they wished, spending whole days exploring the Devon coast from Teignmouth to Brixham although most evenings they spent in Torquay.

One night he was having a pint with Jim in a pub near the pier when a couple of middle-aged civilians offered to buy them drinks. They turned out to be the *stars* in the show at the theatre on the pier. They were surprised the two soldiers hadn't heard of them.

"Where are you being posted to?" they asked.

"The Far East," Steve said. "Possibly Korea."

They bought more drinks and offered them complimentary tickets for the show the following night. Jim, more suspicious than Steve,

9

cried off. On his own Steve waited for them in the pub where they'd met, but only Arthur, a fat balding comedian turned up. In his reassuring BBC accent he told Steve the pier-show had been cancelled that evening, but offered to show him around the theatre. He was witty and urbane so that the hint of suspicion Steve felt was allayed. Not even when he was taken to Arthur's dressing-room and shown his stage costumes did alarm bells ring. A drag artist, Arthur's wardrobe was full of female garments and wigs.

"Here try this on," Arthur said, handing Steve one of the wigs.

"No thanks," Steve said.

"Go on, just to please me." Not wishing to seem churlish, Steve complied. "My God, you look beautiful!" Arthur exclaimed. "Come and look at yourself in the mirror." The image of himself in the wig was disturbing. He did indeed look feminine and pretty. "I wish I could dress you up as a woman and take you out on the town tonight. You'd be a knock-out."

Brusquely, Steve removed the wig. He didn't like what he'd seen, nor did he wish to think of himself as girlish. He didn't like to think of himself as remotely feminine in any way. He began to feel distinctly uneasy.

They did a tour, not of the pubs, but of some of the hotels in the Torbay area. Arthur plied him with gin-and-tonics, sandwiches and cigarettes. He chatted about his theatrical career. And boasted about the famous people that he knew. Steve told him that he hoped to be a writer.

"I could help you a lot there," Arthur said. "I know loads of playwrights and literary agents."

They ended up in a hotel near the pier. There was only half-an-hour before Steve's bus to Newton Abbot. When he went downstairs to the gents, Arthur followed him. As Steve was fastening his flies, Arthur put an arm round his waist and kissed him on the cheek. Suddenly everything became crystal clear to Steve. He had imagined that Arthur had been enjoying his company and showing him a good time because he was being posted abroad. Instead he'd been attempting to seduce him. What a naive idiot he'd been!

"Get off me," he said, sounding vaguely prudish even to himself.

Medal for Malaya

"Come on lad," Arthur said. "I just want a kiss. What's the harm in that?"

"I'm not like that."

"I know you're not, but I am."

"You're a queer?"

"Homosexual, yes, of course. Surely you knew that. You're not that dumb, are you? Why do you think I took you out tonight? What do you think I spent all that money on you for? Because I found you amusing and your wit stimulating! Don't make me laugh."

"Well, you can just fuck off!"

"Don't be like that, kid. Come back to my room. You'll like it, I know. You'll be surprised how much you'll like it."

"I'm catching that last bus."

"Damn your parochial little bus and your provincial attitudes. Come back with me."

"No fucking thank-you."

"Well, at least you can do something about this," he said and to Steve's astonishment fished out his semi-erect prick. "Please," he said. "Just hold it a minute. Give it a little suck."

Apprehensive in case anyone came down the steps into the urinal, acutely embarrassed, Steve shoved Arthur away, watched him stagger back, then fled. He bolted up the stairs, out of the hotel's swing-doors and across to the bus-square where plenty of people were milling about. He saw Arthur emerge from the hotel and look around, searching for him. Steve ducked into the queue for the Newton Abbot bus. A few minutes later he was sitting upstairs in a double-decker, heading out of Torquay.

After three weeks at the Transit Camp, at the end of June, Steve embarked on the SS Dilwara, white and gleaming against a blue sky. Once aboard the troops were jampacked below decks in the stern of the ship with narrow gangways between rows of three-tiered hammocks that folded back when not in use. Most of the ship was off-limits to Other Ranks. They had access to the open deck at the stern, the canteen, a saloon bar that got so crowded they had to queue for their beer, the library and the medical room.

David Tipton

Once the Dilwara entered the Bay of Biscay sea-sick soldiers increased the discomfort on E-deck. Fortunately Steve was never sea-sick. The moment he began to feel the slightest bit queasy he went onto the open deck. And he ate well for the food was good. There were daily fatigues – cleaning the ablutions and sleeping-area, swabbing the decks or working in the canteen, but there were so many soldiers aboard that it was possible to dodge such jobs for days on end.

Algiers was their first port-of-call. Once ashore Steve, Jim and Jock Robinson headed for the kasbah. The teeming crowds, the parrot-bright clothes, the exotic market and the narrow streets up the hill, the vibrancy and colour, were not just a revelation but a culture-shock to the troops, including Steve, who had never been abroad before. A few hours later, steaming across the blue Mediterranean, Steve could scarcely believe the reality of what he'd witnessed.

The Mediterranean was smooth as a mill pond, but certainly not wine-coloured as he'd been led to expect. He sunbathed on deck and read a clutch of novels he'd obtained from the library. His letters home were full of vivid descriptions of Algiers.

It was early one morning when the Dilwara approached Port Said, its minarets and mosques rising almost like a mirage from the bluish haze over the sea. Once they had docked, Egyptians in tarbush and fez, rowed up in their bumboats, selling their wares. For political reasons the troops weren't allowed ashore. Only those soldiers, including Jim Melville, being posted to the Canal Zone disembarked.

For a couple of days after leaving the port the Dilwara steamed in a leisurely way down the Suez Canal. It passed oases and date palms, women carrying pitchers on their heads, dhows with lateen sails in the lakes, the white town of Port Suez at the entrance to the Red Sea where the coastline was like a grotto of strange pinks and mauves at sunset. By now the heat was intense and the troops were allowed to sleep on the open deck.

One afternoon Steve was leaning against the rail watching the coastline – an unbroken stretch of sunbaked rock the colour of cakes fresh from the oven, the sunset gradually turning the mountains pink, when suddenly the Red Sea – really red in the late sun – was alive as

Medal for Malaya

a huge school of dolphins approached their ship. Their greyish-blue bodies, streamlined and beautiful, churned the water as they played round the hull, leaping and splashing in vivacious abandon. Soldiers ran across to the rail to watch. They shouted in a familiar way at the dolphins, enjoying the performance, and when the last dorsal fin had cut away, were thoughtful and meditative. On deck there was a faint smell of food from the galley, sweat and a trace of vomit. Cigarettes disintegrated into orange shreds along the scuppers and the Dilwara chugged on through the warm night.

A few days later they steamed into Aden. The buildings near the harbour were British in style. A Union Jack was flying above the military HQ. Once ashore the soldiers found the place intensely hot and dusty. A few tall Yemeni Arabs were selling silks and trinkets at the harbour gates. Steve avoided them and walked into the town itself. Invisible from the bay, its buildings were whitish-grey nestling in a depression of ash-grey volcanic rock. The landscape seemed lunar-like; the town blending into it. Beggars followed the soldiers around. Hawkers tried to sell them blankets, sandals, leather goods. There were donkeys and camels in the streets. Although the sky was overcast the heat was enervating. Their tunics were soon black with sweat while the thin Arabs looked cool in their long white robes. The women were heavily veiled, shapeless bundles of black yashmaks covering all but brown soulful eyes.

Returning to the Dilwara, the sky vermilion yet hazy, the soldiers discovered dozens of lobster-pink insects, dead or dying, scattered about the decks. Locusts, they were told. More hit the rigging as the ship moved out of harbour towards the glassy blue Indian Ocean.

It took a week to cross over to Ceylon. Sleeping on deck, the night dark velvety-blue studded with stars, Steve smoked and watched the occasional shooting-star illuminate the sky. During the day he'd sit in the stern watching the flying fish, dolphins, or the odd shark glide away from the hull.

They docked for an afternoon in Colombo, but Steve was detailed for fatigues and unable to get ashore. He stood at the rail looking out to the city beyond the docks, a mass of redbrick buildings that once again looked British in style. Close to the jetty was a line of palms,

13

their green fronds hanging down limply. Rusty-coloured gannets were scavenging round the harbour. Dark-skinned Tamils came alongside in boats selling pineapples, bananas and ornaments carved out of ivory. Wafting tantalisingly on the light breeze was the smell of hardwoods, perfume and spices.

Five days later the Dilwara was cruising off the coast of Sumatra into the Malacca Straits. A couple of days out of Singapore, all the troops who were disembarking there were ordered to assemble on deck, Steve's name among them. They were briefed by an RAEC officer who told them something about the Island's history and its political situation. Communist terrorists were still active in Malaya, but not in Singapore itself although there was an underground subversive organisation present in the city which made it dangerous at night, especially in the out-of-bounds areas which were clearly designated and should be avoided. Individually they were informed of their postings. Steve was going to 3 Base Ordnance Depot at the Alexandra barracks.

The following morning the troopship was hugging the Malayan coastline, palm-fringed and vivid green with strips of white sand contrasting sharply with the turquoise sea. All day it cut through calm water towards the tip of Malaya. As it neared the land its fragrant smell assailed them. By mid-afternoon the Dilwara entered Singapore waters, threading its way between small emerald islands with pagoda-type buildings red against the greenery. Sampans and junks were plying the narrow channels.

They disembarked a couple of hours later and were shepherded into trucks. The late afternoon was humid, oppressive like an electric-blanket over the city. They were driven through the centre and from the back of the truck had a series of cinematic glimpses of houses with wooden shutters, tip-tilted roof cornices, Chinese pictographs on gaudy adverts, washing festooned across streets on bamboo poles, symbolic dragons or tigers above shop fronts. The streets were full of Chinese dressed in blue or black pajama-type costumes, wearing shallow conical hats. On the warm gusts of air that filtered into the truck came the odour of burning charcoal and joss-sticks.

Medal for Malaya

Tanglin barracks, the Royal Signals HQ, was a transit camp for their detachment. It was set in gardens of tropical greenery and vivid blossom. That night after a meal in the canteen they stayed in the barrack-hut. At lights out, in their sky-blue pajamas, they lay on the narrow bunks with mosquito-nets spread around them. From outside came the sound of cicadas and bull-frogs in the monsoon ditches and fireflies flitted about in phosphorescent zig-zags.

"God, this is a fantastic place," Steve said to the soldier smoking in the next bed.

"Are you crazy! I just wish I was back home in good old Blighty."

"But this is an adventure," Steve continued. "Go east, young man, some writer advised. Well, we've done just that."

"And we're stuck here for eighteen fucking months."

The following morning they were transported to their units. 3BOD off the Alexandra Road to the west of the city, was near the military hospital. A longish drive led to the guard-room. Beyond it, to the left, was the parade square and several large rectangular corrugated-iron roofed buildings where stores were kept. On the right were the NAAFI and four three-storey white buildings, the barracks. The Royal Signals block was in the centre. Along with two surviving acquaintances from Catterick, Lance-Corporal John Norris and Bill Sissons, Steve was allocated a bed and locker on the first floor.

Archways led onto a verandah that encircled the block. Below them were the kitchens and canteen. Behind these was a steep jungle-covered slope that led up to Mount Faber, the highest point on the Island. Steve was put in an office with a tall gangly regular soldier, Lance-Corporal Rick Walker. The office was mainly staffed by civilians and Steve's section was presided over by a middle-aged matronly Eurasian woman, Sally Managua. Though he seemed intelligent, Rick Walker gave the impression of being thoroughly bored. He was twenty-three and had been in the Army for six years.

The work was routine. They dealt with stock – filing cards, checking stores, receiving and handling orders. Sitting in the office, sticky despite the fans whirring overhead, getting clammier as the day passed, they worked in desultory fashion. Rick cracked laconic jokes, joshed Steve for his initial inefficiency and teased Sally for her loyalty

15

to the British and enthusiasm for the Royal Family. Outside the sun beat down on the bare backs of the drivers and infantry while in the office trivial conversation alleviated the boredom.

Singapore never ceased to fascinate Steve. It fuelled his imagination as no place had done before. When he went into the city with Norris and Sissons on paynights, however, they usually drank at the Britannia Club or the Union Jack Club or went to the cinema in the black Cathay building.

Steve did, though, explore parts of the city alone. On Sundays he took the bus and then walked for miles round the Chinese areas. And on Wednesday afternoons he climbed up the steep jungle-covered slope to Mount Faber. From the summit he could see right across the Island and out to the Straits of Singapore. He watched junks and cargo ships threading their way to Keppel harbour, the sea a startling blue. He also explored the ruins of an old and elegant colonial house where, he was told, Japanese officers had been billeted during the War, eight years before. Many of the civilians in the office remembered the Japanese occupation although few of them would talk much about it.

Steve knew that the terrorists in Malaya had fought alongside the British against the Japanese. Now they were fighting for an independence they believed they'd been promised. Though the political conflict didn't really concern him, he vaguely realised that the British Empire was in a state of slow dissolution and that National Servicemen were scattered round the globe to help preserve the status quo.

From a military point of view, Singapore was strategically essential to Britain, the gateway to the Far East, but Steve also knew that British interests were largely upper-class interests. And like most of the soldiers he couldn't really care less about them. But in the office such opinions shocked Sally Managua. She imagined he was a communist sympathiser. Which, of course, he was not.

Chapter 2

Along with the other new arrivals at 3BOD, Steve was interviewed by the CSM. Red-faced, paunchy, in his mid-to-late thirties, he had recently arrived from Korea. He gave them his customary peptalk about pulling their weight and knuckling down to their duties.

"I'm not keen on National Servicemen," he said. "They're a bit of a nuisance in fact. Here far too short a time and often don't take the Army seriously. But if you keep your noses clean I'll try and control my prejudices. If you don't, you'll find yourselves up shit creek. Is that understood?"

"Yes, Sir," they mumbled.

"One more thing," he added. "Keep away from the wog women. You may have noticed out-of-bounds signs around Singapore. Never go beyond them. That's where the brothels are. Do you know what I mean?"

"Yes Sir."

"Well, they're all poxed-up to the eyebrows, the whores," he said. "That apart, MPs patrol such areas so you're sure to be caught. Should your urges get too demanding, have a stiff wank in the toilets. It's cleaner and safer. I know one soldier in Japan who thought he knew better and ended up with the black syph. That's incurable. And he's still out there. Won't let him back to Blighty. So just remember: a blobby knob stops demob."

Steve dismissed this advice at once, but he kept his mouth shut. At the same time he was interested to learn the real significance of those little red out-of-bounds signs which might just as well have said: this way to the brothels. Disease was an inhibiting factor, but virginity seemed more of a problem.

David Tipton

Not long after the interview, Steve went to the New World, an amusement park in the heart of the city. He went by taxi along Jalan Besar, a street jam-packed with people and lines of stalls selling Chinese fast-food. Washing hung on poles protruding from balconies lit by lanterns. Women in sarongs and tunics, or wearing silk cheong-sams thronged the pavement. An enticing odour of joss-sticks and spicy food assailed the nostrils.

In the New World, apart from some of the expected entertainments, there were numerous bars where girls, their cheong-sams slit half-way up their thighs, served Tiger beer, flirting with the soldiers, showing tantalising glimpses of honey-coloured flesh, trying to entice them into a ten-dollar short-time. Steve bought a sheaf of tickets at one such place and danced with a number of taxi-girls under the rainbow-flashing lights. The New World seemed mildly dangerous, but exciting.

The following night, on guard, locked in the caged walk that ran round the perimeter of the stores, he could hear radio music from the barracks:

> "*Seven lonely days make one lonely week,*
> *seven lonely nights make one lonely week.*
> *Ever since the time you told me we were through*
> *seven lonely days I've cried and cried for you ...*"

Sweating, sticky in his uniform, cradling his rifle, he could see the lights from the barracks. The sound of insects came from the monsoon ditches and three or four miles away was the red glow of the city, evoking images of the New World.

In the sultry heat he began to visualise the Chinese girls in the New World, then one in particular, Dolly Wong, in the skin-tight red silk of her cheong-sam. He felt the stirring of a hard-on and quickly, the smell of rifle-oil on his hand, masturbated. The radio was still playing pop-music, the rifle hard at his side. He wiped himself clean with a handkerchief, caught a whiff of sperm, then lit a surreptitious cigarette. Next time he was in the New World, he promised himself, he would go with Dolly Wong.

Parading in front of the barrack-block the following Thursday, he thought of little else. The sun was still hot while a kite swooped in one

Medal for Malaya

long sweeping curve towards the sea. Steve's name was called. He marched up to the officer sitting at his table and was handed four red ten-dollar notes. He saluted and was dismissed. In the barracks the dhobi-wallah was waiting with his laundry, beautifully washed and starched. Steve gave her a couple of dollars. Ali, an Indian who had been with the Army for years, and who cleaned their gear every day, was waiting for his payment. Steve gave him three dollars and went to the canteen for tiffin. Afterwards he showered, changed into civvies and met his two friends Lance-Corporal Norris and Signalman Sissons.

They checked out of camp at the guard-room and strolled up the road to the taxi-rank. Bullfrogs croaked in the monsoon-drain and fireflies flitted about in the undergrowth. An Indian at his stall was smoking a hookah; Steve imagined it contained opium. Behind it, the Indian looked serene, passive, his face illuminated by a small charcoal fire.

Picking up a taxi in the Ayer Rajah Road, they went straight to the Britannia Club in the city-centre. After a couple of beers there they took another taxi to the New World, wandering around for a while before sitting down at the stall where Dolly Wong worked. A slim, slip of a girl in her red cheong-sam, she spoke in an odd mixture of pidgin and army slang.

Steve bought her a beer and she sat down at their table, smiling and flirtatious, a gold filling glinting between her white upper teeth. "You want to come with me, Johnny?" she said. "You want jig-jig. I good – ten-dollar short-time. Cheap." Steve nodded.

"Don't be stupid, Revill," Norris said. "You could catch a dose. It's just not worth it."

Out of some bravado, though he felt butterflies in his belly, Steve became more determined. Dolly went over to the owner of the stall and got time-off. Steve could hardly back out though he felt more nervous than ever once it was decided. Together they slipped through a side-gate out of the New World and he followed her as she trotted along a narrow back alley. She went into a non-descript Chinese hotel where she quickly arranged a room. An old Victorian lift took them up to the third floor. The room was virtually empty except for a

19

mattress. Dolly stripped off in a few minutes. Naked on the bed, she looked young and fragile. In his underpants beside her, Steve's desire began to ebb away. She tried to rouse him.

"What's the matter?" she said impatiently. "You not want?"

"No, it's not that." But he couldn't explain that it was not the lack of desire, but anxiety. In the end they got dressed. He gave her ten dollars and they walked back to the New World. He felt ashamed of what he regarded as his inadequacy. Norris and Sissons had already left, so he caught a taxi back to camp. As he fixed his mosquito-net, he calculated that he had a mere ten dollars to last him until next pay-day.

Over the next few weeks he avoided the city. Office work continued to be a drudgery, but was enlivened by the companionship of Rick Walker. He had bought a motor-bike and together they took a few trips up the Bukit Timah Road, and across the Island. But Steve's routine in the barrack-room was becoming disturbed by a big slob from Liverpool, Taggart. About four-stone heavier than Steve, he'd begun bullying him, demanding cigarettes and money. They'd already had two scraps, wrestling bouts in reality, in which Steve had come off the worst. The second time Taggart had lifted him bodily and dangled him over the verandah. Only a brusque order from Corporal Walker put an end to the incident, but Steve knew that he himself would have to do something about it eventually.

It came to a head one lunch-time. Steve was lying on his bed, smoking a cigarette, irritated by a minor prickly-heat rash on his back.

"Heh, Revill," Taggart said, leaning over his bed. "Give us a fag. Come on." White-skinned and fat-bellied, the sweat running in rivulets down his slack pectorals and trickling into the waistband of his shorts, he smelled of engine-oil from the MOT square where he worked.

"Fuck off, Taggart," Steve said. "I'm busy."

"Come on, give."

"Help yourself then," Steve said. "They're there. On my locker."

"You give me one." Taggart began punching the top of Steve's arm, not hard, but enough to be irritating. Several soldiers in the room were watching, one or two of them grinning. "Come on, you little prick,"

Taggart said. "Get those fags down." It was clearly some sort of power game, Steve realised, the attempt to exercise some authority over anyone he considered weaker than himself.

Steve got up slowly as if resigned to the inevitability of the demand. He was shaking imperceptibly with a sudden rush of adrenalin. He turned to his locker, then whipped round and punched Taggart hard in the soft part of his belly. He felt the blow sink into flesh and noticed the look of absolute incredulity on Taggart's face. All this was more or less instantaneous for before Taggart had time to react he landed a right-hook to the side of his chin. Taggart ended up on his arse on the stone floor. Corporal Walker and Lance-Corporal Robinson came running across.

"I'll kill you for that, you bastard," Taggart said, sitting up.

"All right," Walker said. "That's enough. Break it up or you'll both be on a charge."

"I'll get you one of these days," Taggart said.

"And we'll all know who's responsible should anything happen to Revill," Walker said. "Anyway, you asked for that, Taggart. You've been on his back for weeks." He turned to Steve. "Not bad," he said. "I didn't know you'd got it in you."

"I'll get you, Revill," Taggart said, still cursing away.

"Here have your cig," Steve said and chucked him one. Taggart caught it, dropped it on the floor and ground it to shreds with his boot.

"Don't worry about Taggart," Walker said. "I somehow doubt that he'll bother you again."

That evening Wilson, a tall thin lad with A-levels who spoke in a posh accent, came over to Steve's bed-space. He'd also been bullied by Taggart who regarded him as a queer, probably because when he went for a shower, Wilson shocked some of the others by strolling through the barrack-room stark naked. And, that apart, he kept himself to himself.

"Congratulations," he said. "That's exactly what Taggart deserved. It was a delight to witness. Just be careful. Cowards are often cunning."

About a week after the Taggart incident, Steve went to the Britannia Club with a group of soldiers from the unit. They had a swim in the

21

pool and watched the dancing in the ball-room. It was full of Eurasian women and nurses accompanied by officers. Vaguely it depressed Steve. He knocked back four pints of Tiger beer and since he was not accustomed to such quantities felt quite drunk when they emerged onto the street. With him was an Irish radio-operator, Paddy Murphy. They were hailed by a trishaw driver. "Heh, Johnny," he called. "You want girls, yes? I take you good place."

"Let's go, mate," Paddy said.

"Are you sure it'll be OK?" Steve said. "I've never been in one of these trishaws before."

"Of course it will. Come on."

They tumbled into the trishaw and took off, not in the direction of Jalan Besar, but towards the docks. For ten minutes they travelled along by the sea, palm trees silhouetted against the night sky. They passed the railway station and came into a district Steve didn't know. It was ill-lit except for braziers at the roadside and paraffin burners flickering in some of the houses.

Finally they turned into a sidestreet crowded with Chinese. There were several bars between the dingy houses. The trishaw stopped outside one. Almost immediately they were surrounded by Chinese women, several of whom seemed to recognise Paddy. Relaxed, self-assured, he disappeared upstairs with one of the women almost straight away. Without actually selecting her, Steve allowed himself to be spirited away by a plumpish woman in green trousers and top. She was laughing and relaxed. Steve put an arm round her waist as they went up the stairs. An aroma of joss-sticks pervaded the place. Despite the beer, Steve was sure things would turn out as they had done with Dolly, but he didn't care. The room was tiny so, taking off his shoes, Steve sat on the edge of the bed. Still smiling, the woman slipped out of her trousers, went over to a basin and sponged herself between the legs, then clambered beside him on the bed.

She was more skilful and patient than Dolly, unfastening his trousers, slipping her hand in, doing more subtle things with her fingers. Almost without realising it, with the woman astride him, he was inside her, enclosed by female flesh, for the first time – a warm moist unique sensation. He felt exhilaration and relief. He was all right. He was home – and away on a tidal wave of excitement. Instinctively, he put his hands round her buttocks, controlling her movement. The pleasure was so intense he came quickly. Afterwards he paid her five dollars, kissed her on the cheek and followed her downstairs. Paddy was already waiting. The women, still laughing merrily, waved to them as they left.

They returned to the Britannia in the trishaw, had a couple more beers, then got a taxi back to camp. Under his mosquito-net in the humid night, Steve felt quietly elated. He'd rid himself of that irksome encumbrance: virginity. And in the end it had been so easy. He smiled to himself about his own doubts and anxieties. Probably he wouldn't have recognised the woman if he were to see her in daylight, but he was grateful towards her.

Partly because of the Taggart incident, and, of course, the hours they spent together in the office, Steve's friendship with Rick Walker became closer. Steve didn't push it, but let it take its course. He was aware of Rick's habit of turning against people who took him for granted. Sometimes he'd assume an aloof attitude and sneer at those NS soldiers who stayed in camp, whining about the Army, chalking up the days, weeks, months to demob, idealising the girls they'd left behind, being sentimental about their mothers. It was as if he'd deliberately blunted his sensitivity – or six years in the Army had.

"You're bloody stupid," he'd say to those who stayed in camp, "dreaming of some woman eight-thousand miles away. What do you think she's doing now? Staying at home waiting for your return. Don't be daft! She's out having a good time. With your best friend most likely. Getting screwed. You should do the same. Go into town. Try the local women."

"Fuck off, Walker!" they'd say.

"Well, at least I'm getting laid, not wanking away in camp. Come on, Revill," he'd add. "Get your arse off the bed and let's go into Singapore."

He'd start whistling, *I wonder who's kissing her now*, as he got ready to go out. He wasn't popular, but he was a dominating presence in the barrack-room.

His comments were sometimes disturbing to Steve. He knew his ex-girlfriend was going out with his old friend, Mike, back in Birmingham, and perhaps with others in the crowd who had so far escaped National Service. But then they were not committed to each other and he was free to sample the sexual provender Singapore had to offer.

One night Rick and Steve went to the Military Hospital where there was a dance. They met a couple of nurses and took them out the following paynight. But it was clear the nurses didn't enjoy themselves much. Rick was furious.

"Fucking typical!" he said after they'd gone. "English women! There's so much competition here, they can afford to be choosy – out with ex-public school second lieutenants or damned doctors. We've got little to offer them. Not enough bloody money for starters. I prefer the whores. At least they're honest. It's a straightforward transaction with them. Come one, let's get the motor-bike and go back into town."

Steve had been uneasy with the nurses, but Rick Walker who had behaved similarly, had tried to cover it up with a brash line of talk. They walked round to the hospital car-park and zoomed into town on the motor-bike. Their sweat evaporated in the rush of cool air created by its speed.

"I know a place just off the Racecourse Road," Rick said. "Let's go there."

They drove along Racecourse Road, then turned right into a narrow alleyway. A few yards down was a cluster of women in a doorway. They were all smiling, clamouring round, offering their services. Steve selected a slim Chinese woman in a red silk-dress. She led him up a winding staircase to her room. Rick had disappeared with another of the girls.

"Wait by the bike," he'd said as they split up.

The room was pungent with joss-sticks and perfume. Silk drapes festooned the walls. The woman urged Steve on, but with a smile. They lay down on a single mattress on the floor. She was delighted that he was already semi-erect. For a Chinese she was quite tall, about Steve's height. Raising her hips and swivelling them round in a slow circular movement, she knew exactly how to excite him quickly. Their bodies were scarcely touching; the focus of their contact was genital. To Steve, a novice, it seemed extraordinarily novel. He came in a few minutes, got dressed, gave her a green five-dollar note and, following her, made his way back down the spiral staircase. He'd just lit a cigarette when Rick appeared, smiling in his wry and cynical way.

"That must have been quick," he said.

"Well, she had this unusual trick."

"*Lekas, lekas*, eh?" Steve smiled and nodded.

In the office Rick and Steve compared notes about the women in the brothels they visited. In his letters home, Steve now inserted descriptions of the city's night-life. He felt no nostalgia for the intellectual pursuits he'd once followed. He felt he was living in the present, acquiring experience he might exploit in fiction later. After receiving their pay, Thursday evenings followed a routine. Once they'd had supper, showered and changed into civvies, they'd speed into Singapore on Rick's motor-bike. Several times they ended up in the brothel off the Racecourse Road and each time Steve went with the slim Chinese woman who had the ingenious hip-swivelling movement. But one night she wasn't available so he went with an older Chinese woman in her thirties. He was getting dressed afterwards when he heard Rick shouting.

"Steve, hurry up, for Christ's sake, it's the MPs." Followed by a couple of the women he burst into the room. Laughing and evidently entertained, the women rushed them down a staircase at the back of the house, out of a side door and into the alley where the motor-bike was parked. The MPs saw them and shouted, but they jumped onto the bike. Rick kicked the starter and they were away, weaving erratically along the alley which was thronged with pedestrians. In their jeep the MPs were unable to follow. They tried to cut round from the right and head them off in Jalan Besar. But once on the main road, full of trishaws, buses and people, Rick was able to avoid them. He sped out of the city and back towards camp, laughing demonically at the close-shave, but keeping his eye on the mirror for the distinctive light-formation of the MPs' jeep.

One Friday evening, a week later, after a tropical storm, Steve went to the army cinema in the Royal Engineers Lines. It was cool after the rain as he walked along the camp road. Outside their shanties the Indians who worked in camp were sitting in what appeared to be the lotus position smoking their hookahs. The monsoon drain gurgled with rainwater and the palms drooped, heavy with moisture. A thin sliver of moon appeared through ragged cloud. He could hear a pariah dog barking in some nearby kampong.

The cinema was a makeshift affair, half-full of soldiers, families from the married-quarters and a few locals employed by the Army. Several fans whirred overhead in a feeble effort to cool the place and the audience continually shifted its weight about on the wooden seats. The film seemed unreal; its Hollywood issues incongruous. Half-way through Steve became aware of a damp patch on his pale-blue trousers and at the interval went to the Gents to investigate. Standing at the urinal he saw that the head of his prick was rashed with whitish spots and a yellowish discharge seeped from the urethra. He didn't stay to watch the rest of the film, but hurried back to camp.

Once in the barracks he checked again. Yellowish pus like snot. He put up his mosquito-net, slipped under the sheet and tried to sleep. He failed. Sweating, he lit another cigarette. Someone was snoring and everyone else appeared to be asleep under the flimsy pyramids of their mosquito-nets. Finally he too drifted off into a fitful half-sleep.

He woke at dawn, instantly recalling his problem. He told Rick that he was reporting sick and wouldn't be in the office that morning.

"What's the matter?"

"I think I've caught a dose."

"Let's have a look," Rick said smiling broadly. Without much hesitation Steve showed him. The symptoms looked worse in broad daylight. Rick laughed out loud. "Heh, fellows," he called out. "Come and look at this. Revill's got the clap." Several curious soldiers came over: not even genital infections were private in the barrack-room.

"Ugh! Keep away from me," someone said.

"Dirty bugger," added another.

"That's what comes of screwing whores," one of the stay-in-camps observed.

"Better get along to the MO," Rick said. Steve's complaint was the subject of much ribaldry which in fact made him feel marginally better.

The MO took one quick look and told him to report at once to the STD at Alexandra hospital. Back in the barracks he packed some belongings as instructed, laid out his sheets and blanket and locked his bedside wardrobe. With his small pack slung over his shoulder he walked up the main drive to the hospital. The last time he'd been there was when Rick and he had taken out the nurses. Once in the elegant cool white building he found the STD quickly. Soon he was in front of the MO there. He described his symptoms.

"When was the last time you had a contact?"

"A contact?"

"Went with a woman."

"About ten days ago."

"Right. Drop your trousers."

He felt vulnerable in front of the MO and the two orderlies. His penis retracted, but the MO took hold of it, tugged gently, then squeezed it. An orderly took a smear of the discharge and transferred it to a slide. Afterwards he had to provide a urine sample.

"Distinct threads," the MO said. "Look!" Steve glanced at the container. He could see whitish filaments floating around in the yellowish liquid. "We'll call you back in twenty minutes," the MO said. "Corporal Jones will take a blood sample first, then wait outside."

Half-an-hour later he was back in front of the MO. "Well, Signalman," he said. "You've got an NSU – non-specific urethritis."

"What's that, Sir?"

"The symptoms are similar to those of gonorrhea, but it can be more difficult to treat. I'm going to put you on a course of streptomycin and then I'll check you again in five days."

"What's the blood for?"

"We check for syphilis. That's routine though I doubt whether there's anything to worry about."

Relief flooded through him. Syphilis was the one soldiers really feared. The non-specific label seemed to indicate that this disease wasn't in the most serious category. He went to the ward in an almost jaunty mood. He wondered what the other twenty or so patients there had, but didn't ask. He knew it would have been bad form to have done so.

After a couple of shots of streptomycin, as if by magic, his symptoms disappeared. Simultaneously his depression disappeared too. He even began to enjoy the time in hospital. He went to the library and took out some novels. He wrote a few letters home – and even a few poems in his notebook. One of the poems was about the anxiety and remorse he'd initially felt contracting the disease. Another of the soldiers in the ward read it and liked it so much he copied it out. He wanted to send it home in a letter as if it were his own. He gave Steve a couple of packs of Lucky Strike for the privilege.

One afternoon new patients were asked to fill in a questionnaire describing their contacts and indicating, if possible, the place where they had met them. Steve couldn't be sure who had infected him, but thought it must have been the Chinese woman he'd last gone with in the ramshackle four-storey brothel off the Racecourse Road. He filled in the form as accurately as he could although some caution stopped him being specific about the location.

That evening a couple of MPs came to the ward. Six of the patients, including Steve, were ordered to put on their shoes. Still in pajamas and hospital dressing-gowns they were taken outside to a waiting truck. From the back Steve could tell they were going towards the city. Soon they were in the heart of the redlight district.

They stopped at the place which he had described in his questionnaire. Flanked by the MPs he was ushered inside. There were shouts and scuffling from the women who tried to get away. Several managed to evade the MPs and make their escape. The rest were herded together. The MPs ordered Steve to identify his contact. He didn't recognise any of the women though several looked familiar. Under pressure from the MPs, he pointed out the woman he thought had been the one. She cursed him in a stream of Cantonese.

"Are you sure?"

"No, not one-hundred percent."

The MPs asked the woman for her yellow card. This proved that she was registered and reported for medical check-ups at hospital.

One of the MPs made a note in his book. Then to the accompaniment of jeers from the women they left.

A couple of days later, his course of antibiotics completed, Steve saw the MO again. Ten minutes later he was pronounced clear of infection.

"You're discharged," the MO said, "but you'll have to report back once a month for the next three, just for a check-up. In the meantime, no sex and no alcohol."

Steve packed his few possessions and walked back in the hot sun to 3BOD. The palm trees were motionless. Above them a kite hung suspended in the air for a moment, then glided down in a wide arc towards the sea. Back in the barrack-room he showed some of the off-duty soldiers his Part III paybook, as the medical card was called.

"You can still keep away from me," one said laughing.

"None so pure as the purified," Steve retorted. Another of the soldiers gave him a cigarette.

"Good to see you back," he said. Steve smiled. He was glad to be back in the good-humoured squalor of the barracks.

On paynights Rick and Steve got into the habit of playing Bingo in the NAAFI. They'd devised a simple strategy; they didn't drink, remaining sober while the majority of players got steadily drunk. They sat at different tables and once either of them had a win, they left and split the money. Most Thursdays they were able to double their pay.

With the supplement they'd check out of camp and go into the city on the motorbike. They'd drink at Chinese bars where they were anonymous and later go on to a brothel. The experience of the STD hadn't put Steve off; rather it had assuaged his anxieties because with antibiotics infections seemed easy to cure. Most of the places they visited were not in the least memorable; most of the women quickly forgotten. It was the thrill of the forbidden, the adventure, that heightened the occasion. And it was like a drug to which they became quickly addicted.

One evening, after a particularly good win, they went into Singapore by taxi, had a few beers, then hailed a trishaw.

"You want girls?" the driver asked.

"Yes, beautiful girls," Rick said. "I want the most beautiful girls in Singapore."

"Beautiful girl expensive."

"That's OK."

They weaved through the traffic into the labyrinth that was Chinatown, eventually stopping outside an hotel. It was like a poorer version of the Raffles, all hardwood and rattan inside. A smooth-faced plump Chinese fellow ushered them into the foyer. They sat in cane chairs at a bamboo table. Beers were brought and their glasses filled. Then the women came into the room. They watched them glide down the staircase, smiling and, indeed, beautiful – Malay, Chinese, Indian. They paraded in front of them, each with a silver chain round her waist. For a while the girls chatted with them and shared the beer. But in the end they had to make a choice which was difficult as they were all so attractive.

Finally Steve chose a small, but well-built Malay girl who looked no more than fifteen or sixteen. She had been the least talkative, the shyest. They went into one of the many rooms off the foyer. It was cool with a fan and spotlessly clean, the bed as in most Chinese hotels, a mattress on a low wooden frame. The girl undressed shyly, modestly. She was dark-skinned with a lovely figure. But while Steve was making love to her, she remained passive and unresponsive, as if relying entirely upon her physical beauty to turn him on. Which it did.

He dressed and met Rick in the foyer. He was looking bored and quizzical. Steve guessed that the woman had not impressed him and to conceal his feelings he'd assumed a cynical expression. They paid the proprietor, not the girls. It cost them forty dollars which seemed expensive to them. On the way back to camp they wondered whether the girls were in bondage to the hotel in some way and discussed the possibility of rescuing them – an act of chivalry that seemed ludicrous the following morning.

On another occasion, after winning at Bingo, they visited a huge kampong to the east of the city. Most of its inhabitants were Malay; the sexual provender on offer various. They were accosted by young boys, transvestites, and scores of women. Steve went with a Malay woman, following her along a maze of paths to her shack. All around

Medal for Malaya

were palm trees and huts. The night was humid and sticky. Separated from Rick, he felt some trepidation. Soldiers, he knew, had been mugged, or even knifed, in such places. Even the MPs stayed out.

Inside the place, pervaded with the smell of pungent perfume, she led him to where curtains partitioned off her sleeping area. A couple of small kids, he noticed, were asleep in the main part of the room. They sprawled out on the cushions and, unlike most of the Chinese women he'd encountered, she wanted to participate more actively. She laughed a lot and talked softly in Malay. Inside her, he felt that she was slack, probably a result of childbirth. Nor did he know exactly what she wanted him to do. After he had come, she was sarcastic, even contemptuous.

"You come? You finish?"

"Yes."

"Ha! You too young. You no good for love. You just little boy. You know nothing."

He paid her five dollars and got out fast. As he stumbled back through the darkness of her kampong, he could hear her laughter. He told Rick how the woman had responded and he compounded Steve's doubts by laughing too. Despite all the whoring he hadn't learned much about women – or their physiology, it was true, he thought.

31

Chapter 3

At the end of October a new CSM was posted to the Royal Signals detachment at 3BOD. He turned out to be a Christian fundamentalist and a disciplinarian, a martinet. Within the week he'd decided that they were a sloppy outfit which he intended changing. The troops sneered at his intention and took no notice. They were on active service; they had essential occupations. They were not greenhorns straight from Catterick. They'd put some service in. And they intended doing sweet fuck-all to change. Two fingers up was their initial response to his brand of muscular Christianity. The first thing he initiated was a two-week course of infantry training for all soldiers doing sedentary jobs. For a while Steve who played rugby football for the unit escaped this.

A week after the CSM's arrival, Steve had a run-in with him that he felt would condemn him to infantry training soon enough. He was awoken by the CSM bellowing in his ear. "Get up, soldier. Rise and shine. Let's have those feet on the deck." Instinctively Steve pulled the sheet over his head. It was ripped aside violently. "That means you, Signalman. Where do you think you are? A holiday-camp?"

His face was close to Steve's. It looked red and burnished. He smelled of shaving-cream and toothpaste. The time was six-thirty. Unheard of to rise so early at 3BOD. No other duty-sergeant checked the barracks until seven-thirty. "What's your name, Signalman?"

"22756964, Signalman Revill, Sir."

He made a note of this in a little black book he took from his tunic. A thin smile appeared below his crisp black moustache.

Once dressed Steve found soldiers queuing at the latrines and ablutions. Downstairs they were queuing for breakfast. Steve missed breakfast. He wanted a shower. He didn't want to rush, start sweating and risk a prickly-heat rash. There had been a minor epidemic over the previous month. The secret of avoiding it was to remain shirtless for as long as possible.

On Thursday, a day later, they finished work early and paraded for pay. The whole battalion lined up in the hot sun. Dust entered their pores and sweat glistened as it trickled down naked backs. A regimental policeman called out their names. At last he came to Revill. One-two, quick march. He halted in front of the officer and saluted. The officer doled out forty Malayan dollars. Steve saluted again, turned and marched off.

In the barracks there were two letters on his bed – one from his brother, Jonathan, and one from his old girlfriend, Dorothy. He put them in his pocket and set off up the hill behind the camp. The path was ill-defined, muddy from recent rain, overgrown with scrub jungle. There were snakes in the area. He'd seen several small ones himself. He didn't know whether they were poisonous or not. It was said there were cobras, too, but he'd never encountered one.

As the slope levelled out and the vegetation thinned away into fern and brush he could see across the Island to the city sprawling away to the east, hazy and remote. On the southern side the slope rolled down to the Keppel Road. From the top there was a panoramic view of the harbour entrance, narrow and strung with islands. He watched a white yellow-funnelled ship steaming towards the Malacca Straits. It left a thin white line in the blue water.

He found a clear patch of coarse grass, sat down in the warm sun and read the two letters. They created a twinge of nostalgia for industrial Birmingham, friends, family. They gave him the sensation of being in exile although the news and gossip they imparted seemed unreal; missives from a distant world.

Back down before sunset he went for supper, had a shower, changed into civvies and found Rick Walker. He was anxious to explore a different part of Singapore that night. "Let's check out Geylang and the Happy World," he said.

They zoomed off on the motorbike, stopping first at the Britannia Club. The beer there was cheap; the toilets immaculately clean. They lingered for a while watching some Eurasian women dancing with officers.

"Come on," Rick said finally. "This place makes me sick. Fucking officers! Just look at them prancing about on the dance-floor. I'd love to tell them exactly what I think of them – with their posh uniforms and pockets full of dollars."

"The women are sexy."

"That makes it worse. I prefer an honest whore. At least you know where you stand – five, ten dollars and a fuck."

Steve was used to Rick's diatribes whether they were directed at the military hierarchy or the wimpish soldiers who stayed in camp. He could empathise with his anger – or envy, but somewhat more ambiguously for some of these officers reminded him of boys, prefects perhaps, he'd been with at school.

Masochistically, as if to compound his irritation, Rick insisted upon trying to get into the Raffles Hotel. He'd tried to gatecrash it before, but this time was immediately accosted by the Sikh doorman in white uniform.

"I'm sorry, Sir, but Other Ranks are not allowed in," he said.

"We're lieutenants," Rick responded.

"May I see your paybooks."

"Haven't got them with us."

"Then I'm sorry."

"Ah, come on," Rick said to Steve. "Jesus, how can they always tell? Do we look so unlike officers?"

"I suppose we must."

"Yeh, no white tropical suits, no fucking cummerbunds."

After leaving they headed straight for Chinatown, stopping at several bars on the way. Rick was drinking Kummel chasers with the beer. He'd got the habit from Steve who'd picked it up from a Hemingway novel. By the time they crossed the Rochore Canal and the Kallang river, its smell rising from the murky waters near which were a mass of junks, sampans flanked by go-downs, they were already drunk.

They went to a bar in Katong, then drove down the East Coast Road in the direction of Changi. There were a multitude of

Medal for Malaya

restaurants and bars in the suburb of Bedok. They parked by an Indian cinema and went into the nearest. Outside a thin bearded Sikh was sleeping on a rickety charpoy. Another was squatting against the wall, smoking his hookah. Steve stepped cautiously over the monsoon-drain, bracing himself against lurching. Inside, a juke-box was playing Indian music.

They ordered plates of curry and rice, simple but delicious. The night as always was very warm and humid. Sweat rolled down their faces and backs. Their shirts stuck to their skin. Outside again Steve lit a cigarette. Sweat beaded over his forehead. There was no breeze from the sea to evaporate it and the street seemed air-less. When Rick emerged they set off once more on the motorbike, driving around Bedok, trying to sober up. Then it began to rain, gently at first, but soon developed into a torrential downpour. It bounced off the tarmac, forming a white carpet a foot high.

Immediately the night began to cool. They drove on, soaked to the skin, laughing, the rain dripping off them. The storm abated and the air felt much cooler although their clothes began to dry soon enough. Steve could smell the ozone on the faint wind that drifted in from the sea. They set off along the East Coast Road again, but this time towards the city.

Rick stopped beside two out-of-bounds signs nailed to tall palm trees either side the entrance to a kampong. As they dismounted a number of women emerged from the shadows. Rick pushed the bike inside the compound where it couldn't be spotted from the road. Several women began admiring it. Another came over to Steve. She was wearing a tight white dress that showed up in the darkness. Close-to he saw that she was probably in her late thirties. He put his arm round her waist. She felt soft and warm.

"You drunk," she said in a low voice.

"No, I'm OK. At least I don't feel drunk, not now."

"You smell beer. Ugh! Very bad boy." She smiled and her teeth flashed white.

"Let's go inside," he said.

"You want jig-jig?" she asked. "You too drunk."

"I'm fine."

They went into the shadow of some palms. Beads of rain dripped from their fronds. The woman led him into a small hut that had a corrugated roof. Inside two candles were burning, throwing shadows on the walls. She gave him a towel. He dried his hair with it and sat on the bed watching her undress. She was quite fat, her breasts big and brown. He lay back and she climbed clumsily beside him, leaning her weight against him, kissing him on the mouth.

"You very drunk," she said smiling, sniffing dubiously. Drunk or not, not having had sex for over a week, his reflexes were quick enough. She straddled him, fingers facilitating penetration. Astride him, moving slowly at first, she felt soft and smooth-skinned. He put his hands round her heavy buttocks, steadying the rhythm. When he came, he pulled her face down to him, kissing her. For a moment she buried her head in the crux of his neck and shoulder, then sat up and rolled off carefully.

"What's your name?" Steve asked.

"Julie."

"Are you Chinese or Malay?"

"I Siamese, I Thai woman."

"How much do you want, Julie?"

"How much you give? Five dollars?" He gave her a five-dollar note, wishing he could have given her more, feeling mean for she had been patient and gentle in the semi-darkness.

"You come see me again?"

"Yes, of course."

"Wait," she said and getting a flannel from a bucket gave him a quick sponge down. "There," she said. "That better." He dressed and went outside to find Rick who approached on the arm of another woman from another direction. They got on the motorbike, waved, and headed back.

"I liked that place," Steve said.

"So did I."

"We'll have to go back."

It was ten days before Steve returned there. Rick was on duty so he went alone. He got out of camp on a Saturday afternoon without signing the book in the guard-room and went first for a swim at the Britannia Club. After a few beers and a nasi-goreng at a cafe he took a taxi to Katong. It dropped him at the entrance to the brothel in the East Coast Road. Immediately a cluster of women surrounded him.

"I'm looking for Julie," he said. Someone shouted her name, then he spotted her himself in the shadow of the palms. She came over. "Do you remember me?" he asked.

"Ha!" she said. "Long time you not come. Long time no see."

"It's only about ten days or so."

"Last time you plenty drunk. No good," she said shaking her head and wrinkling her nose. "Come here." He moved closed. She sniffed at him. "You drink plenty beer again."

"Only a few Tigers."

"You want short-time or all-night?"

"All night."

"It fifteen dollars."

"That's OK."

"We go my place."

"Fine." She stood at the side of the road and hailed a taxi that was parked nearby. They got in and Julie gave some directions to the driver.

"Ha!" she said when they were in the backseat of the taxi. "I too old for you. You very young."

"No, you're not. You're fine. Anyway I'm nineteen."

"Nineteen! Very old," she said laughing. "Silly boy, I tease you."

She sat back and leaned her body against him. He put his hand on her thigh which felt warm and plump beneath the thin cotton fabric of her dress. His mind went almost blank for a moment with the sharpness of desire. Anxieties and doubts disappeared, sunk without trace as if in a swamp. The taxi turned right at the traffic-lights into the Tanjong-Katong Road, then first left, bumping along a narrow sidestreet. They stopped. Steve paid the driver, then followed Julie through a gate into a court-yard. A dog began to bark as he followed her up a stone stairway that spiralled round the outside of a building. Above them the stars were vivid and a thick palm tree overhanging the wall swayed gently in the breeze.

Inside he followed her through a stone scullery lit by a single candle. An old Chinese woman in black trousers and blue tunic was crouched in the corner. Her wrinkled face, bronze in the half-light, cracked into a leer when she saw him. She said something to Julie who laughed, fumbling with the lock of an inner door.

In Julie's room the first thing he saw was a wide double-bed which took up a third of the space. The windows were green-shuttered. An old-fashioned dressing-table covered with bottles and jars of cosmetics stood in the far corner and next to it a rattan table piled with glossy magazines. Over the bed was an oleograph of the Queen and Duke of Edinburgh and on the far wall a reproduction of the Buddha next to a photograph of Bangkok. There was a wireless set and a small cooker in another corner separated by a fretwork partition. A few greenish lizards darted across the ceiling. Julie went straight to a chest of drawers and fished out a black-and-white check sarong.

"Heh," she said. "You take."

"Thanks."

"You like room, yes?"

"Yes, it's nice."

"Rent, it very much. I pay plenty dollar for room. You wear sarong, I go make tea."

He undressed and wrapped the sarong round his waist. Sitting on the side of the bed, he lit a cigarette and watched one of the lizards hunting an insect. The room felt cosy and private after the barracks. In a few minutes Julie came back with tea and rice cakes. After she'd eaten, she began to undress. Steve watched her.

"You not look," she said.

"Why not?"

"No good – I not like."

He put his hand over his eyes to satisfy this strangely modest request, but caught glimpses of her through his fingers. Finally she put on a purple sarong, switched off the light and came over to the bed. He put an arm around her. She touched him and smiled for he was already aroused and she didn't seem interested in preliminaries.

Almost immediately afterwards she fell into a deep sleep. Steve lay there in the darkness wondering about the strangeness of this transition from the English midlands to Katong. When he awoke on Sunday morning the sun was high above the palm tree outside the window and Julie was already up. The room still looked clean though shabbier in the harsh light. He felt as if he were on leave and only hoped that his absence from the barracks hadn't been noticed.

Julie brought in coffee and an omelette with some toast. He ate with relish. Afterwards she drew him over to the bed and they made love again. The sun was glaring into the room and soon they were both slippery with sweat. She was quite different in her response than she had been the night before. Steve got the feeling that she actually wanted to make love. She insisted on trying various positions novel to him and this made it last longer. He tried to hold back his climax as long as possible, prolonging the pleasure. Though he didn't think she had come herself, he thought she had enjoyed it. This again was something new.

"You come wash now," she said.

"Not yet, I want to sleep a bit."

"You dirty boy, not wash all day. I give you shower."

She led him along the passage outside into a cubicle next to the scullery. The shower consisted of a rubber hose tied by string to a tap. He swabbed himself down in the cold water while Julie soaped him. The hose sprayed them both. They kissed and he caressed her slippery body. By the time they'd finished showering he was aroused again.

"Naughty boy," she said laughing.

Back in the communal area outside her room several of the women from the brothel were gathered. With them was Rick Walker. He laughed when he saw Steve in his sarong.

"Taken to wearing skirts now," he said.

"What brings you here?" Steve asked ignoring the comment.

"I got here late last night – to see Lucy. She told me you were here. Word gets around."

By now the women were sitting cross-legged on the floor and dealing out cards. They began playing what Steve assumed was mah-jong. They gambled with small stakes and got very excited about it. He tried to fathom out the game but found Julie's explanations merely more confusing.

"Let's go for a drive," Rick said.
"Right. Where to?"
"What about Changi?"
They explained that they were going out for a while. "You come back tonight?" Lucy said.
"Sure, we'll be back."
"OK, I give you key," Julie said. "Come back eleven to my room. Be good boy. Not drink too much beer. It no damn good."

They drove along the East Coast Road, the Straits of Singapore to their right, through Bedok into a world of palm trees and kampongs, then inland past Changi prison – infamous from the Japanese occupation a decade before – towards the leave-centre, a collection of atap-thatched huts just above the beach. All afternoon they lay on the sand, a hundred miles north of the Equator, and swam in the greenish-blue water which was like a lukewarm bath. Beyond were several off-shore islands motionless and very green in the heat; the distant ones blurred to a mauvish haze.

At sunset, the sky a lurid red although there had been cloud all afternoon, they rode back to the Tanjong-Katong Road, found a cafe and had plates of nasi-goreng. Afterwards they went to a small bar and had a few beers. At eleven they returned to the house. The night was warm; the moon clear. Steve left Rick at the bottom of the spiral stairway, arranging to meet him there at six the following morning.

"We must be back before reveille," Rick said. "Just hope that no one's noticed we're not there and booked us AWOL. That new CSM worries me."

Finding Julie still out, Steve lay down on the bed and watched the lizards hunting mosquitoes. He thought of home, the friends he'd known there, of Dorothy. It all seemed a long way from Singapore. He felt a bit drunk, but clear-headed enough. Unlike at home life seemed simple here. There had been nothing simple about his relationship with Dorothy. It was good to be without emotional attachments, he thought. To have women without the complexities of love. He didn't want to fall in love again. It could be too painful. You got hurt. He relaxed on the bed. Smoke from his cigarette wreathed upwards in blue rings. A lizard flicked across the wall. Then Julie came in.

"What've you got there?" he asked.
"Tiger beer. Plenty bottles."
"That's great."
"I drink all day – samsu, beer. Lucy she bring samsu. Your friend give Lucy plenty money. She very happy. You not give money. Why no money? Come, tell."
"I gave you fifteen dollars yesterday, but I'll give you a bit more now."
"No, I fine. I not care, I no want money." She was rather drunk, her eyes narrowed, wrinkles at their corners. "What your name, I not remember."
"Steve."
"Girls call all soldiers Johnny. What you want, Johnny? You want short-time?" He went to the chair and took five dollars from his trouser-pocket.
"Here Julie, have this."
"No."
"Go on, take it."
"It not enough."
"It's all I've got at the moment. Next week I'll have more."
"Come on, Johnny, you drink beer." She poured two glasses and handed one to him.
"Take this green-spot," he said. Her talk of money had embarrassed him.
"OK, Johnny, I take." She smiled and took the note, her face softening, dimpling. They drank the beer sitting on the bed. She looked older when she was tired, but when she smiled her age didn't seem important.
"Heh, Johnny!"
"Steven."
"Steven, you go back camp now, understand? Go camp."
"Why?"
"Go camp now. Please."
"But I'm supposed to wait for my friend, Rick. He's taking me on the motorbike early tomorrow."
"I no good you."

"Don't be silly."

"I too old."

"That's nonsense."

"I no good pross. I hate pross," she said and began to weep. He put an arm round her shoulders, embarrassed again, not knowing how to handle the situation, not understanding it. "I hate pross," she said. "All soldiers come, give money and I must love. Must speak good with them."

Now nothing seemed uncomplicated. It was ironic, he thought. He just wanted to leave, to escape now. "All right, Julie, I'll go back to camp. I can get a taxi."

"No, you not go. You stay. I want you stay. You diff'rent."

"I'm just like all the others," he said.

"No, you diff'rent, I know this. Come, sleep now. Please."

They lay side by side on the bed, not even covered by a sheet. Julie was soon fast asleep and eventually Steve dozed off too for a few restless hours. It was dawn when Rick Walker shouted up for him. He dressed quickly and met Rick at the foot of the spiral stairway. They sped back to camp and were in time for reveille. No one seemed to have noticed their weekend absence.

For the next few weeks Rick and Steve went into Katong every Saturday night. Rick stayed with Lucy and Steve with Julie. Their place became a species of sanctuary from the camp and its details became etched on Steve's mind: the charcoal-burning lamp at the entrance to the courtyard; the stone steps that spiralled up to the house; the old Chinese woman in the scullery grinning toothlessly, chewing her betel nuts and spitting out a jet of crimson at regular intervals; the stone alcove where they showered; Julie's room.

It was always spotlessly clean with crisp white sheets on the bed; her dressing-table a mass of cosmetic bottles, most of them manufactured by the Tiger Balm company; and the thin fretwork partitioning that divided her kitchen from the rest of the room and which was painted in a pastel shade of yellow.

Back in camp one Sunday, Steve discovered that he'd been put down for two weeks infantry-training. It was Catterick all over again, but in

Medal for Malaya

equatorial heat. He managed to attain his rifle-flash and finished the route marches which they made at night when it was cooler. They completed the twenty-mile march on the last day. They had been driven to Nee Soon in the north-east of the Island where the day was spent on the range, then marched back to camp. Steve found the stamina to complete it though soldiers were dropping out all the way back; trucks picking up those who collapsed at the wayside. After the lethargy of the office, Steve enjoyed the physical activity of the fortnight. Only the CSM marred it.

Not long after his arrival in camp at 3BOD, the CSM had initiated church-parades on Sunday. The first time they paraded he'd gone round each soldier asking what his religion was and telling them where they had to worship.

"What's your religion then, Signalman?" he'd said to Steve.

"I'm a Buddhist, Sir."

"Well, I've heard it all now," the CSM said. "I'm up to all the tricks, but I must confess that that takes the biscuit. A Buddhist, my arse!"

"It's true, Sir."

"Listen, Signalman, no one pulls the wool over my eyes and gets away with it. I'll ask you once again: what's your religion?"

"I'm telling you the truth, Sir. I'm a Buddhist. It's in my paybook."

"Let me see." Steve took the brown paybook from his pocket and proffered it. The CSM read the single word: Budist and gave Steve an old-fashioned look as if to suggest that no one fooled him. "Where do you worship?" he asked coldly.

"There's a temple in Katong," Steve said. "I usually go there." There was in fact a temple near Julie's place. He knew of it because she'd told him she often attended it.

"All right, soldier. You better get moving if you're off to Katong. Dismiss."

From that moment Steve realised he'd be a marked man; his turn for infantry-training had come up not long after the incident. And during the first week when they'd been drilling in the midday heat, Steve made a second error of judgement. They had halted for a moment beneath the palms and frangipani when the CSM called out his name. "Signalman Revill," he yelped. "Fall out."

43

Steve turned right and stepped out of the ranks. "Over here, Revill." He marched across to where the CSM was standing. "Let's see how you handle a bit of responsibility. I'm putting you in charge of the platoon."

Some of the others laughed. They didn't expect a clerk, rusty since basic training, to make a good job of it, especially not under the CSM's eagle-eye.

"Squad, by the right, right turn," Steve began. There was sporadic laughter as the platoon turned. "Quick march." They set off down the road. Steve quickened his pace to keep up with them. "Squad halt!" The platoon came to a machine-gun clattering stop. The CSM sneered.

"You can do better than that," he said. "Your voice must be loud and clear and contain a tone of authority. Carry on."

"Squad!" Steve yelled on an impulse. "Squad, dis-miss! Five minutes smoke-break." Laughing, the soldiers broke ranks and wandered over to the grass verge. The CSM failed to react for a moment or two, then exploded.

"Corporal, arrest that man!" he shouted. He marched up to Steve, thrusting his face close. "Soldier, you're under close-arrest. Corporal, get to the guard-room. I want a couple of regimental police."

Five minutes later the police arrived and Steve was marched at the double to the unit guard-room. Twenty minutes later he was in front of the CO charged with: Conduct to the Prejudice of Good Order and Military Discipline. The CO listened to the CSM's evidence, then ordered Steve to provide an explanation.

"I was put in charge of the platoon, Sir. I thought the troops needed a break. We'd been drilling for an hour in the sun. So I dismissed them."

"It was a deliberate attempt to undermine the CSM's authority," he said. "An extremely provocative act which I regard very gravely."

"It was tantamount to mutiny," the CSM piped up.

"May I say, Sir, that I think the CSM has been picking upon me," Steve said. "It's because I'm a Buddhist."

"What on earth are you on about?" Steve explained about the church parades and his visits to the temple in Katong. "He probably doubts that you're a genuine Buddhist at all. I certainly do."

Medal for Malaya

"I *am*, Sir."

"Well, it's beside the point and if I were in your shoes I'd retract my allegation."

"Yes, Sir, I think I was just being a bit paranoid. Sorry."

"Are you prepared to accept the punishment I'm going to mete out to you?"

"Yes Sir."

"Seven days confined to barracks! March him out, Corporal."

Being on jankers as well as infantry-training meant that Steve was on the go from 6AM to 10PM. Defaulters had to report, smartly-dressed in full-kit at six-thirty in the morning, then again at eight o'clock. From eight-thirty until five in the afternoon there was the infantry stuff. Off-duty in the evenings he had to report every hour to the guard-room from six until ten. In between inspections were cookhouse fatigues, stripped to the waist, washing up greasy pots and pans.

They were allowed a twenty-minutes NAAFI break after the CSM's inspection. One evening Steve bought a couple of Tiger beers, but not having time to finish them, poured what was left into his water-bottle. That night the Duty Officer, a fastidious man, shook every soldier's water-bottle as he passed down the rank of defaulters. Steve's was the only one not empty. As the officer shook it a disturbing sound of beer sloshing around inside was audible to everyone. The officer stood in front of Steve who held his breath for it was actually against orders to consume alcohol while on jankers.

"Good man," the officer said. "You're the only soldier here who's correctly-dressed. You can be dismissed. The remainder will report again at ten-thirty. And this time anyone with an empty water-bottle will be on a further charge."

Another evening, on an impulse, Steve decided to break out of camp after the 10PM inspection. As it was impossible to get past the guard-room at the main entrance, he took the route up the sharp incline behind the barracks. He knew the path well and his only worry was about snakes in the darkness. Once at the top the jungle became scrub and the escarpment sloped down to a kampong which, he thought, was possibly more risky than the jungle, but he quickly reached the

45

main Keppel Road. There he took a taxi to the redlight area near the docks.

He had a couple of beers at a bar and went to the brothel where he had lost his virginity some months before. He chose a small Chinese girl who only asked for three dollars. He gave her five, then took a taxi back to the kampong.

He walked past the now dark shacks, dogs barking, the adrenalin pumping. Once on top of Mount Faber he could see the lights of 3BOD below him. He found the path easily enough. The impulse was to rush down through the dense scrub and get to the bottom as soon as possible, but the last thing he wanted was to attract attention. Controlling his mild panic, he pretended he was a guerrilla fighter making a lone foray into the camp. The moon was up and he could see ahead fairly well. Silently as possible he made his way down. No one saw or heard him. Within fifteen minutes he was in the barrack-room having a shower. In bed he felt exhilarated as if he'd been on some patrol.

One morning during the second week of infantry training the CSM had Steve's platoon in the gym. He split them up into pairs according to size and got them to box. Steve, who was just over nine-stone, had done some boxing before. His father had taught him the rudiments of the sport although he didn't enjoy it much. But the CSM seemed impressed. He called him over.

"You surprise me, Revill," he said. "You might be a lousy soldier, but you can box a bit. Here, come and have a go with me." Boxing seemed to be an integral part of his muscular Christianity but sparring with him didn't appeal to Steve as the CSM looked to be about twelve stone. "Come on," he repeated. "Here's your chance to put one on me. I bet you'd like that."

"No, it's all right, Sir."

"Go on, have a shot, Stevey," one of the soldiers said.

"No, thanks."

"Get up here," the CSM said. "That's an order."

Steve slipped between the ropes of the makeshift ring, put his fists up and began to move around cautiously. The CSM was smiling. Steve didn't trust his expression. "Come on, let's see what you're made of.

Try and hit me." He was dancing around, feinting, sparring like a professional. Steve followed him, throwing a few tentative left jabs. "Come on," he exhorted. "I hardly felt those. I want to see whether you've got a punch."

The other soldiers were cheering ironically. Steve began to really box. He managed to get a good jab to the CSM's face and he dropped his guard fractionally. Steve spotted it and cracked him with a solid punch. He could see it had hurt him a little. His smile disappeared. The soldiers cheered. Steve saw the reddish mark on the side of the CSM's face, just above the jaw-line. Now he was serious. Much heavier than Steve he came in with a rush. Steve ducked and weaved and got off the ropes. He tried to use his speed jabbing him off, but eventually the CSM trapped him in a corner. Steve's chin was tucked in, his arms and elbows close to his body. He ducked one of the CSM's hooks and swayed back, missing a straight right. Then the CSM caught him with a punch above the left eye and, following up, hit him to the body a couple of times. Steve went down. The soldiers counted him out in unison. He certainly wasn't out, but he had no intention of getting up.

The CSM looked happy, smiling, sticking his arm up in a victory salute, a burly enough figure in his track-suit. He came over, helped Steve to his feet. He must have felt that he'd evened things up after the incident on the drill-square.

"OK lads, get changed quick. On the parade square in five minutes." Steve got ready to follow them. "Not you, Signalman," he said. "Come with me."

With some trepidation he followed the CSM into the small office off the gym. He could feel a lump above and below his eye. "Bit of shiner you've got there," the CSM said smiling. Steve touched it gingerly. "Still you're not bad. Get on those scales a minute." Steve did as the CSM requested. "Nine-stone six," he muttered. "Good, good. With a bit of hard training we'll get a few pounds off. Get you down to the feather-weight limit. You know, Signalman, we're always short of the lighter weights."

"I didn't know that."

"Plenty of welters and middles."

"I suppose so."

"You're on the short side but you're quick enough. You'll be OK."

"What for, Sir?"

"For the team – for 3BOD. The FARELF championships are coming up soon. I want to get a few boxers into the finals. And I want to field a full team. You're in."

"I don't think I'm too keen on being in the boxing team."

"Don't disappoint me, Revill. Of course I can't order you to box. Just let me say it's in your best interests. I shan't be happy if you turn the offer down. You've been on jankers, haven't you? Not pleasant, is it?"

"No Sir."

"The boxing team will not be on jankers, not as long as I have a say in the matter. Certainly not while the tournament is on."

"Well, OK then, Sir."

"Good. At the gym every evening – at seven. Starting next Monday."

That was how the CSM volunteered Steve for the boxing team. Of course, news of his bout with the CSM got back to the barracks ahead of him.

"Heh, he got you then, did he?"

"We knew he would one way or another."

"You're going to have a black eye there."

As it turned out he only fought three times for the team after he'd got down to the feather-weight limit. Their first opponents were from the RAF in Nee Soon. Surprising himself, Steve won that contest on a points decision. He used his left jab to keep his opponent at a distance and landed two or three solid combinations. Their next match was at the Royal Navy base in Selangor. He won his contest again – same tactics. And more by good luck than judgement he put his opponent on the canvas. He had walked into a right hook which probably clinched the contest.

In the semi-finals he came up against a southpaw. He was the most difficult opponent Steve had met, extremely awkward to box against. Steve was unable to score regularly with his jabs and discovered that although the southpaw led with his right, it was also his hardest punch. Steve tried to get inside and take advantage of his weaker left-guard. It didn't work out. The southpaw was taller than Steve, stringy-looking but tough.

In the second round, trying to get inside, Steve ran into a straight right that caught him on the side of the chin. He went down with a wallop on the canvas. A sharp pain as if some nerve had been caught shot up from the side of his jaw straight into his head. The referee counted him out. He wasn't unconscious, but he couldn't get up. He was helped to his corner. He was glad later to hear that the southpaw had gone on to win the FARELF feather-weight title.

For the six weeks he was in the team the CSM didn't trouble him. He might even have protected him from minor infringements of army discipline for he treated all his boxers in a paternalistic manner. In the barrack-room, on the other hand, he met some envy and contempt, especially from Taggart who'd never forgotten that Steve had once decked him.

"Think you're a hardcase now, Revill, don't you? Heh, kids, Revill's a hardcase. He's in the boxing team."

"Don't be stupid," Steve said. "It's not the same as brawling outside the NAAFI. I only box with blokes my own weight."

"You're still chicken aren't you?"

"If you want another fight, let's go to the gym. I can arrange it."

"No, here, right now."

Steve always refused. Heads, feet, bottles, anything to hand were usual in such encounters. He was determined to keep out of them.

"You can't really punch your way out of a paper-bag," Taggart said.

"Well, he put you on the floor," someone shouted out.

"Because I wasn't ready. That just shows what a coward he is."

"Go with him to the gym," Rick Walker said.

In the end Rick arranged the fight. The CSM agreed to referee it. By this time Steve was considerably fitter than Taggart. Over three rounds, if he could avoid his heavier punches, he'd win. He danced and jabbed for the whole six minutes, scoring points all the time. Taggart never hit him, never was able to get in close. Steve hit him solidly to the body with a couple of rights while one side of Taggart's face was reddened from the jabs that had connected.

When the final bell went the CSM declared Steve the winner and warned Taggart that he'd be in trouble if the feud continued, but Steve knew he'd still have to be on his guard, especially when Taggart had been drinking.

Because of the infantry training Steve wasn't able to get out of camp – apart from the one illicit occasion – for three weeks. Letters from home seemed to become more significant during this period. His father wanted to know all the details about the boxing tournament. His mother hoped he was taking care of himself and being careful when he went into Singapore. She'd heard it could be dangerous. His old friend, Alan, enjoyed Steve's descriptions of the place. They created a vivid atmosphere, he wrote to him. Dorothy said he sounded the same as ever – full of self-justification and rant. She was sorry their friendship hadn't turned out better. "We were just too young," she concluded, "too immature". She finished up with a postscript: "Don't romanticise debauchery, it's old-fashioned ..."

On his final evening of infantry-training Steve strolled through the local kampong to the swimming-pool in the Royal Engineers lines. It was a sticky night, but cool in the water, watching the stars in a dark blue sky. Afterwards he had a couple of beers at a cafe in front of the silk-store where soldiers had their trousers and jackets tailored and saw the old Indian who worked in their barracks. He was crouched on his haunches, smoking. Steve waved at him and smiled. He wondered how he managed to tolerate arrogant boys ordering him about, yelling for clean boots and badges, showing no respect. Perhaps he was beyond it all, for he'd been working with the British Army since before the War. He could remember its rout by the Japanese.

At another stall the fruit-vendor was slicing pineapple and throwing pieces into a tub of iced-water. Wailing music issued from the cafe and the Chinese waitress shuffled around, wiping the tables. Steve finished his beer and strolled back to the barracks. The cicadas, bullfrogs and sundry other insects croaked and buzzed near the monsoon-drain. It was an alien, but somehow a comforting sound. A dog in the kampong howled – at the moon perhaps. On Saturday afternoon he'd be free to go into Katong, Steve thought, free to see Julie again for the first time in weeks.

Chapter 4

Steve took the bus to Katong. Few Europeans used the service, but he liked it. Changing at Geylang, he caught a rickety single-decker that crawled along the East Coast Road. At the Tanjong-Katong traffic lights he got out and walked. The palms were motionless and the heat shimmered off the softened tarmac. Aromatic smells of spices and joss-sticks assailed him. By the time he reached Julie's place he was sweating freely.

He climbed up the familiar spiral staircase. Plaster flaked from the walls and in the harsh sunlight it seemed a drab building. Only the green and rust of the palm fronds retained their colour. At the top the wooden door was open so he went through. Inside it was cool and dark for a moment. The old Chinese woman, crouching in her habitual corner, gave him a toothless grin, her mouth as usual crimson with betel juice. She shouted something and within a few moments Julie appeared, wearing an orange-and-purple patterned-sarong fixed above her breasts. She exchanged a joke with the old woman and beckoned to Steve.

"Where you been?" she asked once they were in her room. "Long time no come. I wait all the nights. What you do."

"Didn't my friend, Rick, tell you? I asked him to. I've been on a course of infantry-training. Then I was on jankers at the same time. Afterwards I had to train with the boxing team."

"He tell but I not b'lieve."

"It's true."

"He came paynight. Why you not come? I wait all night and you not come."

"I was on guard. I had to stay in camp."

"You not stay in camp. You not infantry. You not jankers. I think you go with young Malay girl in Happy World."

51

"Of course not."

"You go Happy World. You not tell true. You lie."

"No, honestly."

"I think you say: Julie old woman. I sleep her buckshee so I give money Malay girl."

"They're too mercenary at the Happy World. They've got inflated prices and inflated egos too. I don't bother with them."

"What you say? I not understand."

"Nothing, except that I like *you*."

"You speak crazy."

She smiled and he kissed her. The sarong slipped to her waist, releasing her breasts. He slid his hands down her back, pulling her close. She felt big and soft and womanly. She smiled again and led him towards the bed. They made love while the sun, a huge red sphere setting behind the palm trees outside the window, cast a reddish glow over the whole room. The lovemaking was as brief as the sunset. Lying side by side they watched the room darken. After sharing a cigarette with Steve, she switched on the light and went to prepare something to eat, coming back half-an-hour later with a plate of nasi-goreng. After they'd eaten and smoked another cigarette with their sweet black coffee, she turned towards him looking very serious.

"Steve, I speak you now. Tonight, you know Steve, I must go Katong."

"To Katong – why?"

"Yes, I go soon."

"But why?"

"Tonight Saturday, yes? I make plenty money."

"But Julie, I'll give you some money."

"Look, Steve, how much you got?"

"I've got at least fifteen dollars."

"No, you keep money. I not want your money. It not enough. Much rent to pay here. I not want money from good friend. You good friend. It OK tonight, I get plenty."

"Stay here, I'll give you what I've got."

"No, you take key and go for drink. Come back twelve. I come back then. Please."

Medal for Malaya

There seemed no alternative. He turned on the radio while she began dressing. She sat in front of the mirror surrounded by an assortment of Tiger Balm lotions and perfumes. He watched her brush her hair until it looked sleek and glossy. Then she applied a greenish cream to her face, smoothing it in. She added lipstick. Her face was pallid with the cream, her mouth scarlet. He was fascinated watching her. On the radio a girl was singing: *Rose, Rose I love you*, in Chinese. Julie began trying on various dresses, western in style, all a bit tight. For a moment Steve wondered what on earth he was doing there, watching a plump Siamese woman he'd just fucked getting dolled up for the night's work. He'd hang around until she returned, then make love to her again. That was the reality of his situation.

"I look OK now?" Julie had selected a yellow dress and finished her preparations.

"Sure, you look beautiful," he said.

"You not speak true," she said scornfully. "I old and fat. I not beauty."

"You're lovely."

"But I good for love, yes?"

"Very good."

"I think you like me here," she said pointing to the apex of her thighs.

"I love you there," he said. "That's your best point." She smiled and for a moment her face was transformed, almost beautiful.

"I go now, Steve. You not forget. Come back twelve."

She gave him a key to her room, pecked him on the cheek and left. He lit a cigarette and stretched out on the bed. It was a stroke of luck that they'd posted him to Singapore. He'd certainly travelled a long way in the last few months. Less than a year before he'd been in Birmingham, full of self-pity about Dorothy. Even on the Dilwara his nostalgia for the time prior to the Army hadn't completely disappeared. Sentimentally, he'd seen himself as a failure sailing halfway round the world to escape the pangs of despised love. Not now though. Each anonymous encounter in this city had helped to obliterate those feelings and had restored some of his self-confidence.

It was nine o'clock. Three more hours to kill. He decided to go out for a few beers. Outside it was cooler with a faint warmish breeze

53

from the sea. He went into a local bar and ordered a Tiger beer. While he was there the place remained empty; he was alone with the melancholy sound of Indian music. After seven or eight small beers, he left. Feeling relaxed, glad to be on his own, he strolled back to Julie's along an avenue lined with palms.

Though it was nearly midnight she hadn't returned. He changed into the black-and-white sarong and lay down on the bed. He wished he had a book to read; he'd scarcely read anything since coming out of hospital. A mosquito whirred about his ear. He flicked at it, then it bit him on the arm. He killed it as it feasted on his blood, making a red splodge. A lizard squeaked on the ceiling above him. He watched it hunting insects, deftly defying gravity. Suddenly it moved and a fly vanished in a flash. He allied himself with the lizard in a crusade against the insects, but the lizard retired behind the oleograph of the Queen, presumably to savour the fruits of victory.

He stretched out on his back and the room seemed to shift a little to the left. He closed his eyes and it began to revolve in slow motion. He held on tightly as the revolutions accelerated. A few seconds later, or so it seemed, someone was shouting his name. He couldn't breathe, couldn't move, began to suffocate, to drown. Then he woke up with a jolt. Julie was leaning over him, holding his nose.

"What's up?"

"You sleep very much. Long time I speak you and you not wake."

"I thought I was drowning."

"You pleased to see me?"

"Sure I am." She looked tired and there were wrinkles round her eyes.

"I very tired," she said. "We sleep now, OK?"

"Not now you've woken me up."

"I think we sleep now."

She began to undress and he watched her. Then she turned off the light and he could only distinguish her dark shape fumbling around before she settled heavily beside him. He was wide awake now and curious about this woman he was lying next to. He sensed that she too was wide awake.

Medal for Malaya

"Julie," he said, "don't think I'm prying or being critical, but how did you get to be a prostitute?"

"What you say?"

"How was it you started going with soldiers? Was it just for the money?"

"I hate pross," she said. "I speak you before, I hate pross."

"Sorry, it was a stupid question."

"Not you sorry, I sorry."

"I'm just sorry I asked."

"What else I do? I happy one time, Steve. I young girl Bangkok. I marry young Singapore boy."

"You were married?"

"Sure, I marry long time with Singapore boy. He young like you. Much money like you. Then come war with Japan and my husban' – how you say?"

"Husband."

"My husband, he fight for British. I very happy with him. Then one day, finish. Pff! Japan plane kill him."

"I'm sorry."

"I hate Nippon. I love Singapore boy and then bang, pff! Finish. No good the Nip."

"Bastards."

"Sure, they lousy bastard. Leave me no husband, no money, nothing. What can Julie do? All the time I think about this. One time I give rice and papaya to English prisoner in Changi. Nip camp there. And Nip, he hit me plenty. Very bad time, you know, Steve? Very bad time. English woman she help me. I get better. I work with English nurse."

"You mean you worked for the Red Cross or something."

"Yes, I work for Red Cross. They very good, but after War, finish. I nothing to do. No write English, no work for me. I work in shop for Chinese man, but money, it not much. Very hard work, little money. I think I go back Thailand, see family, you understand?"

"They're still in Thailand?"

"Yes, so I must get money quick. How, I speak? In War I see many girl go with Nippon. Sure, Steve, I speak true. They get good time.

Plenty rice, no work. But Julie she hate Nippon and not go. You listen me, Steve. I not speak this to English soldier, but you nice, I like you. Listen me. After War finish I think I come pross. Plenty English soldier here, some nice like you, so I come pross. Get money, then go back Bangkok."

"Why haven't you gone back, then?"

"One day I go."

"It's eight years since the War."

"Steve, you not understand. It hard for Thai woman. Always rent for house. Always money for plenty things. But I finish pross, yes? Maybe I come amah."

"That's a good idea."

"I like kids. Me good amah, I think."

"I should think so."

"You like me amah?"

"I like you now."

"No, Steve, I too old for you. You want nice English girl and I amah for you, for your children, yes?"

"And I could still fuck you."

"No, not then."

"Well, now then."

"No, I speak plenty too much. Very tired now. We sleep, yes?"

"All right."

Steve lay back wide awake in the darkness, too sober and too clear-headed for sleep. He lay like that for sometime. Then Julie spoke to him again.

"Steve."

"Yes."

"You want make love? I want now. Come here." Taken aback, he turned to her. She clung tightly to him, kissing his mouth, breathing heavily. "Steve," she said. "I like you." She pressed closer, rolling on top of him. With the aid of her fingers he penetrated almost at once. She moved above him rhythmically. "Slow, Steve, please slow. Wait. You please wait." She was moving more quickly, breathing harder. "Now, now quick," she said. He felt her body go rigid for a moment. She moaned, gripping him to her, still rubbing against his pubic bone.

Afterwards she smiled and kissed him. He'd never tried to make her come before. With whores it was inappropriate; usually impossible to tell whether they were faking it, or not, when they displayed symptoms of orgasm. But Julie hadn't been faking, not that time. She'd wanted to make love. She'd shared in the pleasure. And at that moment he felt a rush of affection for her.

It was about ten o'clock when she woke him next morning. He put on a sarong, borrowed her leather flip-flops and went for a shower. The cubicle smelled faintly of urine, but after he'd sluiced down he felt refreshed. While Julie was dressing he smoked a cigarette. She was adjusting a purple-and-gold sarong that fitted tightly round her waist beneath a red tunic. In these clothes she looked like a Thai woman in her Sunday best. Almost matronly.

"Where are you going?"

"Steve, I must go temple. Speak Buddha, you understand? I speak him plenty things and he say, Julie, you plenty bad woman, but you sorry, your heart not bad."

"You're a Buddhist?"

"All Thai girl Buddhist. Like you Christian."

"I'm not a Christian."

"Yes, you Christian, Steve."

"OK, if you say so."

"You good English boy, Steve. Come, I give you present." She went to the dressing-table and brought back a pocket-sized image of Buddha carved from green jade. "Here, Steve, you keep. It plenty lucky. It keep away bad things. You not get trouble now. Not get sick from dirty girls."

"Thank you."

This was a strange Buddhism, he thought, this belief in prayer; this animistic faith in amulets and charms against the evil-eye. It bore little resemblance to the pragmatic, rational system that he'd read about.

"It very lucky," she said. "Steve, I go now. You want to stay here?"

"I'm going out for the day, but I'd like to come tonight. Perhaps I'll walk to the temple with you. I've never been inside a Buddhist temple."

"No, Steve, you go now. I go after. Not come with you. That no good. Plenty people see English boy with Thai woman and they say: there go pross with young soldier. He give her plenty money and the old pross must laugh. You understand?"

"Not really, but it doesn't matter."

He left, descending the spiral staircase, out into the dusty alley and hot sunlight. On the Tanjong-Katong Road he caught a bus to Changi. It crawled along the seashore, passing innumerable kampongs half-hidden among palms. When he arrived he found that Rick Walker was already there. Immediately they went for a swim, spending the afternoon in the tepid sea or sunbathing on the white sand. Beyond the breakwater, the sea was a limpid turquoise and strung with islands. A junk with a lateen sail moved along the narrow channel. Some Malays were fishing from a sampan off the nearest island.

That month, December, Steve spent every weekend with Julie. He began to be regarded by the other women in the place as Julie's regular and she continued to refuse his money. Just before Christmas he got a batch of letters from family and friends. There had been a fall of snow in Birmingham and everyone was anticipating a white Christmas. Steve could imagine it – the sprawling industrial city with its factories, gasworks, canals and redbrick estates gloomy under snow. He could visualise the cream-and-navy trams, steamy and damp, threading their routes towards the centre; the streets slushy with piles of dirty snow in the gutters; the hurrying crowds of people dressed in charcoal, brown or navy and huddled into overcoats; the stores decorated with tinsel and balloons. He recalled the wood-panelled hall in his old school, the boys singing carols – usually in Latin. He imagined his parents' house full of Christmas cards, holly and mistletoe; his mother making mince-pies and pudding; his father bringing home the turkey, bottles of port, sherry and gin. Momentarily it filled him with a sharp pang of homesickness, but it passed quickly. Somehow the images he'd conjured up didn't concern him at all. He was eight-thousand miles away from all that. And he preferred the tropics to the industrial Midlands. In Singapore Christmas was somehow a chimera.

Medal for Malaya

Festivities began early at 3BOD. Work in Steve's office finished at two o'clock on Christmas Eve. The civilians had organised a party. With the sun at its hottest, sweat filmed and glistened on their faces despite the fans. Glasses of warmish Tiger beer were passed round and the women distributed bowls of savoury rice, curry puffs and samosas. Some Chinese girls from the YWCA sang carols and the soldiers listened with mild embarrassment. Outside the palms fronds hung motionless in the heat.

That night the depot was entertained by a detachment of American sailors from an aircraft-carrier on a goodwill mission. The beer flowed endlessly and bottles kept arriving at the table where Rick and Steve were sitting. They were outside the NAAFI, under a palm tree. Above them the sky seemed full of stars and distant palms were black silhouettes against a jade horizon. They could see the reddish glow of the city a few miles away.

During the next few hours they worked their way methodically through the beer until the sky blurred and seemed to cascade with diamonds. An occasional bottle crashed on the concrete. The confident drawl of American accents mingled with gruff Yorkshire, sharp cockney and incomprehensible Glaswegian. With the clink of glasses raised in mutual toasts there were no fights that night, but Steve felt a little envious of the Americans – they were so much better-off than the British and their uniforms were smarter. It gave them a confidence the British seemed to lack. In the end sentimentality reigned. A few hundred voices in rough unison began to sing, sporadically at first, then continuously, the sound vibrating round the camp, obliterating the sound of insects.

Much later Steve decided he'd had enough and left. On his way to the barracks he stumbled over the prostrate body of a soldier near the monsoon-drain. The rest was welcome; the location propitious. After relieving himself of some excess beer in the drain he managed to stagger up the stairs to the barracks. *Hark the herald angels sing, Glory to the new-born king* gyrated round the camp. Steve went into the ablution area and took a cold shower. The sensation of numbed drunkenness collided with the cold water and retreated a little, leaving a hollow ache behind the eyes. Still damp he climbed into bed and

59

pulled the mosquito-net over him as Christmas went spinning around in the warm night with the odour of beer and the ephemeral hymns, revolving into a circle of sleep.

On Christmas morning the orderly-sergeant brought the troops coffee laced with rum. It removed some of the stale-beer taste from Steve's mouth. He had a hangover, but after another cold shower it began to shift. The barrack-room was in a state of semi-chaos, scruffy with clothes that had been flung off at random and littered with empty bottles. Sweat-dried garments hung from a makeshift line that crossed the room and a distinct smell of sluggish humanity pervaded the place.

When the NAAFI opened everyone began drinking again. Beer bottles clattered on tables already slopped from the night before and a hundred or so tousled soldiers drank away their hangovers on a hot morning a hundred miles north of the Equator. Lunch was served by the officers; benevolent smiles and red impatient faces as the plates of turkey were passed around. A Chinese photographer snapped them in groups against a background of palms and Christmas decorations. Grinning faces peered from behind pint glasses and pushed towards the camera; fish-dull eyes unsmiling in a smile of alcohol.

"Let's get out of this place," Rick said after lunch. "It's beginning to get me down."

They zoomed on their motorbike down the deserted Pasir Panjang Road, past Keppel harbour and the Empire docks, into the city. The cool rush of air evaporated their sweat. They slowed down going through the labyrinth of the Chinese quarter, people thronging the streets. They crossed the Kallang River, a motley collection of shanties and go-downs tilted at precarious angles above the oily-green water. Steve glimpsed a Chinese woman in blue tunic and black trousers carrying slop-pails on a bent bamboo pole slung across her shoulders. She was shuffling along the deck of a rotting hulk abandoned there and converted into accommodation with strips of tarpaulin and bamboo.

Once through Geylang, they drove straight along the East Coast Road, turning left where it crossed the Tanjong-Katong Road, then into the sidestreet where Julie lived. They went up the spiral stairway. The door at the top was open. Once inside they were assailed by the sound of women's voices. Steve called out and in a few moments Julie appeared. She was draped in a sarong that emphasised her matronly figure.

"You come early."

"It's a holiday."

"Clissmas, I know this. You come my room. Good friends play cards and drink. Plenty beer for you. And samsu."

In Julie's room they were greeted by the other women who were squatting on the floor playing cards. They sat beside the women and studied the game. Rick poured out glasses of beer and put a record on the player. *Seven lonely nights make one lonely week ...* The women were drinking their rice wine and arguing loudly over the few cents staked on the cards. They laughed when they won and pulled faces when they lost.

"Well, I think this takes the biscuit," Rick said. "My idea of a decent Christmas – gambling in a brothel!" Steve laughed. "And a big improvement upon camp. A fucking unhealthy spot, the barracks. Enough to drive anyone crazy."

The afternoon was sticky, the sun shafting through the green window shutters. It *was* good to be shut off in this room, Steve thought, detached, with the lizards on the ceiling, the women playing cards, the palm tree just visible outside the window, the cigarette smoke twisting round the electric fan, and the image of Buddha smiling serenely or grinning obscenely at his navel or at the oleograph of Queen Elizabeth above the rattan table. Julie was laughing. Steve watched her brown flesh bulging where the sarong was drawn tight. She was talking in rapid Malay and pointing at him. The other women began to laugh. When they'd stashed away the cards and left, Rick disappearing with Lucy, Julie came over to Steve.

"You kiss me now. Pliss."

"What were you laughing at?"

"You angry me? I not laugh you."

"What was the joke then?"

"I tell them: go. I say Julie want make love now an' they say: your boyfriend, he good for love? And I say: sure, sure, he very good for me and they laugh because happy for me."

"You said that?"

"Sure," she said putting an arm round him.

"You're drunk," he said smiling.

"Sure, I drink plenty samsu. Now want jig-jig with you." She laughed, pulling his face down to her breasts, loosening her sarong so that it slipped to her feet. "I tell girls you very strong. All night bang, bang, bang. I always tired, I tell them. They think very funny."

"They're probably jealous," he said, intending irony.

"Yes, they jealous," she said and kissed him again. They half-tumbled, half-collapsed onto the bed. Her unexpected eagerness was exciting. It aroused him quickly. But he wanted to linger, to take his time. He wanted to memorise the exact sensations, register the texture of her body, but she was impatient for him to come into her. She felt warm and wet, loose then tight, clamping and fluent. Her breath came in gusts, smelling faintly of garlic and wine. Then he was no longer thinking, but immersed in sensation: the sharp sweet sensation, just that, coming and holding and coming, just the continuous sensation, then her body twisting, going rigid, sucking him to her, stretching and pushing away, then slowly slackening, the sweat in rivulets between them. They separated clumsily, clammily, her breasts making a sucking sound. It had happened so quickly that he wondered whether she'd come, or not.

"I love you, Steve," she said. Her eyes were brown, dilated; her voice soft. He wanted to tell her that he loved her too, but hadn't learned the small lies that make people happy, reassuring them after sex. He kissed her on the mouth instead. Outside the sun was setting, the rectangles of sky between the shutters blood-red, darkening. He felt a kind of sadness that he couldn't account for, but which was strangely pleasant. It had something to do with the sombre reddish glow that permeated the room; related to a vague sense of transience.

"What you thinking, Steve?"

"Nothing," he said. "Well, about a girl I knew in England and how badly I made love to her. How badly I treated her."

"You very good."

"If that's even partly true, it's because of you." He could remember the episode when he'd had the opportunity of making love to Dorothy

Medal for Malaya

in front of the dying embers of a coal-fire and had, he thought, failed pathetically. He wouldn't be so inept now. He had learned something from Julie – this Siamese woman who appeared to love him. She didn't really, of course. She'd just been a bit drunk and sentimental. But she had actually *wanted* to make love. And that was indeed something. If it was all that there was to it, he was glad. He wanted it to stay that way too.

Rick and Steve stayed in Katong over the Christmas, but Steve was glad, finally, to get back to camp. The flat off the Tanjong-Katong Road was confined and confusing. It limited his horizons. Singapore was a big city and he didn't want to make Julie's place the centre of his activities. The slightest emotional commitment made him nervous and worried him. But any resolve he might have had to see less of Julie crumbled on parade the next day. The white rectangular barrack-block invoked the monotony of military routine. Standing in the sun, holding himself rigidly to attention as the CO inspected the ranks, he felt himself tighten into a stubborn knot of defiance.

"Get that cap-badge cleaned, Signalman," the Sergeant-Major said after the CO had muttered something to him. "It's going green with mould."

"Sir!"

The CO passed down the row of green shorts, navy-blue berets, set bronzed faces blank and expressionless, the steel of bayonets glinting in the sunlight.

"Parade, atten....shun!" barked the Sergeant-Major. There were five or six seconds of perfect silence. "To your duties, dis...miss!"

The silence was shattered by the sound of boots on concrete, the slap of rifles, the murmur of voices. Overhead a kite circled the camp and against the hill a cluster of flowers was scarlet and blatant.

Chapter 5

Early in the New Year Rick Walker sold his motorbike to Jack Matthews, a corporal who'd just been drafted to 3BOD. Partly because he wanted to retain access to the bike, he became friendly with Jack, simply changing his status from that of driver to pillion-rider. In the process Steve's friendship with Rick began to deteriorate.

Matthews was a stocky red-faced bloke in his late twenties. A regular soldier he'd fought in Korea and been stationed for short spells in Hong Kong and Japan. He sported the blue-and-white United Nations ribbon and the Korean General Service ribbon on his tunic. He claimed to have been a professional boxer and certainly had a broken nose which, with his blond crew-cut, gave him a tough bullet-headed appearance. He was constantly bragging about the action he'd seen in Korea, the places he'd been to and the various ways of making money each had offered. He was anti-anything intellectual and regarded Steve as a middle-class snob who put on superior airs. Steve found him boring and predictable. Rick probably felt the same about him, but pretended otherwise. Moreover, he changed towards Steve, treating him with some of the contempt that Matthews did.

For a while Steve still tagged along with them. They would leave on the motorbike and he'd take a taxi, meeting them in Singapore. One evening he was sitting with them in a bar at the Happy World. Matthews and Walker were discussing the racket potential of Singapore; Steve was watching the Malay dancing. The circular platform lit up by fairy-lights was raised above the ground and the dancers gyrated elegantly around without touching their partners, swaying to the rhythm of a slow drum-beat. One of the hostesses, a slightly-built Malay girl, who had danced with singular vitality came over to their table.

"Hi soldier," she said. "You have good time here?"

"Sure baby," Matthews said.

"I not baby," the girl said pouting. "I know plenty. Heh, you buy me beer. Come on." She looked about sixteen and vaguely reminded Steve of some of the girls he'd gone out with in Birmingham.

"I'll get you a beer," he said.

"Thank you," she said demurely, giving him a pert smile, showing her gold fillings. She was dressed in a purple tunic and a red sarong.

"What's your name?"

"Salmah. And yours?"

"Steve."

"Heh Steve, you like me? You think I beautiful girl?"

"Like hell he does," Matthews said, butting in.

"Heh, you shut-up," she said, then turned to Steve, "Your friend he no like me. Give me cigarette, Steve." He gave her one which she lit, first pouting again, then smiling and blowing out smoke in an inexperienced manner.

"He always talks like that," Steve said. "He doesn't really mean it."

"He not like me." She scowled.

"Bloody right I don't," Matthews said.

"What's up with you?" Steve asked.

"Come on mate, this gold-digging little whore leading you up the garden path and you ask me that kind of dumb question."

"Don't you like women or something?" he replied. "You act as if you can't stand them."

"What do you mean by that?"

"I mean for all your talk about the women you've had, you don't seem to really like them at all."

"I don't know what you're getting at, but you better watch what you say. You're the pansy around here if anyone is."

"That's your opinion," Steve said. "Anyway I fancy this girl and she seems all right to me."

"She'd pawn her gold teeth, given the chance. Trade her own grandmother. I've seen her type before," Matthews said. "They're all the same in this place. All they want is for you to ply them with beer

Medal for Malaya

65

and fags and rice, then they'll refuse to fuck unless you've got a wallet-full of money."

"She's probably syphed up to the eyebrows," Rick added. "Just leave her alone."

"Your friends no damn good," Salmah said.

"Leave her," Rick said. "Let's go down to Katong."

"Yeh, come on, kid, I've never been there."

"You two go. I'll get a taxi back to camp."

"Meet us in Katong – and leave that gold-toothed little slut alone."

"She reminds me of a girl I used to know."

"For fuck's sake!"

"Anyway I like it here. It's an interesting place. The orient in a nutshell."

"Well, we're off to Katong," Rick said. "Come on, we're not leaving you in her clutches. Besides, what about Julie?"

"Julie? Who Julie?" Salmah said. "Your girlfriend?"

"Are you coming?" Rick said.

"I don't fancy Katong tonight."

"See you later then. Be careful with that one. She's an expensive way of getting the clap."

Steve was glad they'd left. He preferred to be alone when Rick was with Matthews. He ordered another beer, sat back in the bamboo chair and watched the dancing. Salmah was on the platform again. She danced with an impatient almost jerky rhythm and smiled when he caught her eye. He totted up his money. He had enough for thirteen beers, twenty cigarettes and the taxi to camp – or three beers and half-an-hour with Salmah.

She returned to the table, walking with an exaggerated wiggle of her hips. "I very hungry now," she said. "You want supper now?"

"No, I'll have a beer."

"Buy rice for me, please."

"OK," he said. "Can I come back with you tonight?"

"No Steve, not tonight. I have to see old friend tonight."

"What friend?"

"My uncle. He taking me to see family and I happy about this."

"Can't you see them tomorrow?"

Medal for Malaya

"No Steve, why? You not jealous, no?"

"Of course not."

She laughed and wrinkled her nose. "Look, Steve, I going soon. You go back camp. I see you Sunday, OK?"

"But I'll be broke on Sunday."

"That's OK," she said. "We go pictures. I see you outside Cathay. You know that place?"

"Sure."

"I see you four o'clock." She showed him four o'clock on his watch. "You come then, you sure?"

"Yes, I'll be there." Of course, he was sceptical. Girls like Salmah didn't make such dates. She probably had no intention of turning up. It was all part of a game, an act. He had one more beer while Salmah ate her rice. Then he took a taxi back to camp.

In the barracks later that night he was woken up by Matthews and Walker. They were talking in gruff whispers and stumbling around in the darkness. There was laughter, then someone began shaking his mosquito-net.

"Heh, are you awake, Revill?"

"Yeh, you've just woken me up."

"Have a fag." There was some fumbling for matches, then the red glow of a cigarette, the flare of a light. "I met that woman of yours," Matthews said. "Julie, isn't it?"

"That's right."

"She's pretty good. A really good fuck."

"You mean you went with her?"

"You don't care, do you, Revill?"

"You're a bastard, Matthews."

"Did you hear that?" he said to Walker. "Did you hear what he called me?" They were both chuckling. "She's a whore, kid," Matthews said. "She goes with anyone who pays here. She's not your exclusive property."

"Yes, but you picked her out deliberately – because I'd fucked her. That's weird. It's perverted."

"He's crazy," Matthews said laughing again. It was clearly a big joke between them, baiting Steve with the incident. He had a fleeting image of Matthews groping around in bed with Julie. Of course, she went with a great many soldiers, but they were anonymous. Matthews had merely given them a sort of reality.

"What you do is your business," Steve said. "I just don't want to be woken up and told about it, that's all."

"Ah fuck off!" Matthews said still chuckling. They went over to the balcony. Steve finished the cigarette. Some men seemed to get a kick out of sharing women. All good mates together, comparing notes afterwards. Of course, Matthews was right. He had no special claim to Julie. And he didn't really care whether Matthews had fucked her or not. He just had the feeling that if he had done so it was more to try and humiliate him than it was because he'd fancied Julie. After all there were a dozen or so whores at that brothel between the out-of-bounds signs on the East Coast Road.

Working in the office the following afternoon, bored and uncomfortable because of the humidity, Steve decided to go and see Julie. He didn't bother about tiffin, but showered and changed into civvies. Dark clouds were piling in from the South China Sea, a black mountainous mass over the Island. There was going to be another monsoon storm. It would clear the air and lower the temperature for a while. Such storms always did. He watched for the first flash of violet lightning, listened for the crackle of thunder as the cloud seemed to crush and suffocate the place. Finally it came – twenty minutes of torrential rain lashing down, bouncing off the tarmac, forming a carpet a foot high that gave the illusion of snow.

Afterwards it was cooler, refreshing. He left camp and walked to the taxi-rank in the Ayer Rajah Road. The ground was soft underfoot and there was a pungent aroma of sodden vegetation. He took the first taxi that came.

It seemed a long time since Christmas when he'd last seen Julie, but in fact it was less than three weeks. Climbing the spiral staircase in the shadow of the palm tree, he was struck by the familiarity of the place. It was like returning home on leave. The door at the top was open and the old Chinese woman was crouched in her place by the charcoal fire. Steve smiled at her and she returned the compliment with a toothless grimace. Everything was as before. It was as if there had been no time

Medal for Malaya

lapse since his last visit. No reason, of course, why things should have changed, but he'd half-expected things to be subtly different in some way. He knocked on Julie's door and could hear her shuffling around inside. Then she opened it. She was wrapped in a brown sarong and as plump as ever.

"Hello Steve," she said. "Long time no see. Where you been?"

"Confined to camp," he lied.

"You stay camp?"

"Yeh, I was in a spot of trouble."

"Why you not come see me?"

"I told you – I couldn't get out of camp."

"I know why. You sit down, I make coffee."

"Thanks."

"You go see Malay girl, eh?" she said smiling.

"Of course not. I don't know any Malay girls."

"You not like Malay girls?"

"Not specially, no."

"You lie, Steve," she said. "You bloody lie, you no good English bastard."

"But Julie ..."

"You lie," she began to shout – a string of abuse in her pidgin English, employing the expletives of the barrack-room. The sweat beaded over his body. He could feel it prickling his back. "You no damn good, Steve."

"What the hell's the matter?" he said finally as she began to calm down.

"I see your friend last night. He tell me. Oh Steve, he say, he go with young Malay girl, Happy World. Young pretty Malay girl. He no come see you, Julie."

"Julie, it's not true. Anyway you went with my so-called friend."

"Yes, sure, he give me plenty money," she said raising her voice again. "Plenty money and you no money, always no money. Sure I go with your friend."

"Well, I didn't like that much."

"Ha! You not like. Hah!" She laughed shortly. "I like very much. He give me plenty money and he good for jig-jig."

"He's a bloody idiot," Steve said.

"Sure I go with him. It different for me. It not the same. It my work. You, you just butterfly."

"OK, OK, I'm going."

"Heh, you come back now."

"I'm off."

"Come here, Steve." She ran towards him and put her arms round him. "Steve, I like you, I sorry. You still angry me? I jealous and you not come and see me."

"I'm sorry too, but it wasn't true what that bastard told you, believe me."

"I b'lieve. He no bloody good anyway." She smiled and mimicked the antics of someone drunk. "He very drunk. No good, he no good. He keep coming out, then not find me."

"It's all right, Julie."

"Kiss," she said.

He held her and kissed her, thinking that it was all finished, over, and that he was a coward and a hypocrite and all the pompous things he disliked in people; thinking this and caressing her. He hadn't intended making love to her, but she was warm and soft against him. He did want her. Wanted her body. Had wanted her all the time really. They crumpled onto the bed, clinging to each other and for a moment it seemed all wrong because of Matthews, but he was no longer a reality and the images he had of Matthews' drunken love-making were obliterated by his own excitement. To hell with Matthews! To hell with everything! It didn't matter, nothing mattered, nothing except the urgency of the moment.

That Friday he walked out of camp with Matthews and Walker. They wanted to have a quiet drink at a cafe near the hospital. They'd decided not to go into Singapore. It was a decision that arose, Steve thought, from Matthews dislike of women. He preferred boozing with the lads. With Walker in particular. He was also jealous of Steve's friendship with Rick and trying to undermine it. Whenever the three were together, Walker sided with Matthews and seemed like a different person.

That evening Steve felt on the periphery and was debating whether to leave. They both seemed intent upon teasing him still over the episode with Julie. And he couldn't resist swallowing the bait.

"I went into Katong the other afternoon. To see Julie."

"Ah I see," Matthews said. "You thought you'd inspect the goods after I'd irrigated her. Excited you, did it?"

"Mixing your metaphors," Steve said. "Again."

"You what?"

"Anyway she told me all about your visit."

"Did she tell you how much she'd enjoyed a big prick like mine after your tiddler?"

"As a matter of fact she described the incident in detail. She said you were far too drunk."

"I'm never too drunk."

"Not according to her."

"Lay off it, Revill," Rick said. "We don't want to know. We're not interested. So just shut your mouth."

"She said you were so drunk," Steve said ignoring Walker, "that you kept slipping out and losing your hard-on."

"Knock it off!" Walker said.

"Not much good boasting of a big prick if you can't maintain an erection."

"You're a fucking liar – or she is. I never suffer from brewer's droop."

"Not what she said."

"Fuck off, Revill, you snidey bastard," Walker said.

"Yeh, I'm off. You piss me off, Walker. Don't imagine I don't understand why you support Matthews. It's only so that you can still go about on that motorbike."

"You little bastard!" Walker said. "Come on, Jack, let's teach the little prick a lesson." They stood up slowly. The Sikh proprietor, hearing the raised voices, came over.

"Take your fight somewhere else," he shouted.

"You think you're a bit of a hardcase, don't you?" Walker said.

"A feather-weight in the boxing team. That doesn't mean a thing to me."

Since Walker was about six-feet two and Matthews was a light-heavyweight, he didn't for a moment think that his feather-weight status on the boxing team gave him an advantage. But he was still fit and quick. He caught Matthews before he was properly on his feet with a right to the side of the chin and got a straight left into Walker's body which clearly jolted him. Then he turned and sprinted.

He could hear Walker running after him, but thought he was faster. He'd just reached the gravel entrance to the bar that backed onto the road when he went sprawling. As he'd slowed up a little, Walker had managed to hook a foot round his ankle and the momentum did the rest. He could feel the grit burning in the cuts on his hands and knees. As he tried to scramble to his feet Walker lashed out with a kick. It caught him above the eye and for an instant he saw stars. The kick threw Walker off-balance too, but seeing Matthews coming at him Steve ran like hell.

"Bastards!" he yelled, but glancing round he saw that they'd given up the chase and were standing at the end of the path, showing him two fingers. He reached the taxi-stand, got in the first taxi and headed towards the city.

"Fuck them to hell!" he was muttering. "Bastards!" It wasn't just the scrap that angered him; it was the sense of loss. Rick and he had been good friends. They'd spent a lot of time together. Now that friendship was in tatters and Steve felt bitter about it.

On Sunday Steve woke with the first pink streaks of dawn, a thin mist floating above the slope of Mount Faber, transparent enough for him to see the jungle glistening with dew. He went for a shave and a shower. He'd got a cut and the beginnings of a black eye from that kick. The abrasions on his hands were still a bit sore. He noticed that Walker was asleep under his mosquito-net, long and lanky. Matthews was snoring. He tried to see if he was marked by the punch he'd thrown, but couldn't tell. He decided to get out of camp early and go for a swim.

He spent all morning at the local pool near the Royal Engineers' lines, swimming and relaxing in the sun. By midday the place was crowded with families from the married quarters and resembled a seaside resort. He got changed and went to a nearby bar for a beer.

Afterwards he wandered round the stalls that sold souvenirs, catering for the soldiers' fondness for mementoes. Steve was bored but didn't want to return to camp. Sunday there would be too depressing. Unfortunately, he had very little money. He bought a slice of pineapple and another of papaya from the fruit-vendor who kept it cold in a bucket of ice. The juice trickled down his hand and into the dust, drying almost instantly. He threw the rinds onto a heap of garbage. In the gutter he saw a small black snake which, galvanised into motion, wriggled away into a crevice.

There wasn't a lot to do in Singapore without money except to explore the place. He decided to catch the bus into Chinatown and do just that. He could walk from the terminus into the city and check whether the Malay girl from the Happy World had turned up as promised. He didn't expect her to. Such appointments were of an honorary nature, but it would give the trip a destination. And there was nothing better to do. At least four o'clock outside the Cathay was an objective.

He caught the next single-decker which rattled slowly into the city, then walked to the centre. The streets were crowded and the trishaw drivers, their faces impassive, pedalled furiously in and out of the traffic. Older Chinese, dressed traditionally, frowned at the younger ones in Western-style clothes. Girls with a doll-like beauty, hips swaying, thronged the pavement. Conversations in Cantonese sounded shrill and staccato.

Once outside the cinema he looked for Salmah. She wasn't there, but then he hadn't expected her to turn up. He hung around for a while looking at the captions that advertised forthcoming films.

"Heh, Steve, where you been? I buy two tickets and you not come." She'd emerged from the cinema with the first-house crowd. She was wearing a purple dress with a scarlet sash round her waist. Long gold ear-rings hung down to her shoulders.

"You said four o'clock," he told her. "It's only a quarter-past now."

"I say two o'clock and you not here. I wait long time and nearly miss film."

"I'm sure you said four."

"No, I say two." She stamped her foot impatiently.

"What do you want to do now then?"

"We go bar for drinks. You take my arm. Let Malay boys see me with English soldier."

Salmah, head in the air, swinging her hips, looked delighted with herself. Some students sniggered and a British soldier whistled. She obviously enjoyed these attentions though they embarrassed Steve. In the bar she ordered Coca Colas and Steve bought a pack of Lucky Strike. It left him with four dollars and a few cents.

They strolled along the seafront, the harbour and off-shore islands to their left, hazy in the heat. The tall palms along the promenade swayed almost imperceptibly in the slight breeze.

"I'm afraid I haven't got much money," Steve said. "In fact I'm practically broke."

"I not care," Salmah said laughing. "I got lots of money. Last night my uncle, a good friend, he give me lots of dollars. Come on, we go to Geylang. I take you see my mother and father. We go by bus."

They caught another rickety single-decker. It threaded an interminable route through the city. Steve wondered whether this 'uncle' of Salmah's was a boyfriend, an admirer, or simply a customer. On the bus he discovered that her moods were mercurial. One moment she was ebullient, talkative; the next, apparently bored and sulky. At last they emerged on the Geylang Road, north of the Happy World and the suburbs began to thin out. They were in a land of kampongs and shanties with endless vistas of tall swaying palms, their fronds fanning out in the breeze.

Finally they got out in front of a cluster of Chinese shops. Here Salmah determined to have their photos taken. They went into a shabby studio where a dapper Chinese photographer snapped them together and separately. He insisted upon Steve wearing a tie, bringing out a selection for him to choose from. Salmah paid and they waited an hour for his assistant to develop them.

When they arrived they became a source of amusement for Salmah. She looked very young and pretty, but darker skinned than she actually was. Steve, too, looked young and vulnerable like a schoolboy, he thought, and would have preferred to have looked the way he felt – an experienced and rakish traveller.

Medal for Malaya

Afterwards they walked along the Geylang Road, then turned down a narrow path that led into a vast and sprawling kampong. Salmah was still chuckling about the photos.

"I very beautiful, no?" she said. The question seemed almost rhetorical. "Very pretty Malay girl with handsome English boy," she added. "What you think, Steve?"

"Yes, you're beautiful," he said.

It was getting dark, the night descending quickly as it always did in Singapore. Steve liked the darkness in the tropics. It was friendly, soothing, cooler, full of vague promise. Several lamps flickered between the palms and a thin crescent moon threw a pallid light on their fronds. Green fireflies glowed in the bushes. From one of the huts came the sound of someone playing an instrument like a guitar, children's voices, the oddly exotic Indian-style singing. He put his arm round Salmah's waist and kissed her on the mouth. She averted her face, grimacing.

"You want jig-jig, Steve?" She asked. "Not here, not good here. Too many ant and mosquito. And many people know me. They'll think I bad girl."

She screwed up her face in disgust and her gold tooth glinted. It brought him back to the reality, a reality he preferred in fact. Here he was, almost by accident, in a suburban kampong with a young Malay prostitute. He had four dollars until next payday and was in no position, economically-speaking, to take Salmah out that evening or make the slightest demand upon her. He was dependent upon her whims and caprices unless he returned to camp. And he didn't want to do that.

They arrived at her parents' shack and Salmah led him in. Her mother was young, perhaps thirty-five or so, and attractive. Her father was considerably older. Steve was introduced to them. They seemed shy, but friendly and excessively polite. He offered cigarettes around. Salmah had five younger brothers and sisters and for them Steve was a source of curiosity. One of them brought out some schoolbooks in English. She began to read for his benefit, showing off a little. Her parents listened admiringly, smiling fondly.

Then they all sat in a ring on the rush-matting of the floor and Salmah put a huge platter of saffron rice in the centre. Her mother brought in a big bowl of curry. They urged Steve to join in and eat. He did so; he was genuinely hungry. They all tucked in, using their fingers to make a ball of rice and dipping it in the curry, scooping up the vegetables. Eating this way, Steve was clumsy. They smiled at his attempts and Salmah gave him a fork. She used one too as if she thought eating with her fingers was uncivilised. But in the end she ditched the fork.

"My mother like you, Steve," she said, her mouth full of rice. She smiled at her mother who was watching them with maternal concern. "She say most English soldiers no damn good, but you nice boy."

"I'm afraid she doesn't know me then."

"My mother very clever. She know people quickly."

"Does she know I'd like to make love to her daughter – to you."

"My mother not know that. P'haps she guess, but she not like that. She not want to know."

When the meal was finished, they said goodbye and left as Salmah had to go to work. Steve noticed that she surreptitiously gave her mother some money as they passed through the doorway. On the bus Salmah was quiet, a little sullen even. Steve wondered why she'd engineered the meeting. Of course, there might not have been any motive for it as she appeared to do most things on the spur of the moment, upon impulse.

They went straight to the Happy World where Salmah reported for work at the bar. Steve spent his last few dollars on some beers and put most of his small change in the juke-box. Salmah kept coming over to his table to chat.

"Can you get some time off?" he asked her.

"No, I must work. Why you want me to take time off?"

"I thought we could go to a hotel," he said. "Just for half-an-hour."

"You want jig-jig," she said laughing again. "No, Steve, I got to work. Wait till next week."

"Surely, you can get off for half-an-hour."

"OK, I ask for half-hour. You got some money?"

"No, I'm nearly broke, but listen, next payday we'll go out. We'll go to a restaurant and the cinema. We could spend the weekend together. I'll have money then."

"Next payday you take me everywhere – to the Britannia Club, the Cathay, the Raffles Hotel, OK?"

"Anywhere you like. That's a promise."

"OK, Steve, you nice boy so, tonight buckshee, OK."

She got the time off and took him to a nearby hotel she seemed to know well. They rented a room for a couple of dollars and went up to it in an ancient lift. The room was bare except for a bed with a mattress and a single chair next to it. An electric fan whirred overhead. Without preliminaries Salmah slipped out of her red knickers, pulled up her dress and showed him, laughing, the little pouting mound and its smudge of black hair. She had a slim little body and couldn't have been more than four-feet nine in height. Steve touched her between her slender thighs, but she pushed his hand away brusquely, then lay back on the bed, her legs splayed.

"Come on, Steve," she said. "Come and jig-jig. Quick! Not much time."

There was something simultaneously lascivious and childlike about her gestures that excited him. He slipped out of his trousers, kicking them away. He had a semi hard-on which she grabbed and directed towards her thighs. Smiling, with some dexterity, she inserted it in the precise position for him to penetrate. Once he was inside her, she moved quickly and cleverly. In a few minutes he came. Almost straight afterwards she got up, pulled on her knickers, smoothed down her dress and was ready to leave.

"Steve, you like, yes? You come very quick."

"Yes, I like," he said.

"Good."

Somehow he found her brusqueness touching and felt a surge of affection for her that he tried to suppress. There was also a vague dissatisfaction that always seemed to accompany the blatantly one-sided act. Yet he couldn't complain. He had got what he wanted and was satisfied enough, confident that he would be returning the following payday.

They strolled back to the Happy World. Steve could still feel a glow that emanated from her flesh. He wanted her again, but they kissed goodbye and he started back to camp. He liked her. She made him laugh and he had another twelve months in Singapore. He'd be able to see a great deal more of her.

Chapter 6

The following morning Steve was working in the office when a message arrived: he was wanted downstairs. Idly, he wondered what military regulation he had infringed as he made his way down to the entrance of the building. There a corporal in the Intelligence Corps approached him.

"Signalman Revill?"

"Yes."

"You're wanted at Field Security HQ. My jeep's outside waiting to take you there."

"What's it about?"

"No idea. You'll find out soon enough."

He followed the corporal over to his parked jeep. It was very hot away from the air-conditioning of the office. He began to sweat, his shirt clinging to his back. He clambered into the back and the corporal drove off. The sudden rush of air through the vehicle beginning to evaporate the sweat. As they bounced along he wondered what Field Security wanted to interview him about. Perhaps Walker or Matthews had reported him for striking an NCO. In the office that morning Walker had ignored him except to issue brusque orders.

The rusty-green fronds of the palms that lined the roadside were wilting in the heat; the kampongs they passed seemed locked in a tropical lassitude. Only military personnel were about. Field Security consisted of three rectangular buildings in a grove of palms. Close-by was a pineapple plantation. His mouth watered a little as he recalled the sharp tangy taste of the fruit. He lit a cigarette from a pack of Rough Riders.

"Nub that fag, Signalman," the corporal said. "You'll be in front of an officer shortly."

He nubbed the cigarette and followed the corporal along a white corridor. They stopped at a door marked: Colonel A.T. Phillips and

Medal for Malaya

Major J.H. Thompson, F.S.S. The corporal knocked and a voice invited them to enter.

"Signalman Revill," said the corporal.

"Ah! Good morning, Signalman. That'll be all, Corporal. Thank you."

The voice was cultured and reassuring; the office was large and comfortable, the whole of one wing opening upon a verandah that overlooked a fringe of shrubbery with scarlet flowers. The two officers were wearing civvy clothes; their hair was longer than usual. They were both smiling.

"Steven, isn't it?"

"Yes, Sir."

"Please sit down. Relax, you look a little anxious."

"Well, I am a bit anxious, Sir."

"There's absolutely no reason to be. You're not in trouble, not with us at least. I'm Colonel Phillips and my colleague here is Major Thompson."

"Help yourself to a cigarette," Major Thompson said, pushing a tin of Senior Service towards him. Steve took one and the Major gave him a light. He puffed gratefully.

"This is just a routine check," Colonel Phillips said. And we'd simply appreciate your co-operation."

"Yes, Sir."

"Would you care for some coffee?" the Major asked.

"Please." The Major jumped up and went to the door. Steve could hear him ordering the coffee. It was all disarming, unlike the Army, out of character.

"I've got all your details here," the Colonel said. "I'd like to run through them with you, if that's OK."

"Yes Sir."

"I see you went to a good school. I know of it. Your Headmaster was an army man, I believe."

"I think he was with Montgomery during the War. He came up one speech day and inspected the Cadet Corps."

"Were you in the Cadets?"

"The Naval Cadets."

79

"And you played a good deal of cricket and rugby, didn't you?"

"I was in the 1st XV and played a few games for the 1st XI."

"Are you keeping up those sports over here?"

"I've been playing a bit of rugby, yes."

"Good, good. I believe the Fiji islanders have been in Singapore."

"Yes, we played them."

"And lost, I expect."

"Yes Sir, we were beaten."

"Fine bunch of men," the Major said. "Fine sportsmen. A credit to the Commonwealth ... Ah, your coffee, Steven."

"Thank you."

"I expect you're going up to university after you've completed your National Service."

"Probably."

"To read what – History, English?"

"Or languages?" the Major added.

"I'm not really sure yet."

"But you're a big reader, I believe."

"Not really, at least not since being in the Army. It's difficult to get books actually."

"What do you read? Which authors?"

"I suppose Lawrence was my favourite author at school."

"DH or TE?"

"DH, but the last few months before my call-up I was reading Hemingway and Jean-Paul Sartre. I read quite a lot on the troop-ship coming over – stuff I found in the library – Conrad, Zola."

"Sartre's a communist, I believe."

"I don't know. He's an existentialist." Steve was beginning to enjoy the conversation. They were talking about things he'd not discussed with anyone for over six months.

"Tell me, why didn't you apply to go before a selection board and try for a commission, you have the right qualifications?"

"I *was* interviewed."

"Were you turned down. Let me see. Ah yes, you didn't do too well in the mechanical aptitude tests, it seems."

"I'm not very mechanically-minded."

"The board seemed to find you lacking in confidence, it says, someone who also might not accept authority readily. They should have sent you to us. Most of my NS men come from good schools and have their A-Levels."

"Would there by any chance of a transfer to the Intelligence at this stage?"

"I'm afraid not. You've completed nearly half your service already."

"As a clerk – which I find boring."

"Tell me about your work. You're in an office with a bunch of civilians, aren't you?"

"Yes, there's just Corporal Walker and myself apart from the civilians."

"The person in charge of your section is a Eurasian lady, I believe."

"Sally Managua."

"What's she like?"

"She's all right. Crazy about the monarchy, the Queen and all that. A bit too easily shocked so Corporal Walker and I tend to tease her. She's very patriotic."

"Are you?"

"Well, no, I'm not a chauvinist anyway."

"But you're proud of being British, aren't you, of serving your country?"

"I take it for granted, I suppose. Hardly ever think about it."

"Let me put it another way," the Major said. "You're not anti-British, are you?"

"No, of course not."

"For instance – what do you think our role is here in Singapore and Malaya? In this guerrilla war that's going on."

"I suppose we're protecting British interests in tin and rubber. Trying to preserve what's left of the Empire."

"We're also protecting the Malayans from communist infiltration and Chinese aggression. Strategically, Singapore is the most important port in the Far East. It's the key to our defences. And, yes, it's important for the maintenance of free trade too. That's really why we're here: to keep the Communists out."

"I'd have thought independence for Malaya and the Straits Settlements was inevitable sooner or later."

"No doubt you're right, but that means ensuring that power passes into the right hands. That the right people take over if or when we leave. Those who believe in democracy, I mean. And, I assure you, we'll always maintain a military presence here."

Outside the scarlet flowers seemed to shimmer in the midday heat. A faint aroma of spices floated in from somewhere, reminding Steve that it was lunch-time. He waited for Colonel Phillips to continue. He still had no idea what the interview was about, but had begun to feel a mild sense of importance. He was not just a number, but an individual in their eyes.

"What about your spare time, Steven? How do you spend it when you're not on duty or playing rugby football?"

"I go out a lot, exploring Singapore. I like the city, I find it fascinating."

"You mean you visit some of the out-of-bounds areas." At the mention of "out-of-bounds" places, alarm bells began to ring. It must have shown in his expression. "Now don't worry, we're not the Military Police. We're not going to throw the book at you for that. Such restrictions are bound to be broken by young soldiers from time to time."

"I go to the amusement parks sometimes – the New World and the Happy World." An image of Salmah in her short red dress, serving beer, flashed through his mind.

"You mean the redlight districts, the brothels?"

"A lot of soldiers do."

"And as a consequence you've been in a spot of bother with the authorities and spent a week in the STD at the hospital."

"Well, yes, I did."

"I'm not taking a moral stance," the Colonel said. "That's not our business. Our position is a purely pragmatic one." He paused for a moment. "Tell me," he continued. "What do you do in Katong?"

"In Katong?"

"We know you've spent quite a few weekends there."

"How do you know that, Sir?"

"We have our methods," the Colonel said. "But don't worry, I'm not concerned that you've stayed out of camp or theoretically gone AWOL for the odd night, I'd just like you to tell us about those weekends. Believe me, anything you tell us in confidence won't go beyond these four walls."

"There's a Buddhist temple there. I'm a Buddhist, it's in my paybook."

"We know that, but you've never been inside that temple, not once. You have a friend you stay with."

"Julie, yes."

"She might call herself Julie, but her real name is Mae Wong San."

"I didn't know that."

"What sort of person is she?"

"She's all right. She's a prostitute who would like to be an amah."

"We know that."

"But I don't pay her, not now. She won't take my money."

"She's keen on you then?"

"I don't know."

"She's a middle-aged woman. Almost old enough to be your mother. A bit unsuitable for you, I'd have thought."

"She's harmless."

"Are you sure?"

"I know she is."

"You know, Steven, there's an underground terrorist organisation operating in Singapore – Chinese actually. Would you say that Mae Wong San has anything to do with it?"

"Julie! Good God, no!" he said smiling. "She's a-political, a Buddhist actually and as keen on the Royal family as Sally in the office. She's got a picture of the Queen alongside Gautama in her room. She likes the British. The only people she hates are the Japanese. They treated her badly during the War. She's a simple sort of person. Uncomplicated, I mean."

"All right," the Colonel said. "I'll take your word for it."

"You seem to know a lot about my activities."

"Not much, not really. That's why we wanted to see you. There's just one more thing we wanted to ask you, then you can go." He paused again, waited a few moments, then said: "Steven, are you a Communist, or have you ever been in the Communist party?"

"No Sir, certainly not. Politics don't interest me much, I suppose. My Dad supports the Labour Party, I suppose I do too, but if anything I'm a bit of an anarchist – or I'd like to think so."

"And you know absolutely nothing about any secret terrorist organisation in Singapore?"

"Absolutely nothing. I'd never heard of it before."

"Fine, fine," he said. "Well, I must confess it's been a pleasure talking to you, Steven."

"But what was it all about, Sir?"

"A routine check, nothing more. Periodically we investigate, I mean interview, soldiers on active service, but it's purely routine." He stood up, offered his hand which Steve shook. It was difficult to believe that this affable man in white shirt and lightweight grey trousers was an officer at all. "Just take care, Steven. Try to keep out of trouble. Don't stay out of camp at night. There are real dangers here. Try and find a proper girlfriend – a nurse from the hospital, someone like that. Oh, and why not read some English writers for a change – Somerset-Maugham, Neville Schute, H.E. Bates – they've all written about the Far East. Much more wholesome than Sartre, or even D.H. Lawrence. TE is more interesting. Read *The Seven Pillars of Wisdom*, a fascinating book – and he was a bit of a rebel too. And do a correspondence course, if you get bored. The Army would pay for it. Don't waste the remainder of your National Service."

"No Sir."

Outside the jeep was waiting. He climbed in. The sun was high in the sky, the greenery and light dazzling after the shade of the office. The corporal drove back flat out. He was obviously anxious to drop Steve and get back to his unit for a late lunch.

After work that afternoon Steve climbed up the jungle-fringed path to the top of Mount Faber, overlooking the Straits. He kept mulling over the events of the morning, puzzled still. He couldn't believe that the Army had actually tailed him so wondered how they knew about Julie and Katong. He began to suspect that he himself was the source of their information. Only three people might have told them about his activities – Walker, Matthews or Sally. Of course, it had to be Sally. Because she was so pro-British, so naïvely romantic about the monarchy, they'd teased her. Steve had told her he would like to be shot of the aristocracy and wanted Britain to become a republic; he might even have said, to shock her, that he was a communist. Loose talk, for she probably knew any number of officers.

A couple of days later Corporal Walker approached him. At first Steve thought he was going to make an attempt to resolve their quarrel. "Signalman," he said. "I've got something to tell you." He smiled.

"What about?"

"Well, Revill," he added. "You've dropped a clanger now."

"How do you mean?"

"You're up the creek without a paddle, that's what I mean."

"Cut the clichés and tell me what's up."

"You're being posted, mate, that's what. No more cushy numbers down here in Singapore."

"Where am I being posted? Korea?"

"18th Infantry Brigade, Kuala Lipis, Pahang, wherever that is. Up-country anyway. In the middle of the fucking jungle, surrounded by terrorists by all accounts. You're in the shit this time, Revill, and frankly I can't say I give a fuck."

"When?"

"Tomorrow. The six-thirty train up-country. The Golden Blowpipe," he said sneering.

Steve guessed then why Field Security had vetted him, but was unsure about the sequence of events. Had he been interviewed because he was being posted or was he being posted as a result of the interview? He'd no idea and there was no way of finding out. He wondered how instrumental Walker had been in the process. Perhaps he'd told the CO that Steve was useless at his job and the only way they could get a replacement was by posting him.

"Is this some of your devious work, Walker?"

"Don't be daft! You've brought it on yourself. You were always talking about getting a posting."

85

"To Hong Kong or Japan."

"Well, you've got the Malayan jungle, mate."

That day he was in a bit of a panic. It would be his last in Singapore for ten months or so. He wouldn't be able to see Salmah at the weekend, nor explain why not. She'd think he was a complete arsehole, making all those promises, knowing all the time he wouldn't be able to keep them. She'd never believe that he hadn't known. He'd have liked to see Julie, to find out whether she'd been questioned by the F.S.S. And to say goodbye to her. Up-country, well it was exciting in a way, but left him no time to tie up loose ends.

He sold some lightweight trousers and a silk shirt for ten dollars, thinking he'd need neither in Malaya. After supper in the canteen he booked out and took a taxi to the Happy World. Arriving there, he saw Salmah almost at once. She was sitting with a soldier who was drinking a beer. She smiled in a perfunctory manner and he beckoned her over.

"What you come for tonight?" she said. "I busy and can't see you. You taking me out Saturday, remember?"

"I just came to tell you that I won't be able to."

"Why not? You promise."

"Listen, believe me, I'm being posted up-country, to Malaya, tomorrow evening on the six-thirty train."

"Ha! You lie to me."

"I'm telling you the truth, honestly. It came out of the blue, the posting. I was only told this morning. I think that friend of mine, the tall skinny bloke you didn't like, fixed it. I fell out with him. He told me about the posting. He seemed glad I was leaving."

"OK, I believe you. You get some leave and come see me."

"Sure, I'll see you when I'm on leave, whenever that might be."

"You not forget."

"Of course not. I just don't know when it'll be."

"All right, I go now."

"Look, here's five dollars," Steve said. "For that hotel last Sunday."

"You keep your money. I see you when you come on leave."

She gave him a quick dry kiss on the cheek. He could tell she was anxious to get back to her friend. He was pretending not to look in their direction, but Steve had noticed him giving them surreptitious glances. He looked apprehensive and aggressive.

After leaving Salmah, Steve took a taxi to Katong. He went straight to the brothel between the palm trees on the East Coast Road. There were a couple of the women in the shadows. One of them recognised Steve.

"Ah Johnny," she said. "You want Julie, yes?"

"Is she around tonight?"

"No, she not come. She gone, I think. Perhaps she go Thailand, not come back."

He got back into the taxi and went into the city. He went to the Britannia Club and had a few beers. Coming out he picked up a taxi and directed it down to the redlight area near Keppel docks. It was his last night in the city, in civilisation as far as he knew. He'd no idea what was in store for him up-country.

The Chinese streets that radiated off the Pasir Panjang Road were seedy. The women were all Chinese. Few of them spoke any English. He went with a small slight girl who led him through a maze of corridors to her room. It was bare and only half-lit by a feeble light. It smelled of joss-sticks. The mattress looked grey and worn. The girl wasn't interested in preliminaries and neither was he.

While making love to her, his hand on her back encountered a kind of rash. He stopped and looked. He wondered if it were the symptom of secondary syphilis.

"Mosquito bites," the girl said, speaking for the first time.

The light was too dim to be certain. If she had syphilis there was nothing he could do about it now except hope for a bit of luck. You didn't always catch it from an infected individual, he thought, especially in its secondary stage. When he'd finished, she washed him off with a flannel dipped in a bucket of water. There was the faint smell of Dettol or TCP. He paid her three dollars and she led him back to the street. Once there he caught a taxi to camp.

All Thursday he was busy handing in bedding at the stores, being issued with new items of kit, getting forms signed, having things

87

checked and cleared. He was agreeably surprised to be issued with a pair of jungle-boots, green canvas ones that laced higher up the legs, and a lightweight Mark V rifle, a knife-edged bayonet and a bandolier of fifty rounds of .303 bullets. He began to feel more like a *real* soldier than he'd ever done. It was a good feeling and for the first time he was glad to be leaving. Once he'd been forty-eight hours in Malaya he'd be entitled to a General Service Medal with its green and purple ribbon. That was a bonus. No soldier in Singapore received it.

He felt that he no longer belonged to 3 BOD. The other soldiers had already written him off. Some of them shook hands, cracked the usual jokes and wished him luck. He didn't suppose for a moment that they actually gave a fuck what happened to him. He was going up-country. There were real dangers in that. No one appeared to envy him, but neither did he envy them. He even began to feel the superiority that soldiers posted to an active-service zone felt for those safe in base camps.

At six a driver came for him. He grabbed his kitbag and went downstairs to the waiting jeep. They roared off and Steve never looked back at the Ordnance Depot which had been his home for six months. It was already in the past, a memory. Though the train wasn't scheduled for half-an-hour the driver whipped along the familiar streets as if they were late.

He dumped Steve outside the station. Showing his train-pass he went in and waited. Eventually the Golden Blowpipe trundled in. It was the mail-train to Kuala Lumpur. He put his kitbags inside and went off to buy cigarettes. Then he boarded it.

It was dusk and almost dark as the train crossed the Island. Steve stood on the open platform between carriages and watched the lights of the city recede behind him. Soon there was just a red glow in the south. Back there, somewhere, were Julie, Salmah, the girl with the syphilitic rash between her shoulders, Matthews and Walker. He hadn't seen either before he'd left. He didn't care. He felt utterly alone and free, travelling into the Malayan night. By the following evening he'd be three-hundred miles away. Of course, he knew he wasn't truly free at all; he had to report to his unit in Kuala Lipis, but this journey, this parenthesis, gave him a taste of freedom. He was responsible for no one but himself. And, suddenly, he felt like singing.

They were approaching the causeway that separated Singapore from the mainland. From the train it looked like a narrow strip of metal, cold and smooth despite the reflected lights of Johore Bahru with its waterfront bars and green-domed mosque that rose above the other buildings clustered in its centre. He'd once spent an afternoon there with Walker. They'd gone on his motorbike, then sat at the water's edge watching some Malays fishing from a sampan, the sea green and translucent.

Now with its sparse lights sputtering feebly it seemed like the last outpost of civilisation. The train stopped in Johore for a few minutes, then continued through the straggling kampongs north of the city. From the open platform all he could see was the shadowy black jungle. Occasionally the moon shot into view as clouds raced across the sky and for a moment illumined the jungle, then darkness again save for the flicker of a lamp in some isolated hut.

Steve watched for a while then went inside the compartment, the rifle at his side giving him a feeling of security. During the night they stopped at Gemas on the state border where he had to change. It was one o'clock and his connection to Kuala Lipis didn't leave until six in the morning. It was silent on the platform, hardly anyone about except a porter. He thought about walking into the town itself, but didn't know how safe that would be. He decided against taking an unnecessary risk, but while sitting on a rattan bench he dozed off.

It was dawn when he awoke and his connection was due. When it arrived, lugging his kitbag, his rifle slung over his shoulder, he boarded the train and found a seat. Discovering that breakfast was available, he ordered a fried-egg sandwich from the steward who came round. Soon afterwards the train shunted out of the station. At first trailing mist like delicate puffs of smoke obscured the view, but with the pink and mauve flush of the rising sun it soon dispersed. The train was moving through low-lying swampy jungle. The vegetation was lush with tangles of reed and shrubs like green fans splayed above the water.

After an hour the jungle thinned out and they passed through mile upon mile of rice paddy like sheets of glass dotted with emerald shoots

89

of rice. Water-buffalo wallowed in the mud and Malays, knee-deep in water, were bent at work, their sarongs splashes of red, orange and purple against the metallic gleam of water.

All morning, never building up any real speed, the train rolled northwards. It left the paddy behind and was once again travelling through the thick jungle; tall trees festooned with vines and creepers that formed a green curtain either side the track.

It was a slow trek up-country. The train stopped at every little dusty station along the line – Ayer Hitam, Triang, Mentakab, Kuala Krau, Jerantut and Jemberling. Steve jotted the names down in his notebook. At each stop brown-skinned smiling kids waved and groups of labourers stopped working and stared. Women sold food along the station platforms. Everyone wore bright clothes and despite the heat there was an atmosphere of gaiety.

By midday the train was skirting the edge of mountainous terrain – jungle-covered hills that rolled away to the west. It was sticky in the compartment, but he was enjoying the unyielding green intensity of the views. At Kuala Krau the train ran alongside a reddish-brown river that meandered through low hills, then curved away only to reappear round the next bend in the track. Once he saw a fleet of small sampans gliding downstream and in a creek a number of houseboats, high and dry on poles above the mud bank. Some women waved, their teeth flashing, water dripping from their hair, glistening on brown shoulders and breasts.

In the late afternoon the train crossed an iron-girdered bridge and crawled into a parched little station. It was Kuala Lipis. Steve would have liked to have continued on to Kota Bahru, three-hundred miles further north; he thought briefly about doing exactly that. Instead he gathered his gear and jumped onto the platform. The town seemed dusty, somnolent in the heat. He found his way to the parking-lot where an army jeep was waiting with a wiry suntanned lance-corporal leaning against its side. As Steve approached the lance-corporal spat. The spittle globuled in the dust, then vanished. The soldier lit a cigarette from a nub-end which he flicked away, then shifted his weight from one leg to another.

"Signalman Revill?" he said.

"Yes, I've been posted to 18th Infantry Brigade."
"You from Singapore?"
"Yes."
"Your poor sod," the lance-jack said. "Getting moved to a dump like this from that island of fucking paradise."
"What's it like up here then?"
"Take a look round. See for yourself."
"Yeh, but what's the town itself like?"
"Christ! This is the fucking town."

Steve climbed into the back of the jeep with his rifle and kitbag and the lance-corporal started the engine. They began the drive along a winding jungle-fringed lane to camp. The journey took about ten minutes.

Chapter 7

Brigade HQ, Kuala Lipis, lay on a flat prominence approached via a mud-baked track. Their jeep was stopped at the checkpoint, then waved through. To Steve the camp seemed makeshift, temporary. There were several large atap-thatched wooden-based buildings round a circular parade-square. Palm trees surrounded it. The actual barracks, he discovered, were in a jungle clearing a hundred and fifty yards away down a mud path. Above them were the tents where the Gurkhas lived. Their encampment was separated from the main camp by wire-fencing.

Steve was taken to the canteen where dozens of soldiers were streaming in from various parts of the Brigade. Others were wandering off, in desultory fashion, to the *bashas* as the barracks were called. Fresh from Singapore, Steve was mildly surprised by the scruffiness of their appearance and the apparently lax discipline that seemed to pervade the place. No one hurried; no one looked smart. The camp was in an active service zone and so priorities were clearly different.

The canteen was a rectangular basha with a concrete floor; wood beams supported the roof thatched in dark-brown weathered atap-leaf. The kitchen area was open to the elements except for a corrugated-iron roof. The other main buildings were similar, although slightly more elaborately constructed. The only brick structure was the guard-room overlooking the rough red track that led to the lane into town.

The food was basic, prepared by soldiers from the Catering Corps whereas in 3BOD the cooks had been Chinese. Steve wasn't impressed, but later was to discover delicious Malayan dishes were served in the NAAFI. That evening, eating corn-beef hash and mashed potatoes, he bumped into Jock Robertson, a short wiry intelligent bloke from Glasgow who had been at 2TR with him and also on the Dilwara. It was good to come across a familiar face. Moreover, Jock worked in the office where Steve would be employed.

Jock took him down to the bashas – smallish huts that housed twenty soldiers each and were on the edge of jungle. Steve inherited a bed-space, a locker and a mattress that, he was told, had an infestation of bed-bugs.

"There's a spare one in the next basha," Jock said. "I'll show you. I'd change it if I were you."

Surreptitiously he did so, then Jock showed him the showers that used water pumped from the river, reddish-brown coloured and not potable. The shithouse was a small hut with a plank of well-worn wood with circular holes in it at intervals above deep buckets. Between each there was a thatched partition, but no privacy whatsoever. For a piss, Steve discovered, one could use the pipes planted in the ground, containing a metal dish at roughly the right height on top. The buckets, Steve found out the following morning, were emptied by Chinese women who carried them away in containers balanced either end of bamboo poles they supported across their shoulders. Dressed in the traditional black trousers and blue tunics, wearing cone-shaped hats with wide brims, small and unsmiling, they were obviously strong and dextrous.

That first night, not long after Steve had settled in, darkness descended. Except for the lights in the bashas it was pitch black. As they were in a jungle clearing, the noise of the insects was a continuous cacophony. Luminous green fireflies flitted about in the jungle and once a shit-beetle, as the troops called it, came into their basha creating a noise like a demented bumble-bee with a megaphone, deafening in its panic to escape. Jock warned him to be careful about centipedes which sometimes got into your clothing and, with a wry smile, told him there was a green snake that lived in the thatch of the roof.

"But it's harmless," he said. "We've come to regard it as a kind of pet, a talisman."

After a couple of beers in the NAAFI, back in the basha, the lights out, listening to the sounds from the jungle, Steve contrasted these conditions with the comparative luxury of 3BOD, but he had no regrets about the posting. The discomforts were easily off-set by the strange beauty of the Malayan night – nor was it so humid as Singapore. Here he needed a blanket, he was to find out, especially after the air had been cooled by a storm. And rain it did, frequently, when the soldiers would stand naked outside, soaping themselves and having the cleanest shower in ages.

On his first morning at 18th Infantry Brigade, Steve reported for duty at the Royal Signals Office. There he met Sergeant Vernon who dealt with pay. Jock Robertson was responsible for typing and vetting Company orders while Steve was told to handle records – filling in details on personnel, putting in amendments to Queen's Regulations and, when he had time, helping Jock deal with duty rosters and convoy patrols. In fact there was insufficient work for three people so Steve was able later to spend hours reading through old files and jotting down first drafts of poems, mainly inspired by the scenery, in his notebook.

After he'd been there three days he was interviewed by the CO. Lieutenant-Colonel Mallinson had risen through the ranks and had a reputation as a tough no-bullshit officer who controlled the Royal Signals detachment with an iron fist. Steve's first encounter with him was brief and laconic.

"I'm not going to inquire why you were posted here, Signalman," he said. "I imagine it was for some disciplinary reason. Most of the men coming here from cushier places have some sort of record of indiscipline. It sometimes seems that this unit is for throw-outs, rejects or hardcases who've caused trouble elsewhere. No doubt you're in one such category."

"However," he continued after a pause. "Pull your weight, knuckle down and you'll have no problems with me. If you keep your nose clean I shan't hold your National Service status against you either. Mess about on the other hand, or I should say, mess me about, and your feet won't touch the ground. Is that understood?"

"Yes Sir."

That was it. It left Steve more puzzled than before. Surely not every soldier in Kuala Lipis was a reject from other units. After all Jock had been posted there initially. And was he to assume that he, Steve, had been posted for some disciplinary reason? Had it some connection with his interview by the Field Security people? He didn't know and had no way of finding out. There was nothing in his records; he could check these easily enough himself. At first he suspected a little conspiracy that probably included Rick Walker and others in the 3BOD office, but there was no point getting paranoid about it.

On his first Saturday in the unit, Jock took him into town. They walked along the winding lane, jungle on both sides, the Police HQ on a shallow hill above the railway and the kampong, Batu Kurap, which the troops had re-named. It was hot and by the time they crossed the railway line and entered the town, both were sweating profusely.

Kuala Lipis itself appeared to have surrendered to the sun. A layer of dust had settled over the streets and buildings. Strolling down Main Street, they kept to the shade of the arcaded pavement. Every shop had its shutters up except for the English Store managed by a fat Chinese where they overheard one of the officers' wives ordering groceries. Her upper-class accent was audible twenty yards away. They quickened their pace and dived down an alley leading to what Jock called, the Chinese market, away from the dullest shop in town and posh accents with all their associations.

The centre of Kuala Lipis consisted of three streets running parallel to each other though each had a dog's hindleg as it curved round a promontory above the river. Jelai Street, the lowest, ran alongside the Jelai River about fifteen feet above the water. It was linked to Main Street and Station Street by the market. Most of the shops and bars were owned by Chinese or Indians while the Malays lived in kampongs or houseboats alongside the river. From the far end of town Steve could see the Sultan of Pahang's residence on a hill some distance away. It was partly concealed by tropical vegetation and rolling green hills. The Rest House and Officers' Club were situated beyond the padang above the railway. And out-of-bounds to Other Ranks.

There were few people about but the afternoon smells were pungent. Fruit rotted delicately in the sun and flies buzzed around the fishmonger's store. Food cooking in charcoal braziers gave off an aroma of chilli and coriander. Malay women in brightly-coloured sarongs bartered for pineapple, papayas and bananas. They laughed and flirted with the vendors, moving around with a sensuous poise. Chinese women shuffled along in wooden sandals with that characteristic wiggle of silk-trousered hips. With its decaying fish, poor sanitation, mangy cats and monsoon-drains; with its heat, dust and flies; with its women, it drew Steve to it like a magnet.

Once out of the market they crossed Jelai Street and strolled along the river bank. Below them were the wide brownish-red waters of the Jelai and on the far bank thick jungle, startlingly green. They watched some Malays bathing in the water near houseboats and Steve wondered whether to go in for a swim himself.

"The river's sluggish near the town," Jock said. "And the Malays use it for everything. I wouldn't risk it."

An army jeep accelerated down Jelai Street, kicking up a cloud of dust and scattering some stray chickens that squawked off in a flurry of feathers.

"Let's go and have a drink," Jock said.

They made their way back through the market to a cafe called Tong Kok's. As they slipped through the beaded curtain at its entrance, the sun was beginning to set, the sky gaudy red, giving the jungle on the far bank a bronze hue. Inside it was cool with a simple fan overhead. They sat at a stone table on the lower floor below the level of the street and ordered beers and bowls of rice. When the rice came they helped themselves to the thick yellowish-brown curry sauce that was kept constantly simmering in a huge blackened pot. Ladled over the rice it was the tastiest meal Steve had had since leaving Singapore.

There were several other soldiers drinking in Tong Kok's and Jock told him something about each. "That black-haired bloke," he said. "That's Joe Pierce – he's in the Catering Corps and the guy next to him with the broad shoulders and babyface is Geordie Hood. He's in love with one of the Malay girls who comes in here all the time."

"Who's the other guy?"

"That's Dave Dorman. A bit of a dark horse, Dave," Jock said. "Always staying out of camp, always with some woman or other from the town. But he never says much to anyone. Never boasts about it in camp and keeps himself to himself. A bit of a loner, but the local women seem to like him."

Steve watched him, intrigued. Slim, medium-height, darkhaired with a smile that Steve could see might make him attractive to women, he seemed to speak fluent Malay which was a huge bonus. Steve himself decided he'd have to learn the language too.

They ordered more beer. It was ice-cold. Steve watched it frost up the glass. A plump Chinese woman shuffled around the place, sweeping the stone floor and chasing out some stray cat. She wore a faded blue tunic over black trousers and her bronzed face had an expression of permanent ill-temper. Outside the sunset faded in a mass of reds and golds. Soon it was dark except for the paraffin lamps and the candles of the cafe. It had electricity but the power was unpredictable.

Two women entered the cafe. Swathed tightly in sarongs, they undulated towards the backroom and sat down with Pierce, Dorman and Hood. "The older one," Jock said, "the big woman is called Bongah. She's a dominating character who bosses the other girls around. They call her *mother*. Perhaps because she's got a couple of kids on one of the houseboats near the creek."

"The matriarch," Steve said. "Have you been with her?"

"No, I never go with the local women," Jock said. "But I talk to them when I'm in Tong Kok's."

Steve glanced over at Bongah. She was in her thirties, still attractive, but her companion, Endal, was much more so. No older than Steve himself, she was pretty in a soft sensual way. She was sitting next to Geordie, chattering away merrily in Malay.

"That's the girl Geordie's in love with," Jock said. "He's nuts about her."

"Well, she *is* attractive."

"Yeh, but he wants to marry her and that's crazy – they're all whores who come in here."

Steve watched Bongah. She was beginning to behave in a haughty manner, haranguing the soldiers in a jumbled but colourful mixture of army slang and bazaar Malay. Suddenly her tone changed to a whine

97

as she began a catalogue of recent misfortunes. "Eh you!" she shouted to the soldiers when her recitation had finished. "Buy me beer. Come on. Quick."

"Buy it yourself," Pierce said.

"You no bloody good. You wank, wank, wank, you fucking no-good wanker." The soldiers began to laugh. "Buy me beer," Bongah said turning to Jock and Steve.

"OK," Steve said and ordered two large beers. The Chinese woman shuffled over with the drinks, giving them all a look of profound contempt. Bongah smiled smugly and looked at them as if they were total idiots.

"She thinks she's a hardcase," Pierce said. "Take no notice."

"Do you know what her name means in Malay?" Geordie asked.

"What?"

"Beautiful flower."

"What you say?" Bongah said, picking up on the conversation. "Speak Malayu, I not understand you." Geordie and Pierce were still laughing. "Why you laugh? You plenty funny with me."

"You plenty funny," Pierce said. "Petal." Bongah screwed up her face, snorted and made as if to slap him. "You buy me 'nother beer," she said instead.

"I'll get you a beer," Geordie said. "Four more Tigers," he called to the proprietor. Sitting next to him, Endal smiled blandly.

Two more women appeared in the doorway. Jock told Steve their names. One was Aissa, half-Chinese, half-Malay, no more than sixteen or seventeen, a plump girl with a slap-stick sense of humour. With her was One-Eye so called because she wore a black patch over her left eye which the soldiers assumed was missing.

Steve had a couple more beers with the women, then Bongah left. Pierce began teasing Aissa, something Steve doubted he would have done had Bongah remained.

"What happened when you went to hospital?" he asked innocuously enough.

"*Saya pergi* hospital," Aissa began. "'jections, 'jections, *inila*." She pointed to her plump bottom giggling. Pierce immediately gave it a sharp slap and Aissa wriggled away in a paroxysm of laughter. Then

Pierce tried to pull her onto his lap, but she ducked out of his reach still chuckling. They ordered yet more beer. Through the haze of smoke, One-Eye's black patch seemed to glint enigmatically in the flickering of the oil-lamp, but her face looked crumpled and sallow in the pallid light.

"Come on, let's get back to camp," Jock suggested.

It was still quite early, but there was a curfew in Kuala Lipis which many soldiers disregarded. Not Jock, however, he liked to keep within the law. Outside they went back down the Chinese market for a last look at the river and the black jungle on its far bank. As they strolled along Jelai Street, they saw Bongah on the far side. She was shouting and screaming while a bullet-headed soldier was trying to drag her in the direction of town. Everytime she struggled and attempted to break free from his grasp, he slapped her across the head or face.

"What the hell's going on?" Steve said. "Let's go and help her."

"Leave it," Jock said. "That's Robbo. He's not one to mess about with especially when he's drunk. He's a dangerous character. He'll half-kill you if you interfere."

"Come on," Steve said. "We can't let him beat the shit out of the woman like that." Without waiting for Jock he dashed across the road. "What the fuck's going on?" he said. "Leave her alone." Robbo turned and looked at him with an expression of incredulity and menacing contempt.

"And who the fuck are you?" he said in a broad Glaswegian accent. "I can see you dunno know who you're talking to."

By this time he'd loosened his grip on Bongah who tore free and was off, running as fast as her sarong would allow towards the river bank. Robbo turned and began to chase her. "I'll settle up with you later," he said to Steve. "You fuckin' interferin' Sassenach."

"Let's go," Jock kept saying. "For Christ's sake, leave him be, he'll half-kill you."

Bongah and Robbo had disappeared into the darkness of the jungle that straggled up the bank. Steve felt certain she'd got away from Robbo along the bank above the houseboats.

"You're a damn fool," Jock said.

"What do you mean?"

"He's about the most vicious psychopath in camp. No one fucks him about and gets away with it, I'm telling you. He's notorious and you've made an enemy of him. He won't forget just because he's pissed."

"Don't worry, Jock, I can handle myself."

"He's twice your size," Jock said. "And ten times more vicious than you could ever be. Even the officers treat him with caution."

"Who exactly is he then?"

"He's just a fucking lance-corporal in the MT section. A driver from Glasgow – my city – but there's no-one in camp who's ever beaten him in a fight. And he goes around with two or three others who're similar. Everyone calls him Robbo, but his actual name, ironically, is Robert Bruce."

They were approaching the police check-point by the railway track. A Malay policeman smiled and waved. They crossed over the lines and began walking up the narrow lane with scrub jungle either side. The night was warm; the sound of insects loud. Rounding a corner they saw the dark squat shape of a figure standing in front of them at the roadside.

"Oh God!" Jock said. "It's Robbo."

"I'll talk to him."

Suddenly Robbo ran towards them, moving fast for a heavy man. Jock backed away but Steve carried on walking. Robbo came up with a rush and grabbed him by the shirt.

"Get your hands off me," Steve said.

"Who the fuck are you, you little shit?" He stank of stale beer and as he spoke little gobs of spittle peppered Steve's face.

"Take your fucking hands off me."

"You must think you're a chivalrous little fucker," Robbo muttered. "I was fixing to fuck that fucking whoor when you interfered. You fucked up my fuck, you bastard."

Steve smiled and pushed him off. "It looked more like attempted rape to me."

Naïvely, Steve stood in front of him, face to face. Suddenly, quite unexpectedly, Robbo head-butted him. It happened so quickly he had no time to retaliate. He felt a dull pain and crumpled to the floor. It was the first time he'd encountered the head-butt. Sitting up on the ground, blood pouring from his nose, he saw the light-formation of a jeep coming towards them.

"You better fuck off, Robbo," Jock said. "That's the MPs coming." Robbo disappeared into the shadows of the jungle. The jeep came to a stop. It *was* the MPs who patrolled the town after nightfall.

"What's up, soldier?" one of them shouted.

"It's all right," Jock said. "He's been in a bit of a scrap, but he's OK." Steve was back on his feet, a bit dazed, having already checked that his nose was unbroken and his front teeth intact.

"Are you OK?" the MP asked, shining his torch in Steve's face. "You're going to have a black-eye, I reckon. God knows why you young idiots want to fight with each other. Anyway, smarten yourselves up and get back to camp."

No-one in the office the next morning remarked upon his appearance although his face was a bit bruised. "I'd keep well clear of Robbo in future," Jock advised him. "He won't touch me because I'm from Glasgow too. He's a sentimentalist, but he despises all Sassenachs."

On his way to the canteen Steve saw Robbo working on a jeep in the MT square. Stripped to the waist, covered in oily marks, his skin red from the sun, he was certainly a burly individual, not more than five-nine in height, but about fifteen stone in weight. Steve was two or three inches shorter and about five-stone lighter. Speed could help, but perhaps not enough, he thought. Even if he could get two or three punches in, he wasn't sure he could deck him, let alone knock him out. As he was fantasising about just this, Robbo noticed him, picked up a wrench and jogged over. Steve continued on his way, but Robbo confronted him, his stance aggressive, hands loosely at his side. Crewcutted, he looked remarkably ugly, Steve thought, like a fucking gorilla – insulting a species.

"Thought you'd look worse than you do," he said.

"No thanks to you."

"Look, I'm sorry," Robbo added. "I shouldn't have butted you like that but I get mad quickly – and you fucked things up for me."

"I'd been chatting to that woman about ten minutes before I saw you. You can't go round beating up on women."

101

"Ach! She's only a whoor," Robbo said.

"That's beside the point."

"She's a tough cookie, that one, believe me. She didn't want to go with me so I was trying to persuade her."

"Ten bucks would have done that."

"I never pay for it," Robbo said puritanically. "Anyways, I'm sorry I lost my rag."

"Forget it."

"If you're ever in trouble, give me a shout. No one fucks around with me here."

With a quick smile Robbo was off. He was a complete arsehole, Steve thought, but had detected a sneaky admiration in his attitude. He knew a bit about bully boys. Whatever happened you had to stand up to them. To back off was fatal.

One night, a week later, Steve met Bongah in Kuala Lipis and she invited him back to Batu Kurap. He'd drunk enough beer to accept and she only wanted five dollars. According to Jock, there were dangers in staying out of camp: rumours of terrorists in the area and in theory anyone out after curfew could be arrested by the police. But the only danger, Steve worried about, was being discovered absent in a bedcheck at camp.

He followed her down the lane out of town. They crossed the railway track, passed the Police HQ, then branched off along a narrow path that was extremely muddy from recent rain. As they were in almost total darkness, he floundered blindly behind her swaying sarong-clad figure. The area was low-lying, swampy. Palm trees loomed up out of the darkness. The odd orange lamp flickered from some hut. He knew the MPs rarely visited the place at night. Unless you were with someone who knew the way blindfold it meant a jaunt through swamp and an occasional stumble up to the knees in muddy water. But Bongah knew the track well and Steve stuck close behind her. Individual huts loomed ahead and pale moonlight illumined patches of gleaming water.

They crossed a stream by means of precariously-balanced stepping-stones and arrived in the kampong. Dogs began to bark and one kept

Medal for Malaya

up a continuous whine. He heard scuffling in the undergrowth and the stifled cry of a child somewhere; then they reached her hut. She fumbled with a key and opened the door. Inside she lit a paraffin lamp and the room's features began to emerge.

The floor was baked mud. Old newspapers and sarongs draped the walls. An ancient bedstead staggered in rickety fashion against the far corner and a flower-patterned sarong was thrown over a mattress. Cramped into the remaining space was a bamboo chair piled with clothes, a stack of cooking utensils and a rattan table. The smell of spices lingered in the room. Asleep in a cot on the floor, separated by a partition, were Bongah's two children.

Bongah slipped out of her sarong and beckoned him to join her on the mattress. For a moment or two before she extinguished the lamp he saw her somewhat matronly figure. She wasn't pretty, nor young, but felt good in the darkness, especially as he'd not held a woman's body since leaving Singapore, several weeks before.

He left her at dawn and started back to camp. He needed to be there before the six-thirty bed-check. It was easier finding his way to the road in the first flush of sunrise. He'd left her half-asleep, naked on the mattress as the grey light filtered into the hut through chinks in the thatch. Above the hills the sky was a deep red. A fine mist curled round the palms in the kampong. The world seemed motionless, transformed. He strolled back to camp at a leisurely pace, the ground underfoot sodden with dew. He could see the river like a thread of mercury below him and in the distance the mauve shimmer of the mountains.

Chapter 8

A few weeks after arriving in Kuala Lipis, Steve discovered that he'd got another urethral discharge. It was only slight and he kept hoping it would disappear of its own accord. He wondered whether it was a relapse or whether he'd contracted it from Salmah, or the Chinese girl on his last night in Singapore, or even Bongah. He hesitated to report sick immediately, but eventually saw the MO, a young lieutenant just out of medical school.

He ordered Steve to report to the Military Hospital in Kinrara near Kuala Lumpur. Steve was delighted as it would give him the opportunity of visiting the city and seeing more of Malaya. Supply convoys left for KL every Friday, returning with stores on the Monday. For the drivers this was a regular part of their duties, but convoys always needed volunteers to man the bren guns on the armoured trucks.

The terrorists were in retreat, short of food, medicine and ammunition. At 18th Infantry Brigade they used to watch the helicopters flying over the jungle dropping leaflets. These urged surrender and offered amnesty, then rehabilitation in specified townships. The terrorists were giving themselves up in droves although the conflict lingered on. There was still the occasional ambush but to Steve the dangers of a convoy patrol seemed minimal. The only live bandit he would ever get to see was one who strolled past the guard-room one afternoon, across the square and straight into the CO's office to surrender.

It was still dark the following Friday morning when the guard making the early calls woke Steve up. He got out of bed, lit a cigarette, then had a quick shower beneath the rusty-looking river-water in the cubicle outside. He packed some extra clothes and notebooks in his small pack and strolled up to the canteen as the first greyish streaks of light were edging out the night. There he had some hot sweet tea and a fried-egg sandwich.

The drivers of the convoy vehicles were revving up their engines in the MT square. Steve drew his bren-gun and boxes of ammunition from the armoury and climbed up into the escort vehicle. He fixed the bren on its swivel, slapped a magazine in the breach, checked that the safety-catch was forward to rapid fire. It was still cool in the early morning so he put on his khaki-green sweater. The other soldier on escort-duty, a young Scottish National Serviceman Steve knew by sight, arrived with his bren and fixed it to the swivel on the back.

A sergeant and an officer came over to check. "Remember," the officer said, "there's a minimum speed-limit on convoys and an ambush is unlikely, but if we do meet one, keep your heads down and only fire at an actual target. You'll see the smoke and flashes that give away the enemy position. Fire at that. Your duties are strictly defensive. Understand?"

"Sir."

There was a short delay. Steve watched the coming-off guard being dismissed; the drivers giving a final check to their vehicles. Stray shouts of command echoed across the square. He could still smell frying fat from the canteen. Cigarette smoke mingled with the mist and the dark green trucks looked drab, utilitarian in the greyish light. Then the convoy started, Steve's truck leading, followed by the three-tonner and the jeep.

Soon they cleared the police barrier at the town's limit and speeded up along a straight stretch of road running parallel to the Lipis River, a tributary of the Jelai. On the raised platform at the front of the armoured-truck, the butt of the bren in the crook of his arm, Steve had an unrestricted view over the steel-plated sides to the river meandering in an easterly direction below. On its far banks the jungle swept down to the water's edge, trailing in the shadows and veiled in a thin gauze of mist. It was cool high up in the truck with the wind rushing through his hair, but exhilarating. He decided to volunteer for as many convoy patrols as possible.

105

They were passing a rubber plantation, miles of symmetrically planted trees where occasional groups of Tamils were already tapping for the resin. Then the road curved in towards the river, crossing it at the village of Benta. Below the suspension bridge some Malays were bathing. He could see others huddled in their sarongs, shivering on the bank. The children, naked and splashing about in the water, looked up and waved. Some of the women, naked to the waist, honey-brown in colour, glanced in their direction and threw kisses at the soldiers. Once through Benta the road straightened out again between low-lying paddy and swamp that seemed to stretch to the mauve line of hills, the red disk of sun was behind them, casting bronze light upon the water. Soon it would be hotter and the last traces of the mist dispersed.

At Raub, lying in the shadow of the mountains to the west, at the edge of the pass, it was still cool and fresh. They had travelled about thirty-five to forty miles and it was only eight-thirty. The convoy drew up in the main street and they all poured into a Chinese cafe. Most of the troops ordered buttered-toast and coffee. Steve had a plate of rice, helping himself to the curry gravy simmering away in the usual big vat. It was savoury and warming after the wind-swept early morning drive from camp.

Half-an-hour later they began the long haul through the mountainous spine of the country, the road spiralling in wide curves through the pass. Tall forest, glistening and redolent, sloped away below and above them. The hills were covered in jungle and had the rounded shape of green breasts. As they climbed higher the air became cooler. At each bend they slowed almost to a standstill and at such points Steve could glimpse the road winding below like a sliver of tinfoil that seemed to fashion the mountains into tiers. The vegetation was a spectacularly-vivid green.

At the summit of the pass, the four-and-a-half thousand feet high Pine Tree Hill to their left and Bukit Fraser, a colonial rest-house signposted to their right, there was a cold nip in the air and a panoramic view of rolling jungle-softened hills that changed from green to mauve, the Cameron Highlands in the distance to the north.

On the journey down, travelling south-west, they crossed innumerable streams that tumbled and cascaded down over boulders. At a stone-quarry cut into the rock-face a gang of Chinese labourers was working, the women in blue or black pyjama-type clothes and conical hats, lugging the hewn rock with rope and tackle to the waiting lorries. Unlike the Malays, the Chinese flashed them sullen, even hostile glances. At intervals along this stretch were signposts warning travellers of the danger of armed-ambush.

As they descended the air became warmer again, the jungle denser, redolent of ammonia or chlorine, a strange smell that Steve thought must have emanated from decaying vegetation. Suddenly Steve noticed a ripple in the tree-tops some distance away. As the movement became clear he saw that it was made by a troop of monkeys swinging from tree to tree, swarming away from the noise of their engines.

Once emerging from the pass the convoy sped through the military town of Kuala Kuba Bahru and was on a straight stretch running towards the capital. The jungle became sparser. They passed disused tin mines, clusters of kampongs, white chunks of phallic-shaped limestone, Batu Caves, that Steve was told were infested with snakes. Soon the convoy was threading its way through the outskirts of Kuala Lumpur, passed adverts for Tiger Beer and Tiger Balm products, the occasional traffic-lights, then the eastern part of the city.

The Transit Camp was an ugly sprawling barracks on the main road, a couple of miles from the city centre. With the continuous stream of troops passing through it – soldiers on leave, waiting for postings, on convoy duty, just out of hospital or en route for the UK, it was difficult to keep a check on individuals. On arrival, along with the others, Steve drew some bedding and went for a rest.

Later he strolled down the Batu Road into the city centre. It was a warm night, the palms that lined the middle of the street swaying in a faint breeze pungent with spices and, faintly, bad drainage coming from the direction of the Klang River. Murky and canalised it split the city into halves. Once in the centre Steve could see that Kuala Lumpur lay in a shallow bowl surrounded by jungle-clad hills.

He passed the Lucky World and Rainbow Cabaret. To his left he could see the striped minarets of the mosque between tall palms and in front of him the Moorish domes of the Post Office and Central Station. He noticed that the upper section of the Batu Road was dotted with girls, reminding him of Singapore. He went into a Malay restaurant and ordered a nasi goreng. Afterwards he strolled on to the Union Jack Club and had a few beers before returning to the Transit Camp.

Up early on the Saturday morning he caught the truck that ran to and from the hospital at Kinrara. They travelled through the city, then out towards the west along the road to Klang. The hospital lay between the capital and Klang in flat swampy country, not many miles from the Malacca Straits.

Once in the hospital he was directed to the STD at the far end, almost completely isolated from the rest of the place. The medical rooms were temporary huts and the patients lived under canvas erected over duckboards near the perimeter wire. The verandah was raised above the ground as the area was low-lying and often flooded during the monsoons. He waited with several other soldiers until it was his turn to see the MO, Major Jackson. As he'd expected the MO diagnosed NSU. He was given blood-tests, a smear and urine tests, then a shot of streptomycin.

There were two large khaki-green tents and Steve was allotted a bed near the entrance of the far one. Its sides were rolled up during the day so that the soldiers could see out. Steve unpacked his few belongings and went to the ablution area some thirty yards away. It was a square brick-outpost with wash-basins, toilet cubicles and showers. Later some of the inmates in hospital kit – sky-blue pyjamas – introduced themselves. No one asked him what infection he had. They never did. You might volunteer the information, but it was considered bad form to ask.

After lunch he found the library. It was staffed by the Women's Volunteer Service. He found novels by H.E. Bates, Somerset-Maugham and Conrad. He chose three titles and took them to the desk. The officer there appeared impressed by his choice. She chatted to him about authors and books for some minutes. He told her that his favourite English writer was D.H. Lawrence and that he particularly liked American writers, such as Hemingway and

Steinbeck. "That expatriate set-up on the Left Bank in Paris during the twenties fascinates me," he told her.

"Well, in that case I recommend the work of Ford Madox Ford and, of course, James Joyce," she said. It was the first vaguely literary conversation he'd had since his interview by the Field Security officers a few weeks before.

Finally she stamped his books and asked him which ward he was in. When he told her, her attitude changed. Not once after that did she attempt a conversation, dealing with returned books or stamping out new ones in silence. The "tents" as they were called, were not only isolated from the rest of the hospital, but its occupants were ostracised more emphatically than those suffering from TB and malaria.

Steve soon settled into the hospital routine, however, and it was pleasant enough. Every morning he'd slip across to the treatment compound, provide a smear and receive an injection. The rest of the day was his own. He'd sit outside the tent, read books, sunbathe, write in his notebook or pen letters home. But his NSU was proving obstinate and didn't seem to be responding to the antibiotics. After five days on streptomycin, the microscope still revealed evidence of the organism that was causing the problem. He was then prescribed potassium permanganate washes. These were a nuisance. The permanganate solution was a purplish-pink colour and had to be pumped up the urethra by inserting a nozzle and squeezing a tube. It caused an odd ticklish sensation. When he had to piss afterwards, it hurt and the urine had a pinkish tinge.

After a few days of this the MO saw him again. Steve was still positive. He'd now been in hospital almost two weeks and the MO prescribed *sounds*. Steve didn't know what this treatment consisted of, but found out the following morning. Told to lie down on the medical couch, he watched the MO pick up some steel rods. These were of different sizes and shapes like miniature hockey sticks.

"What are you going to do with those?" he asked.

"We insert them via the urethra into your bladder," the MO said. "In an attempt to scrape any pus from the infection. It can be quite effective."

"They look too big," Steve said, his penis retracting into a stubby sliver of flesh at the thought of this ordeal.

"Don't worry, it doesn't hurt," the MO said smiling. He took hold of Steve's penis and pulled it lightly as if it were a bit of rubber, then delicately inserted the rod. He could feel it pushing bluntly forward somewhere inside him. The sensation was like an acute tickling. The MO seemed to wiggle it about a little and as he withdrew it the sensation was similar to that of urinating. Afterwards when he actually needed to piss, the pain was excruciating, urine spraying out in bursts.

The morning afterwards he had to see the MO again, but when he awoke he discovered he'd had a wet dream though he couldn't recall it in any detail. Through the mosquito netting he could see the camp-bed opposite and the rolled-up khaki of the tent. He got up and went for a shower. It was going to be another hot day though it was still cool with a fine mist over the swampy jungle beyond the perimeter-wire. He put on his hospital gown and strolled across to the huts. On the verandah he waited for the RAMC corporal to call his name.

"Let's be having you," he shouted. "Come on in, Revill." Steve went into the treatment room. "OK, drop your pants." He did so and stood, trousers round his ankles, waiting. The orderly got a slide, lifted his penis and squeezed it gently until some mucous appeared, then dabbed it onto the slide, placing a further slide on top of the first, then filed it in a tray. "Urine specimen in this, please." He handed Steve a small container. "The MO will be seeing you at ten o'clock," he said.

"Will I be discharged today?"

"Depends upon the result of the slide. If you're free from infection, yes."

He went back to the tents, got his knife and fork and went to the canteen for breakfast. On his way back he called at the library and changed his books. He took out a couple of Conrad novels, winking at the WVS officer on duty. She didn't respond.

At ten o'clock he was in front of Major Jackson who was generally reassuring and phlegmatic, but occasionally employed an acerbic turn of phrase.

110

"Revill," he said. "I'm really most annoyed with you."
"Sir?"
"Your smear this morning," he went on smiling a little. "I could see nothing but spermatozoa swimming around. You must have been masturbating."
"No, I haven't, Sir. Honestly."
"How do you account for it then?"
"I had a nocturnal emission – a wet dream, just before I woke up."
"Well, we'll just have to give you a prostate massage," he said still smiling.

Once again he had to slip out of his trousers, bend forward as ordered, resting his hands upon a chair, legs wide apart while the MO put on a rubber glove smeared in vaseline and inserted his finger with some finesse into Steve's anus. It was a strange sensation, almost pleasurable, but when contact was made with the prostate became too acute. Within seconds some mucous appeared on the tip of his penis which the orderly neatly captured on a slide.

"I hope we'll be able to discharge you in a few days," the MO said, examining the slide under his microscope. "It's still not completely clear so I'm going to put you on a five-day course of a newish antibiotic, aureomycin. If you're clear at the end of that time you'll be sent back to your unit to report for duty."

After lunch that day Steve got a blanket from his bed and stretched out on the coarse grass beside the tents. He took his cigarettes, the Conrad novel, *Lord Jim*, and lay back reading. The sun was hot, but he was already nicely tanned. Distracted momentarily, he watched a gecko hunting insects on the side of the tent. Geckos fascinated him: their patience, the sudden pounce, tongue flicking out and the fly gone in a quick flash of green.

The pervasive sound of banal songs issued from a radio in the tent and an African soldier from the Queen's African Rifles was walking obsessively round the perimeter fifty yards away. With the heat and inactivity, a mood of lassitude seemed to descend upon the patients in the tents. Even the sporadic bursts of ribaldry had ceased.

"*Moon above Malaya ...*" sang some woman over the radio. "*Shine down on my sampan ... All alone in a bamboo hut/No one to care if I'm kissing you but/the moon above Malaya ...*"

An hour later he was disturbed by some gruff comments from a group of patients playing cards. They were looking towards the treatment area. Escorted by two orderlies, each supporting him with an arm, limped a small Gurkha soldier. In obvious pain he approached the tents.

"Fucking hell!" someone said. "What the fuck's wrong with him?"

"Fuck knows!" his companion said.

The Gurkha hobbled towards the tents. Inside he was shown to a spare bed and helped onto the mattress where he lay comatose, eyes closed, neither talking nor displaying any emotion.

"What's up with him, Corporal?" someone asked.

"The same as you blokes."

"Which disease, for Christ's sake?"

"I'm not allowed to divulge that."

Having seen the Gurkha safely installed the orderlies returned to the medical centre, ignoring the curiosity of the other patients. Later that afternoon Steve went into the office to have a chat with the Records clerk. Since he'd been in hospital longer than most he had on occasion helped him sort and file documents. He'd enjoyed it and had learned something. A few of the regular soldiers who had passed through Kinrara had lengthy records of venereal infection. One sergeant, not long discharged, who had been through World War II and Korea had contracted syphilis in 1937, in Nairobi. Steve was shocked to discover that he'd been treated with arsenic and bismuth. He discovered too that there had been a huge STD outside Rome at the end of the War. Thousands of Allied troops there had been some of the first patients to be treated with penicillin.

"What's the Gurkha got?" he asked offering the clerk a cigarette.

"Gonorrhea."

"Why was he limping?"

"He's evidently had it for over two years."

"Jesus!"

"Never reported sick. He was on patrol in the jungle and they had to helicopter him out. I don't think he understands what's wrong now. He doesn't seem to know when he contracted it, nor from whom – or he won't tell us. We've got to try and contact his wife, but she's in Nepal."

"But why the limp though?"

"Gonoccocal arthritis. That's when the bacteria attack the joints."

"Is it curable?"

"He'll probably be out of here before you are. It all depends upon how much damage has been done already, but we can cure the gonorrhea itself, no problem."

Later Steve strolled across to the canteen for tea and sandwiches, then back to his blanket and the sun. Thank God, for antibiotics, he thought. There didn't seem to be anything romantic about dying of syphilis or any other sexually transmitted disease although, thinking of Maupassant, Gauguin, Lautrec and other 19th century luminaries, he'd once vaguely thought so.

At six he watched the sun set over the stunted jungle in the distance, the sky turning gold, then blood-red and finally darkening with streaks of pink and green lingering in the west. Despite the hospital and the Army he was besotted with Malaya itself; there was something so romantically exotic about the place. At times he felt that he didn't want to return to the grey austerity of Britain. He wondered whether he could get discharged in Malaya and sometimes considered the possibility of signing-on for a further three years. He was twenty; he could handle the Army now. What was there in Birmingham? The university, a job? He'd be better off in the Far East, in the Army.

Nights were the worst in hospital, in the tents. There was little to do, only the radio, cards, books. Restlessness came like a psychic prickly-heat. There were dances in the main part of the hospital, but the STD patients were barred. The nights were warm, humid and the patients could see the red glow of Kuala Lumpur some miles away, mocking them.

Coming from the canteen one evening, Steve had seen a nurse and orderly embracing near the perimeter. It was a clear night with a lemon moon. The couple were etched in silhouette between postcard-palms. Steve smiled to himself and felt a twinge of nostalgia as memories returned. They compounded his restlessness. Still he'd probably be discharged by the end of the week – back to normal army life, if barrack-room life could be described as normal.

There were compensations, of course, to army life, he thought. You might be lonely, but you were never actually alone. If you wanted companionship it was available. There was an egalitarian lack of selectivity in your friendships, but few demands either. Within a framework of discipline there was also a degree of freedom. You were relatively free of responsibility. You could blow your wages in a single night and still eat for the rest of the week, bum a few cigs and even cadge a drink or two. It was a rough sort of life, but you were also protected. Soldiers weren't critical either. Only if you broke the unwritten code and made things worse for everyone were you shunned or rejected.

Lying awake on his cot, cosy beneath the green canopy, but unable to see through the far side of the tent, Steve began to anticipate his discharge. If he got out the following Saturday there wouldn't be any transport to Lipis until the supply convoy left on the Monday, so he would have two days in KL. There would be women in the city and he could break this enforced spell of celibacy. He'd be free from infection and there was, as soldiers said, none so pure as the purified. If he went with a woman he'd he taking another risk, but everything you did involved risk. He could be ambushed, shot, even killed on the way back to Lipis. What was the risk of a dose in comparison? A nuisance, that was all. It was all a question of luck anyway. Certainly there was no natural justice in such matters.

A friend of his in camp, a cipher-operator and a conscientious soldier with a wife back in Derby, or Nottingham, who never went with women in town, had been chosen to represent the 18th Infantry Brigade on a two-week cruise in the South China Sea – a sort of prize awarded to model soldiers. In Sarawak, or some such place, he'd got drunk and had his only lapse in eighteen months. Three weeks later he noticed a chancre. Syphilis was diagnosed. When he told Steve, he was almost in tears. He believed that he'd ruined his marriage. The MO

Medal for Malaya

had told him that it would be two years before he could be one-hundred percent sure of being cured.

"One shot of penicillin and you're probably cured," Steve said to reassure him. "And you've had about twenty-thousand units of the stuff by now. So don't let it worry you."

"You've got no particular medical knowledge, so how do you know?"

"The authorities try to scare you," Steve said. "As they did on the ship coming over."

Steve was glad he wasn't married, nor had a girlfriend back home, not a steady one at least. After being in hospital twice he didn't give a damn about a dose – or so he tried to tell himself. As the character, Rinaldi, had said in *Farewell to Arms*, it was an "industrial accident." The Army had changed him in that respect; he was less sensitive; able to face risk, or danger with a little more panache because of that. Actually becoming a *good* soldier in military terms, so paradox that. Or perhaps he was merely justifying his future conduct in advance. He'd been in hospital a month. The very thought of a woman was sufficient to arouse him. A sure sign that he was well on the way to complete recovery, both of his health and self-esteem.

He put out his cigarette. Someone else in the tents was still awake. He could see the red pinpoint from *his* cigarette. The sound of sentimental music floated over from the main part of the hospital. Three days and he'd be out – with the freedom of Kuala Lumpur, the key to the city, he thought, smiling to himself.

In fact it was a further seven days before he was finally discharged. "Just remember," the MO said, "no sex for three months and no alcohol. Come back each month for a check-up."

"Sir"

He packed his kit, said goodbye to several acquaintances and walked with a spring in his step to the main gates. There he waited for a jeep or an ambulance to take him to the Transit Camp.

As they raced towards the city in the midday heat he could almost smell the aroma of the place. After nearly six weeks the mere smells were intoxicating. They crossed the Klang River, the minarets of the

115

mosque to his right; raced up the Batu Road with its palm trees, bars and restaurants to the Transit Camp. There he met some soldiers down from Lipis on the Friday convoy. He'd return with them Monday. In the meantime there were forty-odd hours in Kuala Lumpur.

Chapter 9

Back in Kuala Lipis Steve resumed working in the office with Jock Robertson, poring over Queen's Regulations, filing and pasting in amendments. There still wasn't enough work for the two of them although they typed up daily orders and ran errands for the CO. There was the occasional guard-duty when armed with fifty rounds of ammo they did two-hour stints watching the lane that led to camp. If the routine was monotonous, Steve consoled himself with the thought that he'd have to go to KL once a month for a check-up and could volunteer for convoy-patrols as well. He also played rugby for 18th Infantry Brigade which meant trips to other units nearby.

One Wednesday afternoon they played a Malayan school at Benta. The Malays were fast and skilful, but the Brigade managed to win. Playing at fly-half Steve dummied a pass, nipped through a gap and scored a try that looked spectacular, but in fact was lucky as he'd only noticed the gap at the last moment. Early in the second half he hurt his ankle and switched to the wing. After that he didn't see too much of the ball as the heat slowed down the pace. It was always the same in the tropics. They would sweat freely for the first half-hour, then begin to feel dehydrated, slightly feverish running up and down, keeping behind the ball. But the game over, showered and glowing from the exercise, travelling back in the truck, the team felt tired, but exhilarated.

It was almost dark and their convoy was speeding along a straight stretch of tarmac road raised above rice paddy. Crouched with his Mark V rifle, fifty rounds of ammunition in a bandolier round his waist, Steve gazed at the landscape through the back of the truck. In the distance were the jungle-rounded mountains, mauve against the setting sun, and on both sides were miles of gleaming water, green shoots of rice peeping above it. Fringing the cultivated strips was the darker green of the jungle. Every so often they passed a kampong among tall palms. In the shallow water sarong-clad men and women stooped, picking the rice. At intervals he glimpsed water-buffaloes wallowing in the mud.

The brief twilight had a special clarity, but it darkened quickly enough, leaving only a red flush in the west. The armoured truck in the rear had switched on its headlights. He watched their beams and the dark silhouette of a soldier behind the bren above the cabin.

Half-an-hour passed. They were still travelling between paddy fields, but the jungle was closing-in ahead. It was now pitch black and the jubilant rugby players, soldiers again, had stopped singing. A cigarette or two glowed in the shadows of the truck. A match flared and momentarily illumined a pallid face and the gleam of a rifle, then flickered out. Tall trees were weird shapes, then gone. The water of the paddy showed palely though the moon hadn't yet risen. In twenty minutes, Steve thought, they'd be back in camp for supper and a beer or two in the NAAFI.

Suddenly, however, the convoy braked to a halt. Once the engines were silent the troops could hear the insects – incessant, tuneless, somewhat eerie: cicadas, bull-frogs, fireflies, beetles. Wondering why they'd stopped, Steve felt a certain trepidation.

The lieutenant and the warrant-officer who had been in the jeep leading the convoy came round to the back of the truck. The lieutenant had his revolver out and the WO cradled a sten-gun.

"Out, all of you," the WO said in an urgent voice. "Into the cover of the monsoon ditch."

"Keep your rifles dry," the lieutenant added.

"What's up, Sir?"

"There's a tree across the road a bit higher up."

"Hurry! Move yourselves," the WO shouted.

Steve had not seen troops shift so quickly for a long time. They scrambled over the tailboard of the truck and ran towards the ditch. One or two plunged as if at a swimming-pool straight into the sludge below the road. Steve climbed down more circumspectly, remembering to hold his rifle aloft to keep it dry. Within seconds they were all crouched down, up to their thighs in tepid, almost comforting, soupy water. Steve was absolutely sure they'd run into an ambush. Some distance up the road he could make out the black mass of an obstacle across it. The noise of the insects seemed even louder, but somehow emphasised the surrounding silence. At any moment he expected to hear a staccato burst of automatic fire from the jungle. His heart was thudding against the wrist that held his rifle close to his body. Ambushes were rare but they still happened. He'd read about them in documents that came into the office for the CO.

Protected by the side of the stationary truck two shadowy figures moved towards them. "All right, you men," the WO said in a hoarse, but imperative whisper. "I want some volunteers to help remove the tree. Move. Quick!"

No one budged. Their emergence would surely be the moment that the terrorists were waiting for. The WO peered short-sightedly into the shadows of the ditch. "Come on, you wankers," he said. "Move!" The soldier next to Steve snuggled even lower and deeper into the sludge. Peering forwards Steve could see the WO tapping a soldier on the shoulder, then helping him up. "You, yes you, and you," he muttered as he moved along the bank. Steve watched half-a-dozen crawl reluctantly back into the road and move forward at a crouching run. He could hear the water squelching in their boots. Then there was silence again. With the men hauling away at the obstacle in the darkness he expected to hear the rattle of rifle-fire, but nothing happened. Five, perhaps ten minutes elapsed, then the lieutenant came trotting back.

"All right," he said. "Get back in the truck. Quick."

There was another scramble as they clambered, dripping, up the side of the ditch, cutting hands on the sharp reeds, grabbing tufts of grass for leverage, running to the back of the truck, hurling themselves up and over the tailboard. In a few minutes everyone was back in the safety of the lorry. Someone shouted at the front of the convoy and they moved off, the sound of engines a comfort. As they passed the spot where the tree had been, Steve strained his eyes towards the darkness, but could see no movement, nothing.

"Must have been a fucking ambush," someone said. "At least we were set up for one."

"They were there all right," another said. "Just not worth their while – a convoy carrying only troops."

"They're only after fucking supplies."

"The bastards must have fucked off when they saw us."

Recalling the fear and panic they'd displayed, a little ashamed now, everyone laughed, needing to relieve the tension, putting the incident into perspective.

"I don't think there was an ambush at all," Steve said. "It was some sort of practical joke."

"Lieutenant What's-his-name didn't think so. He was shit-scared, you could see that."

"And Sergeant Walton?"

"Not him, he's a Korean veteran."

"He was shitting himself."

"Come on," Steve said. "We all were."

Cigarettes were lit. The conversation petered out. Soon they were in the outskirts of Kuala Lipis, past the police road-block, roaring triumphantly up the dark lane to camp. The bandits, if there had been any, must have estimated the value of shooting-up a convoy of troops, figured it not worth their while and dissolved back into the jungle. The guerrilla war had become more a test of nerves and strategy than anything else. There had been little real risk, Steve decided, not in such a convoy. But in the NAAFI that night a taste of the fear he'd felt still lingered.

Chapter 10

It was Thursday, paynight, but Steve couldn't go into Kuala Lipis as he was duty clerk. Instead he strolled up the muddy path that led to the NAAFI. There he ordered a nasi goreng and a Tiger beer. He took them outside and sat at a table by himself on the verandah. When he'd finished eating, he lit a cigarette from his free-issue tin of fifty Senior Service, sipped his beer and stared out across the parade square.

Beyond the low-built thatched structure of Brigade HQ were the low-lying jungle-covered hills, black now in silhouette. There was a gibbous moon throwing a phosphorescent light over the camp. In front of HQ two palms were etched against a paler sky, their fronds hanging motionless. Despite the loud voices and sporadic laughter from the NAAFI he could hear the buzz of insects. Every so often a firefly flickered in the nearby bushes like a green jewel.

He went back into the NAAFI for another beer. Outside again he was joined by Geordie Hood, the teleprinter operator, and Jock Robertson. They chatted for a while, but soon left for town.

At a nearby table four of the Glaswegian drivers were drinking. They were a tough lot, the drivers, practically a law unto themselves. One night, Steve recalled, a bunch of them had bundled the RAEC sergeant and the guard commander into the unit cells when they'd tried to clear the NAAFI at closing time. The act was tantamount to mutiny and had looked as if it could develop into a nasty incident. The ringleader, an even burlier version of Robbo, Jock Lee, had been shouting and haranguing the crowd of drunken soldiers in front of the guard-room, inciting them to join him and march down to the Officers Mess to make a complaint against the RAEC sergeant. Fortunately, someone had already phoned the Mess and a Captain Fitzgerald, a big dark-haired Irish officer, came up to mediate. He called upon Lee to meet him in the lane outside camp to discuss the situation. The soldiers thought they were going to fight it out between them for Fitzgerald was reputed to be a bit of a hardcase himself. Within a few minutes, however, Lee who had accepted the invitation, re-emerged with the Captain. Together they strolled back to the guard-room, not actually arm in arm, but laughing and joking. As if they were close friends, the two of them persuaded the crowd to disperse, releasing the sergeant and guard commander from the cells. The incident was over and no further action was taken. The "mutiny," as it was later called, became a minor legend in the annals of the camp.

Among the drivers at the table near Steve's were both Robbo and Jock Lee. Steve had already had a second brush with Robbo. A quiet, almost withdrawn character who got on with his work and hardly spoke to anyone, Robbo was unpredictable; drunk, he erupted quickly into violence.

Not long before Steve had been drinking in Tong Kok's with a group of the Malay women when a lance-jack from the Hussars tried to pick a fight with him. He'd grabbed a beer bottle, smashed it down on the table and come at Steve with the jagged top. Broken glass in the face was not a prospect Steve relished. He leaped up, ran to the far side of the room, picked up a stool and used it as a shield. At that moment Robbo, who'd witnessed the incident from the entrance, moving with a speed that belied his bulk, grabbed the Hussar's arm and locked him with his other hand round the throat. Twisting the arm into a half-nelson, he forced the Hussar to drop the bottle-top.

"You daft Sassenach," he said, "What's up with you? If you've got to fight, use your fists."

"OK, OK," the Hussar said, cooling down, scared of Robbo. "It's just that I don't like that arsehole's face." He indicated Steve. "He's too greedy with the women."

"Stupid bastard!" Robbo said. "Steve's not a fighter, he's a lady's man – a pretty boy. Sit down and calm down or you'll have me to deal with."

"I'll take him on anytime with the gloves," Steve said, humiliated by Robbo's description.

Medal for Malaya

"Ach! Sit down, pretty boy," Robbo said. "You don't want to ruin your good looks."

Steve wasn't sure whether Robbo had become an ally or whether this was some manipulative strategy. He disliked his ironic reference to his "pretty looks," but in another sense he was right. He wasn't a fighter, not in the same way some of these Scottish bastards were, ready to use anything to hand. He only knew how to box, Queensbury rules, although he was learning that this was not enough. Physical violence worried him unless it was controlled in the ring or on the rugby field. But his cowardice, or what he imagined might be interpreted as cowardice, nagged at him.

Sitting in the NAAFI, thinking about that incident, he wondered what Robbo's motive had been, coming to his assistance. It was out-of-character, but at the same time disarming. He went into the NAAFI for his third beer. As he sat down again Robbo called to him. "Heh, Stevey boy, come over here and join us. Have a drink on me."

Steve went over to their table. The drivers were all grinning which made him uneasy. He sensed trouble in some guise or another.

"Make yourself comfortable," Robbo said in an almost-menacing tone. "He's as pretty as a lass, isn't he?" he added, turning to the others. They laughed, ugly bastards all of them, Steve thought, the camp's hardcases. Ross had just spent twenty-eight days in the Military Corrective Establishment. During that month he'd spent nine days on a ration of bread-and-water. He'd lost weight. He looked gaunt, wolfish, tougher than ever, older than his years – as did the others, their faces bloated with beer.

"He's a bit of a ladies' man, our Stevey," Robbo said. "A bit of a knight errant, if that's the right expression."

"No, not me," Steve said.

"Stuck his nose in when I was fixing a screw with that bitch, Bongah."

"I was under the impression you were beating her up."

"Beating her up!" Robbo laughed. "She loves it. She loves being slapped around a bit."

"Most of those bitches do," Ross said.

"Bullshit!" Steve exclaimed.

123

"Ah Stevey knows how to treat them," Robbo said, "don't you, Stevey? He's always with one or other of the bitches."

"Dirty little fucker," Lee said. "Dipping your wick in those poxed-up cows."

Steve finished his beer and stood up. The drift of the conversation disgusted him. "I'm off to the bashas," he said. "See you." But Robbo grabbed him with his muscular arm and pulled him onto his knee. "Sit down," he said. "There's no hurry." Steve tried to move but Robbo held him down, pinning his arms. He could feel the tension in his thigh, then the intrusion of Robbo's free hand under his buttocks.

"Nice bit of bum," he said. "Shapely as a lassie's. Come on, Blondie, any port in a storm eh?"

Once again Steve tried to wrench free, but Robbo's grip was too firm. He could smell his breath on his cheek as Robbo tried to nuzzle closer.

"You're a nice looking lad," Robbo said. "And I can see right through you. I know exactly what you want. I've seen you looking at me in the showers."

"Fuck off!" Steve said. "I only like women. I'm not a queer."

"What's the difference?" Robbo said and laughed unpleasantly. "A bit of arse is as good as a bit of cunt anytime."

A figure appeared in the doorway of the darkened NAAFI. It was the duty-sergeant. Robbo's grip immediately relaxed and Steve broke away from him. "Come on, chaps," the sergeant said. "It's gone eleven." He came up to the table. "Heh, Robbo, I want a chat with you. About that jeep. Have you got it running yet?"

Steve took advantage of the interruption and walked off towards the bashas. He was halted by the guard, identified himself, then quickened his pace down the path. Fucking bastard, that Robbo, he was thinking. He's a bloody queer. Fuck him! Then it began to make sense: his treatment of Bongah, his contempt for women; or was it a feeling of power that gave him a hard-on?

Halfway down to the bashas Robbo jumped him from the bordering fringe of jungle. Steve had caught a glimpse of shadowy movement to his left, and tried to run, but Robbo dived, got hold of his leg, then together they crashed to the ground. In seconds Steve was flat on his face with Robbo's fifteen-stone on top of him. With one hand Robbo pushed his face into the soft earth. With the other he was trying to tear off his jungle-green trousers. As Steve struggled, Robbo clouted the back of his head with a fist. Half-stunned by the blows Steve felt the denim material give way. Within seconds his trousers were round his ankles, cool air on his thighs. Ineffectually he tried to push Robbo away, but was pinned down by his sheer bulk.

"Get the fuck off me!" he muttered and Robbo thumped him on the side of his head. "We'll both be in the shit if anyone comes." Another blow caught him on the cheek. He felt the flimsy army-issue underpants tear, then Robbo's stubby hard-on prodding blindly at the cheeks of his buttocks. Any moment he expected to feel the pain of penetration, but quite suddenly Robbo's weight was gone. Steve scrambled up, his trousers round his ankles. Standing silently on the bank above them, small and impassive, aiming his rifle in their direction, was one of the little Gurkha guards who had come across to investigate the scuffle.

Robbo grinned for a moment at the Gurkha, who rammed a round up the breach with an ominous sound, then trotted off towards the bashas, still smiling sheepishly. Steve dusted himself down and tentatively felt the bruises on his face.

"Thanks," he said, but the Gurkha neither smiled nor acknowledged the comment. Skirting the edge of the jungle, Steve found his way by a circuitous route to the basha and safe under his mosquito net, his bayonet under the pillow, lit a cigarette and smoked greedily.

Working in the office the following morning Steve was distracted by a tap at the window frame. He looked up. It was Robbo, leaning against the verandah beckoning him. He went outside.

"Look, man, I'm sorry about last night," he said. "I was fucking pissed."

"That's no fucking excuse."

"You're not going to report it, are you?"

"Of course not. It just better not happen again."

"Ach! Don't be daft. I was drunk, I'm telling you. I'm not a fucking queer."

125

"Nor am I. Just remember that."

"OK, OK," he said grinning. "Someone must have tried it on before, don't kid me."

"They haven't."

"OK, shake hands then," he said. "You're not a bad bloke, quite ballsy for a Sassenach. See you in the NAAFI for a drink, OK? And take care of yourself."

With that vaguely-menacing comment he jumped off the verandah and strolled back towards the MT square – to his oily trucks and spare parts. Steve watched his broad naked back, the big biceps and grease-stained forearms, his reddish skin that never seemed to suntan properly. He went back inside, flinching involuntarily as he recalled the sensation of Robbo's body, the hard paunchy gut, and struggling beneath it the night before. Fucking bastard, he muttered!

To avoid the NAAFI Steve decided to spend his free evenings out of camp in future. He preferred the company of the women in Tong Kok's to the tensions of the Brigade. On Thursday and Friday evenings there were often prolonged card-playing sessions in the bashas. Steve often joined them early on, stayed sober and won a few dollars as most of the others drank heavily. Once he was up a bit he'd leave unobtrusively. Provided winnings were comparatively small no one would notice, or mind if they did.

There was a nucleus of soldiers who would usually turn up in Tong Kok's. Geordie Hood was there as often as money would allow. He was crazy about Endal and wanted to marry her, but had been refused permission by the CO. For once, Steve thought, the CO was absolutely right, but Geordie could neither understand nor accept it. Endal was young and pretty, but was available to any of the soldiers for ten dollars.

One night Steve was drinking in Tong Kok's when Geordie was on duty. When it was closing-time, curfew, Endal invited him back to her houseboat. To reach it they walked out of town, away from the direction of camp, then followed the railway line, stepping on the sleepers, until they came to the iron-girdered bridge that spanned the Lipis River at its confluence with the Jelai. Once there they scrambled

Medal for Malaya

down through the scrub jungle to the houseboats nestling on stilts at the water's edge. Endal introduced him to her mother and her two other kids. They were friendly and invited him to share the supper they were about to eat.

After the meal the kids went off to bed and their mother soon followed. Endal took him to her sleeping-quarter, a small cubicle partitioned by atap and bamboo from the rest of the houseboat. Through an opening like a small door they could see the silvery water of the creek. Above them the black silhouette of the bridge was gaunt and forbidding.

They made love, or rather, Steve made love to her for few of the women participated fully, or were genuinely aroused although they were friendlier than those in the brothels in Singapore. After all, over the weeks, they had become friends. They treated the soldiers' adolescent lusts with jovial humour, laughing a lot, pretending to climax, knowing that the soldiers knew, or should have known, that they rarely did, treating them as boys. Endal, black-haired with a soft slim copper-brown body, was really attractive and Steve could understand Geordie's response to her.

Afterwards, showing off, he went for a quick swim in the creek. Back in Endal's houseboat, drying off with a sarong, he noticed that he'd picked up a couple of leeches on his leg.

"Ugh!" Endal grimaced, then lit one of Steve's cigarettes and touched the leeches with the glowing end. They curled up and dropped off instantly. Not long afterwards, as Endal wanted to sleep, Steve gave her a ten-spot, kissed her on the cheek and ducked out through the doorway. It was about midnight. He clambered up the fifty or sixty feet of jungle-covered bank, following the track made by the inhabitants of the houseboats.

He reached the top, the railway track that crossed the bridge, the stones between the sleepers whitish in the moonlight, and saw someone standing a few yards away. It was Bill Atkinson, a friend of Geordie, someone Steve had played cards with a good deal.

"Hello Bill," he said. "What are you doing here?" It was rare for Bill to leave camp, let alone break the curfew and follow the track to the houseboats where some of the women lived.

127

"I could ask you the same, but I know you've been fucking Geordie's girl. That's Endal's houseboat down there."

He approached Steve. He smelled strongly of beer and looked threatening. Steve might have guessed there was some weird morality involved by the tone of his voice. As he reached the point where Bill was standing, without any warning, Bill let fly with a right swing that caught him above his left eye. He went down like a nine-pin, not unconscious, but seeing a few big stars in front of his eyes.

"You deserved that, you little bastard," Bill said.

"For fuck's sake, she belongs to no-one. She goes with anyone who can give her a few dollars. That's how she makes some money for her family and the kids. Jesus Christ!"

"But you're Geordie's friend."

"How the fuck did you know I was there anyway," Steve said, sitting by the railway track, rubbing his eye.

"I didn't know it was you. Someone in Tong Kok's told me Endal had gone off with a soldier. I thought it was that lieutenant she's been seen with before."

"Jesus, it's ludicrous defending Geordie's honour, or whatever. I reckon you fancy her yourself."

"I suppose I do," Bill said after a pause. "Yeh, I fancy her. God, I'm sorry, Steve, I didn't know it was you." Atkinson jutted out his chin. "Heh, come and take a swing at me. I deserve it." He gave Steve a hand and pulled him to his feet. "Here," he said. "Put one on me."

"Don't be stupid, Bill. Let's just forget it."

"No, come on, I owe it you. One punch. Right on the point."

It seemed to Steve that Bill was not merely drunk, but in a disturbed state. He had been angry enough to take a punch at him, but his demand that he should do so was disarming. "Let's get back to camp," he said.

"No, I owe you a punch. Come on, take a swing at me." He stood, thrusting his chin forward. There was no way Steve could avoid the invitation. Bill was determined. A few inches taller than Steve, Bill stood on the railway track, sticking out his chin and vaguely pointing to it with his index finger. Had anyone been watching it would have appeared a ludicrous sight. Steve went up to him, made as if to punch him on the jaw, but landed a right hard in his belly. Bill didn't go down, but buckled a little, gasped, then looked up smiling broadly.

"Not bad," he said. "Not bad at all, but it wouldn't have decked me even if you'd hit me on the chin. You're not the hardest puncher. Reckon you must have pulled that one a bit."

"Maybe."

"OK, let's go." He put an arm round Steve's shoulders and they walked along the railway track back into town.

Chapter 11

At Easter there were two days' holiday – Good Friday and Easter Monday although Saturday was a normal working-day. Steve was down on the roster as duty clerk, but believed this was of an honorary nature. He didn't think anyone would be in the office after the Friday festivities.

On the Friday, after winning a few dollars at poker, he showered, changed into a civvy shirt, put on a pair of jungle-green army-issue trousers and strolled into town. Most of the soldiers had stayed in camp. A large school of card-players had been becoming more aggressive and vociferous as the beer flowed.

It was a relief to get out of camp on such a night. There had been a storm that afternoon and the jungle was still glistening with moisture while a full moon threw a pale yellowish-light over the fronds whenever it emerged between rain-heavy cloud. Once in Jelai Street he could see across the river and hear the lap-lap of water against the bank and the river-boats.

He walked along the railway track as far as the confluence of the Jelai and Lipis. the iron-girdered bridge and a group of palms were outlined against the moonlight. The night seemed timeless; suspended like beads of rain on the atap leaves. The waters of the river drifted slowly with a steady rhythm. In the jungle nothing had changed for thousands of years, Steve thought. A Malay woman emerged from the path above the houseboats. Steve watched the sway of her hips swathed in a sarong; the sensuous elegance of her movement. He followed her along the track back into town. At the police check-point he caught her up. It was Bongah.

"Give me cigarette," she said by way of greeting. He offered one from his tin of fifty. She snatched a handful, put one in her mouth and secreted the others in the folds of her clothes. "You go to Tong Kok's?" she said.

"Yes."

"OK, you walk in front. I follow." Like most of the Muslim women she insisted upon walking behind, or sometimes in front of a man, but never with him.

Tong Kok's was as busy as usual. Several of the local women were there; One-Eye as the soldiers called her although her actual name was Soldah; Endal with Geordie Hood; Aissa, the sixteen-year old, part Malay, part Chinese wiggling her plump behind in the tight silk-trousers the Chinese wore. And with the group was a woman Steve had not seen before, a stranger in town. She was attractive, tallish for a Malay, wearing a green sarong and red tunic.

Steve got a beer and joined the group. He wondered whether Bill had ever told Geordie about the episode with Endal. Broad-shouldered, heavily-built, fair-haired with a boyish face, Geordie was always smiling, always friendly and, Steve thought, somewhat naïve. He spoke briefly to Steve but was too engrossed with Endal to say much to anyone else.

Sitting by the new woman, Steve tried to break the ice, but she was cool and distant. He bought her a beer and finally she told him that her name was Zenana and she'd come from Kuantan on the East Coast. She intended staying in Kuala Lipis for some months. She mentioned an ex-husband in Kuantan who had divorced her in the traditional Muslim manner. Most of the women in Tong Kok's, Steve had discovered, claimed to have had at least one divorce. He wasn't sure whether this indicated a freedom in relationships or was a result of Islamic law. Most Malays were Muslims, but their religion didn't seem obtrusive. They appeared happy-go-lucky; their Islamic beliefs over-laid by an easy-going hedonism.

Steve was pondering this phenomenon when Pierce, the cook, came in. "There's been a big fight up in camp," he said. "Just got myself away. All the hardcases, the nuts, were playing cards and Robbo was losing a stack and betting more wildly all the time. In the end nobody would give him any credit so he picked a fight with Atkinson. We managed to break it up, but Robbo's round town somewhere, drunk out of his head and looking for trouble."

"The stupid bastard!" Ben said.

"Well, just be careful, he's on the rampage tonight."

Pierce sat down and ordered a beer. A few minutes later Bill Atkinson pushed through the swing-doors. He stood inside the door, hair dishevelled, his uniform open to the waist, a dark trickle of blood from above his left eye. Sweat had soaked through his shirt and formed black patches.

"Heh, Revill, you old bastard!" he yelled.

"Beel," Aissa called out. "Buy me beer."

"Are you coming back to play cards?" he asked, ignoring Aissa's request.

"No way," Steve said. "I'm staying here, it sounds safer."

Atkinson looked round at the women, flashing Aissa a broad smile. "Look Stevey boy," he said. "Lend me a ten-spot, can you? I'll explain tomorrow. Be a pal, mate. You'll get it back – with interest. I'm on a winning streak and I feel lucky."

Steve gave him the ten-dollar note and he left, throwing a half-full pack of Rough Riders onto the table. "Cheers pal," he said. "Here, have a smoke on me," he said to Aissa, but Bongah had deftly caught the cigarettes and the pack had disappeared in the folds of her sarong.

A few minutes after his departure Robbo framed himself in the swing-doors. He swayed heavily, then squared his shoulders, puffed out his chest and stood, legs apart, surveying the scene in the posture of a Western gunslinger. His arms hung loosely in front of him, hands twitching nervously in the region of imaginary gun-holsters. *High Noon* had been an inspirational film for Robbo.

"Where's Atkinson?" he muttered in his almost unintelligible Glaswegian accent.

"Not here," Ben said.

"I can see that, but he's fuckin' been here, don't you try to kid me." Then he spotted Bongah. "Heh Bongah," he called. "Come here, lass. Come over here, you big beauty."

"Tarzan!" she shouted, got up and rushed out through the back-door, closely followed by Aissa and One-Eye.

"Come back, you bitch!" Robbo shouted, but Bongah had vanished into the night. Robbo grinned, impressed no doubt by her epithet and the power his presence had invoked. He gave the rest of them a look of contempt, shook his head slowly to indicate what he thought of them – a shower of shite – and left.

The drama subsided. Ben and Endal were drinking themselves into a mutual jelly of sentiment. Pierce had gone off to find Aissa and Steve was trying to get through to Zenana. After she'd had a number of beers she began to loosen up. Her ambition was to go to Singapore where she thought she could make a small fortune.

"I want to go Singapore," she kept saying. "This place no good. You take me Singapore, yes?"

"Sure, I can do that. When I go on leave."

"*Bagus*. You good boy. We go Singapore, yes?"

"Of course."

"*Ini malam* – tonight you come my room and when you go leave, take me to Singapore." She rambled on half in Malay, but he got the gist of her monologue. If he helped her to get to Singapore, she'd give him a free pass, as it were, to her room.

With Tong Kok's in a soporific state, the Orderly Sergeant and a couple of MPs arrived. The scarlet sash and the red-peaked caps stood out incongruously. Zenana and Endal withdrew down the back steps and went quietly out of the door. The Orderly Sergeant was in the RAEC, an NS man himself. Tallish, wearing glasses, ill-at-ease in the trappings of authority, he appeared embarrassed.

"Look lads," he said. "You must know this bar's out-of-bounds. Personally I don't care if you come here, but I've got to make the gesture when I'm on duty. So, come on, let's have you out, it's after curfew anyway."

With that he left followed by the two hefty MPs, sneering at his politeness. Steve and Ben finished their beers, then followed the trio into the street. Pools of moonlight cast shadows on the pavement. The few street-lamps were flickering off. In the cafes the shutters were being put up, sounding the death rattle of another Malayan night. A policeman shone his torch in their faces, smiled and moved on. In the Chinese market one dingy ill-lit stall was still open. Ben went off in the direction of Endal's houseboat. Steve began walking back to camp. The howl of a dog from some kampong, the scuffling of a cat or a rat in the monsoon-drain and the stifled cry of a child behind the closed shutters of a house mingled with the multitudinous sounds of insects in the scrub jungle. At the end of Main Street Steve turned left over the level-crossing. On the far side someone beckoned to him. As the figure emerged from the shadows he saw that it was Zenana.

"I wait you," she said. "Tonight we go my room."

"I haven't much money."

"*Ti-ed apah*," she said. "Soon we go Singapore. Tonight my room."

He didn't hesitate. He followed her down the lane until they reached the track that led to Batu Kurap, higher up the river. Built in a shallow concavity of land, the kampong was dark on the clearest nights, but Zenana knew the path that avoided pools of stagnant, mosquito-infested swamp. He kept close behind her until they reached the shanties. She fiddled with the lock and they were inside where she lit a lamp and the features of the room emerged.

Within minutes she stood naked by the bed smiling at him. Her tallish body was bronzed and slender. He watched the sputtering lamp cast shadows on her belly and breasts. Then he knelt in front of her, put his arms round her buttocks, burying his face between her thighs. She smelled warm, slightly of sweat, fragrant. The earlier menace of the evening, his own personal anxieties ebbed away. He felt safe, secure as if in his own home.

She made love with a certain passion that belied her status and afterwards, smoking a cigarette, he thought that if he could make love enough with her; if he could, as it were, saturate himself in her flesh, he could purge the bad memories of the last few weeks and his distaste for the vulgarities of barrack-room life.

In the morning, thinking that Saturday was also a holiday, not forgetting that he was duty-clerk, but thinking that no-one would be in the office, he slept on. After all, the keys to the office should be safe enough in his bedside locker in the basha.

They were woken by a loud banging on the door. He heard Zenana talking angrily and the sound of gruff masculine voices. Suddenly two MPs, pushing past her, came into the room. Steve knew them both, bully boys, especially the corporal with the big belly and sandy hair, grins of pure malice on their red faces.

"OK Revill," one of them said. "Get up, you dirty bastard. We've been looking for you nearly four hours."

"But it's a holiday."

"You daft bugger! You were duty clerk this morning."

"It's Easter."

"Colonel Mallinson went up to the office at eight-thirty this morning and couldn't get in. It was bloody-well locked. And you had the keys. You should have opened it up. I wouldn't like to be in your shoes. He was bloody furious."

"Oh Jesus!"

"Sent down to the bashas and found your bed unslept in. Jock Robertson found the keys in your locker, fortunately you'd forgotten to lock it. But the CO went bananas. Called us in and we've been looking for you ever since. You're on a charge, so come on, get yourself dressed."

"What charge?"

"Absent without leave. What else?"

"OK, I'll get dressed – if you two wait outside."

"All right, but don't think you can do a runner, you'll just make things worse for yourself."

"I'm not stupid."

He got dressed, said goodbye to Zenana, kissing her on the cheek, and joined the MPs who were having a smoke outside.

"You're really in the fucking shit this time," the Corporal said. "God knows what you see in these mucky wog women. I know this one. She's just down from Kuantan. And I'll tell you something else for nothing."

"What?"

"She's got the syph."

"Had it, or got it?"

"Got it."

They clambered into the jeep which was in the lane. Steve wasn't really worried about the information he'd just received. The MP was probably lying in an attempt to worry him. He knew this bastard and his salacious curiosity.

"Incidentally, let me correct you about one thing," Steve said. "Zenana is not a dirty wog woman. She's Malay and beautiful. Clean too."

"I tell you she's got the syph though."

"Don't bullshit me."

"I've seen her records at Police HQ. They've got tabs on all these prostitutes."

"I don't believe you."

"I've seen her dossier. She's got it all right – up to her eyebrows."

"Doesn't worry me."

"Always said that little prick of yours would land you in trouble," he said. "Some of you kids seem to think with your pricks. Or I should say: a bit of a hard-on and you lose your minds. All balls and no brains. Fuck anything in skirts."

"In sarongs, you mean."

"You and that Dorman and Ben Hood. All of you are the same. You'd follow your pricks to perdition."

"Fine speech," Steve said.

By this time they were back in camp. The MPs escorted Steve to the bashas and waited while he got dressed in full battle-kit. A few moments later he was in front of the CO, charged with AWOL. The Colonel looked absolutely furious. Steve wondered whether he'd be sent down the river: to the Military Corrective Establishment at Kinrara. Once before he'd been on a charge for failing to salute an officer, a pompous little captain in the Hussars.

For a week or two after that he had plagued the captain by seeking him out, or ambushing him and saluting whenever he had the opportunity. The captain got so fed up that on the final occasion he'd failed to salute in return. Steve had then reported him to the Colonel though it hadn't done any good. He'd been bollocked for his impudence. He imagined that the incident was still vivid in Colonel Mallinson's memory. Now he was standing in front of him between the two large MPs.

The MP on his left was ordered to make his statement. "At eleven-thirty five hours we apprehended 22756964 Signalman Revill in a state of undress with a woman of ill-repute in a hut at Batu Kurap, Sir." The MPs' statement to the CO sounded bizarre to Steve, thinking of Zenana, the kampong he'd just left, the cosy warmth. He smiled.

"This is not funny," the CO said. "And – to quote Queen Victoria – I am not amused, even if you are."

"That was what she said to Gladstone, I think, Sir."

"Shut up and don't act the clown, Revill. You're on a serious charge so what's your explanation?"

"Well, I thought Saturday was a holiday. I didn't realise I should have opened the office, I mean, I knew I was Duty Clerk, but I didn't think the office would be opened today."

"That you were negligent in your duties has nothing to do with going absent which is what this enquiry is about. Your negligence merely got you caught. The question is: why did you spend the night out of camp?"

"I can't really explain that, Sir. I suppose in one sense it was to get away from the barracks for a few hours. To a female environment, the tenderness of a woman. Psychologically speaking ..."

"I'm not bandying words with you, Signalman. You break every rule in the book, spend the night with a town prostitute and have the impudence, no, the arrogance to talk about femininity, tenderness. Psychologically speaking, my arse! Seven days detention! March him out of here, Corporal!"

Seven days in the unit cells were not that unpleasant. During the day Steve worked in the cookhouse, helping Pierce and the Catering Corps soldiers, washing up and drying, cleaning the tables, sweeping the canteen. Sometimes he helped to serve the food. Then after the six o'clock guard-parade he'd be locked up for twelve hours, but he had his notebooks, some novels from the library and those on guard would invariably come by for a chat. Depending upon who was guard commander he could also persuade someone to bring him a couple of beers from the NAAFI. Sometimes they'd even let him out of the cell to chat with the off-duty guards. In fact he quite enjoyed the relative solitude which was available if he wanted it.

Chapter 12

Coming out of detention, Steve found that he'd lost his clerical job and had been demoted to General Duties. This meant working permanently as a Dining Room Orderly. Not being stuck in the office under the eye of the sergeant-major and the CO had its compensations. He had more freedom to come and go. And because it wasn't regarded as priority work he could volunteer every other weekend for escort duty on convoys to Kuala Lumpur. Also, in a mood of defiance allied to the romantic notion that experience of combat would be useful for the novel he intended to write about National Service, he volunteered for a jungle patrol.

Three weeks later his name cropped up on the rota. He was to be attached to a platoon of the Queen's African Rifles. With a certain trepidation he attended the briefing on the operation before they set out. An officer with an Oxford accent gave them the low-down, explaining their position.

"Right men. Intelligence believes there's a group of bandits operating south of Kuala Lipis in a jungle area west of the Jelai River. Obviously, their exact position is not known, but the SAS were parachuted into the centre of the area earlier today. Their objective is to disperse the bandits and drive them out. The infantry – that's us – are going in from various points round an imaginary circle. With the SAS in the middle, the Gurkhas and African Rifles closing in like a net, we hope to be able to eliminate the group."

"For those of you who might be new to jungle patrolling, I want to stress the dangers. It's all too easy to cross paths with a friendly section. The cardinal rule is to avoid firing at the *sound* of movement, but only when, and if, the enemy is actually sighted. If you hear movement you freeze, find cover, wait. We don't want, nor do we take kindly to accidents that stem from trigger-happy, or nervous, newcomers."

"We shall have an experienced jungle-tracker from the Sarawak Rangers as our guide. Treat him with respect. A lot depends upon him and, believe me, the Rangers are expert in jungle terrain ..."

They set off at dawn in a truck that dropped them at the tenth milestone south of Lipis. Jumping from the lorry, Steve felt a vague unease like nausea in the belly. The officer gave some brief orders, his voice clear in the morning stillness. His hands trembling a little as the adrenalin began to flow, Steve moved forward and with the rest of his section took cover at the side of the road. Once the whine of the engine had faded it was very quiet save for the insects.

Their section began grouping ready to move and the African soldiers were chatting quietly amongst themselves. Steve could feel his rifle pressing against his side, the bolt nudging his hip, the bayonet in its scabbard flapping against his right buttock. They somehow gave him a sense of security. He checked the magazine, the bolt sliding easily in the breach, its black metal filmed with oil, the bullets like small ingots of gold. The old cliché slipped into his mind: the soldier's best friend is his rifle. He awaited the order for his platoon to move forward, jungle-hat floppy, its rim soaking up sweat, water-bottle bobbing at his belt. He felt for his tin of cigarettes, safe and dry in a pocket of his pouch.

He watched the African soldiers who came from Kenya or Uganda and had the reputation of being tough with unlimited stamina. They didn't look scared, but perhaps that was because they were veterans who knew the routine. Most of them were practising Christians – and seemed to have much more faith in orders than Steve did. They lacked his scepticism. Certainly they had more respect for their officers. All of them had somewhat unusual Christian names – Samson, Moses, Solomon. As they began to forge ahead through the jungle they seemed to Steve more like missionaries than soldiers searching for Chinese terrorists. Clearly those British Bible-punchers in Africa had done a thorough job of things.

At first the going was easy enough and enveloped in green shade they moved forward at a steady pace. The undergrowth became denser the deeper they pushed into the forest. Vines and ferns entwined the trees. Tangled creepers like green snakes hung down from the branches while the ground underfoot was mushy with rotting vegetation that gave off an ammoniacal odour reminiscent of chlorine. Soon enough they were chopping at the vegetation with their parangs, cutting a route through, disturbing a variety of insects and butterflies.

Steve kept thinking about something his ex-girlfriend, Dorothy, had said to him in one of her letters. She was studying botany and zoology for her A-Levels, probably in fact sitting her exams about this time for it was June, although the idea was hard to imagine.

"Do you get much chance to study the fauna and flora of Malaya?" she'd asked.

The question had mildly amused him. He wasn't a scientist, but, yes, he could truthfully say he was studying it now all right. The jungle was probably a botanist's dream world and he was deep in its flora, sweating, catching a whiff of his own armpits as he raised the parang, insect bites irritating his hands and face. As for the larger fauna, so far they hadn't even seen a monkey. He'd seen hundreds from the armoured cars on KL convoys. Wild pigs often came rooting at the edge of the jungle near their bashas. He'd seen quite a few small snakes in the jungle lanes round camp. And on one memorable occasion he'd even seen a tiger.

Steve and Jock Robertson had been sent to deliver mail to the radio operators who did shifts in a transmitter hut on top of a hill not far from Brigade HQ. There was a broad grassy path that cut through the jungle up the hill to the site. They'd been strolling towards it when Jock had suddenly stopped in his tracks. For a moment Steve thought he must have spotted terrorists, but following his transfixed gaze, saw, about a hundred yards up, the tiger that seemed to be watching them too. Even at that distance it was a thrill to see its orange-and-black striped beauty. They'd unslung their rifles and backed slowly down the path towards the road to the jeep where the driver sat waiting for them. In one swift movement the tiger had disappeared into the jungle as surprised no doubt as they were. Now in the middle of that jungle Steve saw nothing but tropical birds that squawked ahead of them as if announcing their presence.

After a couple of hours Steve's section emerged from jungle into an open stretch, reeds growing evenly. It looked to be much easier terrain, but he could tell from the pungent smell as the soldiers ahead disturbed the mud that they were entering swamp. Soon they were up to the tops of their jungle boots in muddy water, wading against the suction and pull. It was the last thing they needed. Surely the officer in charge should have been aware there was swamp ahead. After all he had a map, a compass and the Sarawak Ranger who should have recognised the signs. Goddamn-it, Steve thought, once this patrol was over – a patrol he'd volunteered for, breaking the old soldier's code: never volunteer for anything, there would be a weekend in Kuala Lumpur as compensation.

On the far side of the swampy stretch the officer called a halt. They slung their packs on some dry ground and sat upon them, lighting cigarettes which even in their tins were slightly damp from the humidity or sweat. One or two soldiers had acquired a leech or two which they touched with their cigarettes until they curled up and dropped off.

By the late afternoon they were bordering paddy fields, close to civilisation again. There were water-buffaloes lathered in mud, grazing near an irrigation ditch. Green shoots of rice sprouted from the watery expanse. Their section was moving along the edge of forest to avoid an isolated kampong, its huts stilted on poles. Somehow it was comforting to see Malays working in the paddy, brown backs bent in the hot sun. When they looked up and saw soldiers, they waved.

As dusk approached, the western sky to their right streaked with red and orange, they were struggling through stunted second-growth jungle. The officer was up front talking to the Sarawak Ranger. Steve watched his neck and shoulders upon which was an intricate network of tattoos. Before it was quite dark they made their camp on the bank of a small stream and had a meal from their rations. Steve had never slept in the jungle itself and felt a bit nervous about it. Two of the Africans had built a fire, coffee was made and they drank it, black, strong and sweet. It was delicious, its aroma wafting around them.

Soon darkness obliterated the jungle. There was no moon and no stars could be seen through the canopy of treetops, only the glowing embers of the fire gave a modicum of light. They did guard-duty in pairs. Waiting for his turn, Steve tried to sleep but the concentrated noise of the insects ground on his nerves. The Sarawak Ranger probably knew the significance of every crackle of twig and rustle of leaf, every alien noise. Steve didn't know and it made him jumpy. At night the jungle was an auditory experience and the various sounds kept him awake. A cigarette or two glowed in the darkness and a face was profiled for an instant, hands cupping a match. Steve hugged his rifle by his side. It was cold comfort now.

He did the midnight until two o'clock guard-shift with an African called Jacob and afterwards must have dozed off for the next thing he knew it was first light, a silver mist rising round the trees, the ground saturated with dew, the jungle redolent of damp vegetation that mingled with the aroma of coffee. After a cold breakfast they continued but the romance was beginning to wear thin.

By midday they'd arrived at a small village on the banks of the Jelai, approximately seven or eight miles south of Kuala Lipis. They relaxed, smoking and watching some Malays bathing in the reddish water. Clearly this village had been their rendezvous as they were soon joined by other sections. A couple of SAS officers were already there, having been helicoptered in. The officers went into a huddle, talking in animated fashion, pointing and gesticulating up-river. When the group split up, their lieutenant came running across to them.

"OK chaps," he said, "we've just received some really important info. The enemy's been located up-river, not far from Lipis itself. We're to make tracks as fast as possible and the quickest way is via the river itself. We'll probably have to commandeer some wog sampans and hire their owners to negotiate us up-stream. Let's be looking lively, you'll get some action soon."

They requisitioned several sampans and a Malay or two and proceeded to paddle up the Jelai. For a couple of hours in the afternoon heat they sat back in the boats, enjoying the sunshine and the tropical beauty of the scenery – vivid green jungle, reddish-brown water and rolling mauve hills to the west. The river was wide and sluggish. Vegetation slanted down to the water's edge. The lieutenant kept urging the Malays to put more effort into their paddling.

Suddenly they heard the harsh, dry staccato sound of a bren-gun. Steve slammed a round up the breach and heard other rifles clicking on all sides. There was another burst of fire; it was coming from the east bank. He could see smoke spiralling in thin columns from the jungle. And the water ahead of them was peppered by small splashes. They were under fire, he realised with a shock. It seemed very close; the sound tense, brittle. Several soldiers in the sampan ducked involuntarily. They rounded the curve in the river, heading for the west side of the bank. There were isolated rifle shots.

"Hold your fire," the lieutenant shouted. Crouching low in the boat as they beached, Steve could see the iron-girdered suspension bridge over the Lipis River where it joined the Jelai, and the houseboats nestling in its shadow. They were scarcely a mile from the town itself.

When the boats were pulled up onto the mudbank they raced for cover. Stray shots still zipped in their direction. Once they were in a relatively safe position they began to fire back across the bend in the river towards the puffs of smoke. Everything but the tension of the moment, the adrenalin pumping round, was forgotten. Dangerous it might have been, but it wasn't really fear that Steve felt, merely a strange excitement. He had no idea how close the enemy bullets had been, nor how close they'd been to hitting the terrorists. Nor did he realise exactly what was happening for it was chaotic.

"Hold your fire," came the urgent command. They did so, watching and waiting. On the far side was a straggling group of Gurkha soldiers moving along the narrow stretch of beach. All the firing had stopped. There was a lot of confused shouting. By this time the Gurkhas had reached the houseboats under the bridge.

"Keeping under cover, make your way round to the bridge," their lieutenant said.

Slowly, keeping to the fringe of jungle they crawled round the headland to the bridge. They could see the Gurkhas on the far side, out in the open by the side of the railway track. There were shouts of greeting from across the bridge and an officer began walking towards them, casually, unconcerned about cover. It was obvious that the skirmish was over. On the lieutenant's orders they emerged from cover and crossed the bridge. Other sections emerged from different points along the headland. Steve hadn't realised that so many men were involved. Rifles slung they reached the town side. It was with a shock that Steve saw that the small Gurkha soldiers were hauling dead bandits up the slope on makeshift stretchers. He counted seven of them, utterly without dignity, or even humanity, hanging loosely from bamboo poles.

He watched as they came closer; the ashen faces, the khaki uniforms stained with blood. Chinese, they'd evidently been surprised on one of the houseboats that belonged to a woman Steve might well have met in Tong Kok's. While he'd been exalting in the experience of combat, intensely alive, aware of the blood pumping through his body, nerves and senses in a highly-stimulated state, revelling in the knowledge that life, at any one moment, was tenuous, seven bandits had died. And being close to the results of a gun-battle was not so pleasant. He watched the slow procession carrying the blood-splashed bodies along the railway line. Life was cheap, he kept thinking. These men, human beings with their complex biology, emotions, thoughts, memories were now nothing but inert flesh, dead meat. It was a sobering thought.

That night the Gurkhas celebrated with special-issue rum. All evening Steve could hear the rhythmic beating of their drums. It was a dubious victory as far as Steve was concerned. He kept seeing the bodies of the bandits draped on poles. The sight had certainly shocked him. He'd never seen death at such close quarters before. He recalled the bullets splashing the muddy water ahead of their sampan, the zipping whine as they flew above him. It created a fear which at the time he hadn't felt. Only hours later did the reality hit him.

They drank in the NAAFI that night. Much of the conversation centred upon the skirmish. They were amazed that the terrorists had been holed up on the houseboats with some local women. Such places were out-of-bounds, but quite a few soldiers were in the habit of visiting them. Now they wondered whether stricter orders would be issued because of the incident. Ben Hood, Dorman and others kept

Medal for Malaya

saying they'd give the houseboats a wide berth from now on. A five-dollar fuck was not worth the possibility of getting killed or captured by terrorists. Steve agreed with them, but within a week or two, the incident forgotten, they were all, once again, taking such risks as a matter of course.

For a few days back in the cookhouse as an orderly, Steve got questioned a lot.

"What was it like then, Revill?"
"Were you scared?"
"Did you see the Gurkhas kill them?"

But soon this stopped too and once he'd got over the shock that had hit him the first evening, he enjoyed the memory of actually having been in action, fired at and firing back. He felt that he'd earned his General Service Medal. But even these feelings turned out to be as transient as the skirmish itself. The Gurkhas, the professionals, had been at the centre of things. If victory it could be termed, it was theirs.

Chapter 13

Back on General Duties Steve was once more relegated to the position of Dining-Room Orderly, but he was able to volunteer every other weekend for convoys to Kuala Lumpur. In a letter home, however, he happened to mention the work he was now doing and his father who was an active member of the Labour Party in Stechford said he felt like complaining to his local MP about a lad with A-Levels being employed in such menial work. Steve wrote back at once telling him not to do that.

One afternoon Steve was having a cigarette in the cookhouse when Geordie Hood came trotting across from the teleprinter office. "Heh, Steve," he said. "This has just come through. It's classified information and should go straight to the CO, but I thought I'd show you it first. Don't tell anyone. Just read it."

He took the telex Geordie handed him. It read: WAR OFFICE INQUIRY INTO THE CASE OF SIGNALMAN REVILL. PLEASE FORWARD FULL DETAILS. Steve was shocked. He realised that his father must have ignored his last letter and contacted the MP, who must have passed it on to the War Office. He knew that Colonel Mallinson would be furious, but forewarned was forearmed, he assured himself. At least he would know what it was all about should the CO want to see him.

For a few days nothing happened, then Jock Robertson came over to the cookhouse. "Steve, the CO wants to see you now." He smartened himself up and went across to the verandah outside the office, hesitated a moment, then knocked on the CO's door.

"Come in ... Ah Signalman Revill," he said. "Do sit down." He placed a chair in front of him, looked searchingly at him for a moment as if seeking an answer to a problem. "Have a cigarette," he said. "You do smoke, I take it." Steve nodded. The CO pushed a tin of

Senior Service in his direction. Steve took one and the CO offered him a light. "Signalman," he went on, "I need to check your background and details," he added, perusing a piece of paper. "I see you went to a good grammar school in Birmingham. I've heard of it. A good institution, I believe."

"Yes Sir, it has that reputation."

"And you got three A-Levels and two Scholarship Level passes. Do you intend to go on to university?"

"I think so."

"I see you also played a lot of sport. Do you play here?"

"I've played rugby for the Brigade."

"What about your hobbies, your interests? Poetry and chess are listed here. Tell me about them."

"Well, I write poetry, Sir. I'd like to be a writer."

"You write poetry?" he repeated, his tone ironic. "I don't meet many soldiers who write poetry."

"I've written some about Malaya."

"Sounds to me, Signalman, as if you're in the wrong unit. You should have been in the RAEC or something."

"I did try to transfer once, Sir."

"All right, Revill," he said and his tone changed from one of ironic interest to one of barely suppressed anger. "Can you explain to me why you've made such a balls-up of your National Service? Why in fact, for an apparently intelligent lad, you've fucked it up completely?"

"I didn't think I had, Sir."

"Signalman, how long have you been at 18th Infantry Brigade?"

"About six months, Sir."

"About six months," he mimicked. "And in that short time you've been in front of me for one disciplinary reason after another. I'd go further than that. In six months you've caused me more trouble than any other soldier in the unit. What's more you appear to have done your damnedest to fuck me up personally."

"How do you mean, Sir?"

"Don't play the innocent with me, Revill. You know perfectly well what I mean. You've been writing to your MP, complaining of your treatment here, haven't you?"

"No Sir, I haven't."

"Look, there's a War Office inquiry into your case which could only have been initiated by some interfering MP upon your instigation."

"I think I can explain, Sir."

"I think you better do so."

"I wrote to my father and said I'd been made a dining-room orderly. He wasn't happy about it. He couldn't understand why someone with A-Levels was doing a job like that. I told him I enjoyed it and I didn't want him to mention it to any MP."

"No, I don't suppose he could understand why his son had been demoted. I don't suppose for a moment that you told him about going AWOL with the local whores and I'm sure you didn't mention your visits to the hospital with VD. Nor do I imagine you told him about being on jankers or in detention either, come to that."

"Well, no Sir, I didn't."

"Soldier, you've tried to make a fool of me and you've made a damned fool of your father too. Imagine what the War Office will write to him, or his local MP, after I've sent in my report. I don't suppose he'll be happy about it. In fact I'm pretty sure he'll feel like a bloody idiot having acted on your behalf – just as I do. And personally, I do not relish being made to look like a fool by some arrogant whipper-snapper, some twenty-year old National Serviceman with a chip on his shoulder. Some boy, I should say. Do you see what I'm driving at?"

"Yes Sir."

"But I'm a fair man, I believe in justice – natural justice, do you understand me?"

"Sir."

"Therefore I'm going to give you a chance to redeem yourself and make amends. In a few weeks Sergeant Vernon, who as you know is in charge of pay, is going on a course for a month. In his absence I want you to take over the job of pay-sergeant. It's a difficult one, I can assure you. It involves care, application and, yes, some intelligence too. I'm going to find out whether you can live up to your own estimation of your ability."

Medal for Malaya

"I think I could manage it, Sir."

"I sincerely hope so – for your own sake. Do this job properly and you'll get your leave plus a decent report from me before you're demobbed. Make a mess of it, or mess me about in any shape or form and I'll make sure you're down the river for twenty-eight days – and you must know what that means."

"Yes Sir."

"I don't want to see you in front of me again for even the most minor infraction of discipline. And let me tell you, Signalman, I don't think you'd survive a month in a military corrective establishment. You'd find out just how tough the Army can really be."

"I know, Sir. I remember Ross doing twenty-eight days in Kinrara. He spent nine of them on bread-and-water."

"Ross is a genuine hardcase, Signalman. He's a regular soldier from a tough area of Glasgow. If it could break him, imagine what it would do to you – because you're not really a hardcase at all. Oh, I know you've been on some jungle patrol and done seven days in the unit cells, but that's a picnic compared to life in the glasshouse. You're just an ex-schoolboy with an inflated opinion of himself – soft as shit in fact. You wouldn't last five minutes in a place like Kinrara."

"I don't know whether that's entirely true, Sir."

"In my book it is. You'd go under. You'd succumb. But you've got a reprieve with Sergeant Vernon's job. You're going to be acting paymaster – and you're going to make a success of it. That's an order. Just remember this: you may only have a few months of National Service to complete but you're still in the Army. And right here, in 18th Infantry Brigade, I *am* the Army. Fuck around with me and I'll make it my business to delay your demob. Do I make myself absolutely one-hundred percent clear?"

"Yes Sir."

"All right, you're dismissed. Just one more thing. Get your arse back into the office tomorrow morning. Report to Sergeant Vernon. He'll show you the ropes and teach you the rudiments of his job before he goes on that course."

Steve saluted and left. He felt thoroughly chastened. Later it dawned on him that the CO had probably pulled off a bluff. He could

149

now claim that Steve was Acting Pay Sergeant – certainly a job worthy of his academic qualifications. He'd got himself off the hook neatly. Now Steve was the one who had to watch his step. Put a foot wrong and the CO would make his life as difficult as possible. He had no alternative but to do the new work well. He'd have to be extremely careful about haunting the kampongs and houseboats. He'd have to wait for weekends in Kuala Lumpur to enjoy himself.

The following morning Steve was re-installed in the office. Sergeant Vernon was a heavy-set taciturn man who knew his job from A–Z. So after a couple of weeks Steve felt he did too. It was easier than the CO had intimated, though it did require accuracy and effort. For the first time in the Royal Signals he had a job that was interesting. And during the next few weeks his stock went up with the other soldiers as they all had queries and problems about pay and were obliged to see Steve about them. As Sergeant Vernon's sidekick he had some small element of power, something he'd not experienced in the Army before. As paydays were on Thursday, his work for the week was virtually finished by then so that he could still volunteer for convoy-patrols to KL. And subsequently must have completed half-a-dozen at least.

There were three girls he used to see in Kuala Lumpur – Meena, Molly Chan and Rukhsana, a half-Indian Muslim girl. He'd first met Molly in the Batu Road and discovered that she was a student, paying her way through university, studying history and economics. She claimed to despise the British, especially soldiers, feigning complete contempt for those who fought for the imperialists, as she phrased it. Far from feeling that she was being exploited, she laughed at the way she could intimidate a young soldier. Her English was excellent and she referred to soldiers as pawns. No matter how much Steve protested that he had little interest in the concept of Empire and no special patriotism, she simply laughed, scoffing at his naïvety.

The first time he went to her room which was immaculately clean and tidy, books, magazines and work-folders neatly filed on bookshelves, she demanded the money in advance and was in a hurry to get on with things. Firmly plump, she had an attractive figure, made sexier by the red cheong-sam she usually wore. Naked, she was pale skinned, lighter than Steve was with his bronze tan. Naturally it didn't take him long to become aroused. Then while making love, lost in his own pleasure, he became aware that she was quietly singing:

> ... "*Seven lonely days make one lonely week*
> *Seven lonely nights make one lonely week* ...",

in a faintly derisive tone, a mocking half-smile on her face. In her hand which was dangling over the side of the bed, she had a cigarette from which she took a drag every few seconds. Half-amused, still inside her, he stopped moving and looked hard at her. She smiled again, but not in a hostile manner, then blew a puff of smoke in his face.

"Come on, Johnny, don't stop," she said.

"But you're singing."

"Sure, that's no problem, is it?"

"Turn over," he said.

"On my hands and knees?"

"Yes."

She gave him a rueful look but did as he'd requested. "You better be quick," she said.

He penetrated from behind, her bum in the air, thrust away and came fast. She turned her head and grinned in a mildly triumphant manner. "Very good, very good," she said sarcastically. He smiled back at her. They uncoupled and he lay on his back and lit a cigarette. Then, unexpectedly, she turned towards him and gave him a big kiss smack on the mouth.

After that occasion he found her irresistible and they became friends – almost – though her attitude in bed remained the same. He liked her for it – the lack of pretence. Another time, while he was in the throes of orgasm, he noticed that she was munching an apple. She was still chomping away as he lay exhausted on top of her.

Meena, a Malay, was quite the opposite, a childlike creature who seemed hopelessly vulnerable. Steve came to feel protective about her, an emotion most of the girls singularly failed to provoke. She loved going to the cinema or for a meal and spending the whole day with a soldier she liked. She made love, too, with an enthusiasm that didn't seem feigned. In fact she demanded orgasm. Once when Steve had come quickly, she gripped him with her thighs, keeping him inside her until the over-sensitivity passed and he hardened again, able to fuck her at the angle she appeared to enjoy.

Often she forgot to ask for money at all. He'd take her to see a film, come back and spend the night with her, slipping a ten-dollar note into her handbag when he left in the morning.

Rukhsana worked as a dance-hostess at the Rainbow Cabaret. She was dark-skinned and pretty. She liked to be treated as a "girlfriend" and didn't like the subject of money mentioned at all. She was slim with slender hips and wouldn't make love if it could possibly be avoided. Steve only managed to do so twice in the few months he knew her and only stayed overnight with her once. Her room was in a kampong behind the mosque. That morning the dawn woke him and looking through the window he'd seen the minarets of the mosque golden in the sunrise and realised that the muezzin's call had actually disturbed him. Between the palms that surrounded the kampong some kids were already playing football in the dust. He caught the faintly insanitary smell of the River Klang that flowed nearby. Beside him, lay Rukhsana, dark and slender, still sleeping, looking very young, indeed no older than Steve was himself.

Steve still had to visit the hospital in Kinrara and just before he was to attend for his last check-up, he discovered he had a couple of sore patches on his penis. He was alarmed. He wondered if they were a symptom of syphilis. He recalled the fat MP who'd told him that Zenana had the disease. At the time Steve had scoffed, but now he was worried.

"Ah Revill, good-morning," Major Jackson said affably. "Everything all right?"

"Well, no Sir."

"Good God! What's the matter now?"

"Well, Sir, I've got these sores."

"Let's have a look then." Steve dropped his khaki-green slacks. The MO examined him carefully, his expression assuming an intense seriousness. "You've been worried, I can see that."

"Yes Sir."

"Imagining you've got the nasty one, I suppose?"
"Yes Sir."
"I can see why."
"Is it?" By now Steve was really worried, but the Major smiled.
"Ah Revill," he said. "You're such a worrier, but this time it's nothing serious at all. Just what are called clinical chancres which we treat with saline washes, that's all. They'll be gone in a day or two. A skin infection, superficial."

Steve was only kept in over the weekend by which time the sore patches had disappeared. And all his other tests proved negative.

One Saturday in Kuala Lumpur Steve was drinking with a tall thin dark-haired Glaswegian, Jim Connell. They'd started at the NAAFI Club and worked their way via a number of bars along the Batu Road to the Rainbow Cabaret. They were sitting at a table when half-a-dozen soldiers from some unit in Kuala Lumpur approached them. It seemed they knew Connell and were out to exact a species of revenge upon him for something that had happened in the past. Steve had no idea how Connell had offended them and never had time to find out.

"Stand up, Connell," one of them said. "You've had this coming to you for ages."

"Fuck off, bastard!" he retorted.

"Heh, leave it alone," Steve said. "Let's just get out of here."

"I'm not leaving because of these bastards," Connell said.

"And you, you little Sassenach," one of them said to Steve. "You better get the fuck out if you know what's good for you."

Steve got up and stood between Connell and their ring-leader. "Leave him alone," he said. Drunk, Connell matched their verbal belligerence with his own. Suddenly one of them clobbered Connell with a punch from the side. He never saw it coming. Then the others started as he crumpled to the floor. Steve ducked out and pulled one of them off. He turned and Steve hit him with a short right. He staggered, then came back at him. One of his mates attacked Steve simultaneously. Steve couldn't see what was happening to Connell, but he was on the deck and the boots were flying. Steve hit his first opponent again with a straight left and a swing to the side of the head.

Someone from his blind side punched Steve in the face. He tripped over a chair and stumbled to his knees. Several of them closed in. He saw stars as a couple of clubbing punches got him while he was down. Liquid – spilt beer – was running down his neck and shirt. He heard glass breaking and saw someone with a broken bottle in his hand. As Steve turned to face him he was kicked in the head. Then he was on the floor, hands, elbows and knees tucked in to guard his face, his body hunched up foetus-like. Someone ran at him as if to kick a penalty. His head jolted back and he managed to crawl under a table. Glass splintered on the wall in front of him. Fortunately, the chaos spread.

It had all happened quickly. The band was still playing, the tempo jazzed up. There was a really cool trumpet somewhere in the band, Steve recalled thinking, incongruously.

"MPs! The MPs are coming." People were shouting and screaming. Everyone began to scatter, making for the exits. When Steve got to the entrance he saw that there were dozens of MPs outside, trying to stop people as they tumbled through the swing-doors. The neons were flickering on and off. He heard the sound of engines revving up in the car-park. Eluding the MPs, he managed to grab a taxi.

"To Nanto's," he said. "*Lekas!*" He'd no idea what had happened to Connell.

In Nanto's he drank a couple of beers quickly. He noticed that people were looking at him anxiously. In the toilet, leaning against the side of the wash-basin, he swilled his face and combed his hair. There was blood in his hair and a bruise below his right eye. He'd also got cuts on both thighs, probably from a bottle or a nail in someone's boot. He cleaned himself up as well as he could and went back to the bar. He had another beer.

Feeling better, he paid, grabbed one of the empty bottles and left. He wanted the bottle in case he met one of those bastards on the way back to camp. He smashed it against the monsoon-drain and concealed the jagged top in his hand.

He walked down a sidestreet. It was quite dark. In front of him he could see the minarets of the mosque and down below, to his right, the Klang River, dark and oily-smelling. Suddenly he thought how utterly stupid all this brawling was. He chucked the broken bottle-top into the river and seconds later heard the splash.

"Heh soldier!"

It was the MPs. He could tell by the distinctive formation of lights on the front of their jeep which was slowly approaching.

"Soldier, you're out-of-bounds."

Steve decided to run and the MPs came after him, but the sidestreets were narrow which made their manoeuvring difficult. He nipped down an alley, saliva sticky in his mouth, only to find another jeep and more MPs blocking his way.

"Christ! You're a mess," one of them said.

"There was a fight at the Rainbow Cabaret."

"Get in. We'll take you back to camp. Where are you from?"

"18th Infantry Brigade."

"Staying at the Transit Camp?"

"Yes."

"In the back then."

They took him back to camp, joking about the state he was in, but there was no charge. Once back, he showered and went to bed. Next morning he woke up sober, feeling battered and bruised. Connell was in an even worse state.

"You bastard!" he said to Steve. "You ran out on me. You fuckin' ran."

"Don't be daft," Steve said. "Look at my eye and these cuts." He showed him the cuts on his thighs, but couldn't convince him that he'd tried to help out. Because Steve had fled when the MPs arrived, Connell was absolutely certain he'd deserted him. They were never friends again.

Back in Kuala Lipis Steve found that the cuts on his legs were not healing properly. Showering in water pumped from the river obviously didn't help. In fact the cuts began to get worse. Steve reported sick, but the MO told him to bathe them in TCP or Dettol. This didn't do the slightest good. The cuts turned greenish. Steve began to worry about gangrene setting in. The lymph nodes in both groins began to swell up and ache. He went back to the MO. He still swore in the efficacy of disinfectants.

A few days later he took his festering cuts back to the MO and demanded a course of antibiotics. The MO said they were not necessary. Steve told him he didn't want to die of gangrene or lose a leg. Finally the MO gave him penicillin. After a couple of thousand units the wounds began to heal. In a week they were better. The only legacy was the scars.

One afternoon, in the medical room for a jab, Steve saw a ginger-headed soldier from the Hussars whom he knew. He was stretched out in bed in the small adjacent room, the door of which was wide open.

"Heh, Revill," he called. "Come over here."

Steve went across to his bed. "What's the matter? What're you doing here?"

"You've been in the STD ward a time or two, haven't you?"

"Well, yes."

"Bet you've never seen a prick like this before." Steve's mind boggled. He wondered whether the Hussar had acquired some strange and obscure disease. "Look at this," he said and fished his prick out of the flies in his sky-blue army-issue pajamas.

"My God!" Steve said. The penis was hugely swollen and inflamed to a vivid scarlet in colour. "What the hell did you do?"

"I was in this jeep, wearing my shorts. We were driving into town when I felt this tickling sensation in my groin. I gave it a scratch and there was this flash of pain like being electrocuted or something. I just tore off my shorts and there was this large centipede in my crotch. I flicked it off, stomped it to a pulp and yelled. My prick felt red hot, on fire."

"It stung your prick?"

"Yeh, two days ago. I was in bloody agony. They gave me some medicines to take and some painkillers, but I was running a temperature. The centipede must have been lurking in the jeep somewhere. It was one of those big orange things with segments the size of ha'pennies. I'll never wear shorts again while I'm here." He was laughing by now. "Always thought I'd like a bigger one, but by God, I just wish it was back to normal rather than swollen-up like this."

"How long are they keeping you in for?"

"They say I'll be fine in a few days. I'll be down town then – to see if it still works OK."

"Do you need anything – cigs or beer?"

"I'd love a beer."

That September an event occurred that shook the whole of 18th Infantry Brigade. Steve's arch-enemy, the bisexual Robbo, got drunk one night, absconding with an army vehicle, a jeep, and going for a joyride. No one knew what had happened until the morning. Evidently Robbo had driven off the road, hit the bank and overturned the jeep. He was found unconscious, but otherwise unhurt, having been thrown clear. He'd finished up, naked to the waist, in some swampy undergrowth.

A week later he was tried by Court Martial. It lasted three days and half the camp was summoned as witnesses. There was considerable speculation about the outcome as the evidence was conflicting and inconclusive. The only certainty was that he'd driven off in the vehicle without permission and crashed. During the trial he was seen to tremble and shake continuously. His teeth chattered so much he could scarcely answer the questions put to him. He claimed to be feeling cold, but the sceptics jeered. He claimed to be sick, but the young MO diagnosed his symptoms as those of shock. Many in the Brigade thought he was simply scared at the prospect of a stint in the military corrective establishment.

Here was the camp hardcase a victim himself at last and giving his enemies plenty to scoff about. In the end Robbo was found guilty on two counts. He was stripped of his lance-corporal's stripe and fined twenty-eight days' pay. His enemies said he'd been lucky, but now he was at large again the scoffers vented their scorn on the quiet. Something of the myth Robbo had himself created still lingered although he continued to shiver and reported sick several times.

A few days after the trial he passed out at work and was put in the sick-bay with a high temperature. At last the MO began to realise that there was something really wrong, but he still didn't know what. Two days later, his illness still undiagnosed, Robbo was rushed to hospital in Kinrara by helicopter.

Twenty-four hours later Geordie Hood received a message on his teleprinter. He came running over to the CO's office. On the way he showed the telex to Jock Robertson and Steve:

DRIVER ROBERT BRUCE DIED 0700 HOURS
SEPTEMBER 23
MALIGNANT TERTIARY MALARIA

They were stunned and so, when the news filtered through, was the whole Brigade. The scoffers realised that Robbo hadn't been bluffing; in fact he'd been dying. They realised that the MO and the hierarchy had made a serious and tragic blunder. The effect through the camp was electric. Robbo hadn't been popular, but he had been respected. Mutinous mutterings were heard in the NAAFI and the bashas. Soldiers talked about taking matters to the press for it was clear the Army intended a cover-up. Rumours abounded and the teleprinters divulged the classified information that came through.

What a tragedy, his enemies said, especially as he only had a few months left to serve in Malaya. Underneath the tough exterior he'd been a nice enough bloke, they claimed, and now he was dead in circumstances that pointed to medical negligence aided and abetted by the Court Martial and MO.

Some people still jeered, of course. He only had himself to blame, they said. He wasn't obliged to strut around minus a shirt, showing off his hunky physique. No doubt it was that night at the roadside, bitten by mosquitoes, which had done it for him. Well, no one was that tough, not with regard to malarial mosquitoes. It just showed you, they said, the Army knew best. Orders were that shirts should be worn after sundown, mosquito nets put up every night and paladrine tablets taken daily. Until Robbo's death nobody had bothered much about anti-malaria precautions. Now everyone was concerned. Discipline in such matters was immediately tightened up. Paladrine parades were held and officers made sure the tablets were taken.

Robbo was given a funeral with full military honours and everyone volunteered to attend as it might mean a weekend in Kuala Lumpur. In the end only three officers and ten selected Other Ranks went. They flew in helicopters and were back in the Brigade by the evening. Robbo was the only casualty 18th Infantry Brigade suffered during the year Steve was stationed there. He often wondered whether Robbo's parents were told the truth or whether he'd been officially listed as a casualty of the war.

Chapter 14

Having performed his duties as acting pay-sergeant satisfactorily, Steve put in for his fourteen-days leave. He had the choice of going to Penang or Singapore. He should have gone north, perhaps, and seen a new part of the country, but he was keen to revisit 3BOD, meet Rick Walker, even Julie in Katong. Besides, Changi Leave Centre was cheaper than the one in Georgetown.

It was early October and payday when he drew his leave money, three-hundred Malayan dollars in crisp ten-dollar bills. It seemed like a lot of money for a fortnight, the thick wad of notes in his trouser-pocket giving the illusion of wealth.

He had a couple of beers in the NAAFI, anticipating his return to old haunts and meeting old acquaintances. In the hot sunlight the beer seemed to sparkle with a gold lustre which added to his glow of pleasurable excitement. He knew, too, that once his leave was over he only had a month back in Kuala Lipis before embarking by ship back to Blighty and demob.

Early in the afternoon he drew a rifle and fifty rounds of ammunition from the armoury, then waited for the duty-driver to run him to the station. In the sunlight as they rattled along the tropical lane to town, he felt light-headed. At lunch-time Kuala Lipis was dusty, somnolent. Steve was sweating and the dust caked in the open pores of his face. As the train wasn't due for an hour he strolled through the market into the back of Tong Kok's and ordered a beer to wash the dust from his throat. It was cool and pleasant sitting in the stone-floored backroom of the bar. And not long after his arrival Aissa and Endal came in. They sat down at his table.

"Hello, Steve, you buy beer, OK?" He pealed off a note from his wad and the two women squealed delightedly, Aissa making a playful grab for the money. "Plenty money," she said. "Where you go?"

"To Singapore – on leave," he said.

"Take me, take me," she said. "You promise. Long time you promise." He had never promised to take Aissa to Singapore though he had promised to take Zenana who, a few weeks before, had returned to Kuantan.

"I can't do that. It's against army regulations."

"What time train?"

"It's in an hour."

"Come then. We have quick jig-jig now. Ten dollars." Steve declined the invitation, but bought them a couple more beers and bowls of rice. When he'd finished his beer, he left, slipping Aissa a five-dollar note as she saw him off at the back entrance. "*Terima kaseh*," she said smiling. "You good boy – *bagus*."

Twenty minutes later he was on the train, moving out of the station, over the suspension bridge above the confluence of the two rivers and into the viridescent countryside. He watched the scenery until late afternoon. Soon enough the sun began to go down over the jungle which was copper-tinted in the fading light.

At Kuala Krau two SAS men joined the train. They came over to where Steve was sitting and introduced themselves. They all played cards and got mellow on the beer as the train travelled south. Kuala Lipis lay a hundred miles behind them and they were moving inexorably towards Singapore. Though excited at the prospect of seeing the place again, he was glad he'd been posted up-country and earned the green-and-purple medal ribbon now sewn onto his tunic.

At Gemas they had to change trains and wait some hours for the connection from Kuala Lumpur. With the SAS men Steve strolled into town for some supper. At a pavement cafe in the tiny square they had curry. It was delicious, but the waiter, a Tamil, clearly disliked British soldiers, his lip curling contemptuously. He began speaking, not in Malay, but in his own language. They could understand the tone if not the words. Then he spat at their feet – a globule of betel-stained phlegm.

"Take it easy," the SAS soldiers said. "If we retaliate, they'll all be against us."

They left, running the gauntlet of disapproving and hostile looks. Such an incident would not have occurred in Kuala Lipis where the Malays were friendly, but to these Tamils it seemed as if the soldiers symbolised the colonial power. They had money, were armed and in their view had no right to the freedom of their wayside town.

The train to Singapore left Gemas in the early hours. As it continued through the darkness, Steve snatched some sleep, awakening as they drew into the station at Johore Bahru. There the SAS lads shook hands and got out. It was a grey misty dawn. Ahead, the water of the causeway looked pallid and motionless. To Steve's right was the pale green dome of the mosque. As the train passed over the narrow straits to the Island, with the recognition of once familiar landmarks, excitement was like a clenched fist in his belly.

They arrived at Keppel Station near the harbour half-an-hour later. Steve found a military jeep waiting. It drove slowly through the morning traffic to Tanglin. Once there he handed in his rifle and ammo, then was taken by another truck to Changi on the East Coast Road. They drove through the centre of the city, past the Dhoby Ghat and Rochore Canal, smelling insanitary as always. The drive brought back memories, but he knew these could be treacherous and he didn't like wallowing in the past. He intended getting to Changi and cauterising nostalgia in the neutral sun.

Changi village was near the sea and the Leave Centre almost on the beach itself. A flavour of World War II still lingered there for the area was strewn with old concrete pillboxes and outcrops of barbed wire, relics, he supposed, of defences erected both by the British and the Japanese.

During the first few days he stayed in the Leave Centre, reluctant to visit the city. The long serene hours blended into each other. They were lazy days, lying on the white sand or swimming to the raft inside the breakwater or occasionally paddling a canoe to the nearest green island. He began to acquire a deeper tan and feel really fit, taking long walks over the sand that felt hot and fluid to his bare feet. At night, drinking beer he'd watch the sun set over the sea, listen to the swish of leaves or someone playing sentimental tunes on a harmonica. With iced drinks on tables beneath a canopy of palms, it was idyllic enough at night, but gradually he began to feel restless. Although he wanted to visit Singapore he still procrastinated about it, fearing that things would have changed.

But on the sixth day he decided that he'd had enough of the sun-and-salt-water cure, he would visit 3BOD. A bus and a taxi took him there. He got off near Alexandra hospital and walked down the road to the camp. Passing the guard-room he saw scores of smartly-dressed soldiers marching here and there or wandering off to the two-storey barrack blocks he'd known so well.

He went upstairs and immediately recognised the old disorder, but saw no-one he knew. He asked one of the soldiers if he knew where Rick Walker was.

"Corporal Walker? Oh yes, he's been posted."

"Where? Do you know?"

"Somewhere on the Island. Pasir Panjang, I think it was."

Eventually he caught up with Rick Walker by taking a taxi to the small Royal Signals detachment in Pasir Panjang. Their old quarrel still between them but unspoken, it was a tense-enough meeting. Rick had fallen in love with a Eurasian dancer from the New World. They wanted to get married. Rick had even been to his CO to ask for permission, but now the Army had decided to post him away from Singapore. He was being transferred to Colombo, Ceylon. Steve was lucky to have found him. Another week and he'd have been gone. Rick told him that he'd considered deserting, getting married secretly and staying on as a civilian in Singapore, but deep down he knew he hadn't quite the bottle to do it.

That evening he took Steve to her home off the Racecourse Road. They had a meal and a few beers. She was attractive, but not the beauty Steve had been led to believe. When he left he wished them both all the best, but outside advised Rick to dismiss any idea he might have of deserting, and go to Ceylon. It would be a new place, another beginning. There would be other women for company – and solace.

"Yeh, I think you're right," he said. "But it's sad."

"Nothing lasts forever."

"She's beautiful, but we do fight a lot."

"Write to me from Colombo." He gave him his parents address in the UK. "I'll be home in a couple of months. Keep in touch."

With Rick standing on the street corner, Steve hailed a taxi, waved a final goodbye, got in and told the driver to go to Katong. Once out of the city it headed along the East Coast Road. Steve got it to stop outside the brothel where he'd originally met Julie. It looked unchanged; the same out-of-bounds signs still nailed to the palm trees at its entrance. And once inside the darkness of the kampong, he was surrounded by clamouring women, but there was no Julie among them and no-one he recognised.

"Hello Johnny," several of them were chanting. "You want short time?"

"I'm looking for someone."

"You want five-buck quick fuck?" another asked.

"Not tonight."

"Why not? I too old for you?"

"No, it's not that."

"Silly boy," she said. "I tell you something. You listen me. I say there plenty good tune played on old fiddle. You want to try?" She laughed. Steve was almost tempted to go with her on the strength of that remark.

"I'm looking for a woman called Julie. Do you know her?"

"Ah, you've got special friend?"

"Julie – do you know her?"

"I know her," one of the others said.

"Is she around tonight?"

"She not here anymore. She gone. Long time she gone."

"You mean that she never comes here anymore?"

"No, she gone. No more prost' for Julie. She got good job with English family. She look after kids."

"An amah?"

"Yes, she amah now, not here. So you stay with me."

"Tomorrow perhaps."

"Tomorrow no good."

He left the women, returned to the waiting taxi and went back to Changi. Watching the kampongs and palms rush by, a moon between trees, the night still humid and sticky, he sat back thinking about Julie and how, sometimes, there was indeed a good tune played on an old fiddle. So Julie was an amah now. It was what she had wanted. She would be good at that too.

The following day he got up late and found a spot on the beach near the breakwater. The sky was a whitish colour, the sea a grey-blue, the islands in the distance a hazy mauve in the heat. Every so often he'd swim out a hundred yards and back. The water was tepid, scarcely cooler than the humid air. He couldn't actually see the sun except for a white glare through the cloud, but it burned none-the-less. He'd seen soldiers just out from the UK get horrendous burns on days such as this, so he was careful.

He didn't know the names of the small islands in the distance, but knew there was a chain of them across the Straits, south-east towards the Java Sea. He thought about the War when the Japs had overrun the whole of the Far East, less than a decade ago, within the memories of most of the Island's population. Changi prison behind him, a gaunt fortress, was a kind of memorial to those who'd suffered and died at their hands.

That evening after a snack in the canteen he sat on the verandah listening to the rhythmic swish of the waves and a soldier singing songs about home to the accompaniment of a mouth-organ. Thoughts of England seemed incongruous to Steve. It was eighteen months since he'd left it, not a long stretch in reality, but it seemed so. He thought about his family and friends, especially those who wrote to him, but somehow his memories of back home seemed abstract. He wasn't in truth that anxious to return at all. He felt he could have quite happily remained in the Far East.

Anxieties about what he would do after he was demobbed and a vague nostalgia evoked by the harmonica made him nervously restless. He decided to get a taxi into the city. He enjoyed the drive along the coastal road, particularly in the evening. To his left was the sea, with the lights of ships – junks and cargo boats; to his right the endless lines of palms in silhouette.

The taxi passed through Geylang, across the Kallang River, and into the heart of the old city. They went through Chinatown, teeming with people and activity, to the New World. Around it was a labyrinth of streets – Jalan Besar, Bugis Street, Lavender Street and the

Racecourse Road; a melange of sights and smells. In upper-storeys of houses people were moving about their balconies, lamps were flickering; there were the smells of a thousand meals cooking and along the streets hundreds of women – Chinese in cheong-sams split to the thigh, Malays in sarongs, Indians in saris, older Chinese in blue smocks and black trousers.

In the New World itself, music blared from a myriad of stalls, dance platforms and beer stalls served by short-skirted Chinese girls. He wandered around, then finally sat down for a beer at a stall near the back entrance. It was a bar he'd frequented when he'd been at 3BOD over a year ago now. The first girl he'd gone with had worked there. He was thinking about that embarrassing incident when he saw a woman he remembered: Polly Wong. She had the sort of figure that attracted male eyes like iron-filings to a magnet: firm smallish breasts, a provocative bottom, the convex curve of a belly accentuated by her tight red cheong-sam and glossy black hair. He waited until she came to his table.

"Hello Polly," Steve said.

"Ha! You know my name. I not remember you."

"I used to come here about a year ago. I've been up-country since then."

"Many soldiers come here. I know many, but you not."

"Sit down and have a beer."

"Sure. And rice? I hungry."

Steve ordered two Tigers and a bowl of rice. "I used to know your friend. Dolly, she called herself."

"My sister, yes. She not here tonight. Heh, wait! I remember. You came with friend – tall boy on motorbike."

"That's right."

"He live with Eurasian woman – dancer from cabaret."

"Yes, I've met her."

"I remember you now. You like girls very much. We call you baby-face."

"Babyface?"

"It joke, OK. You look young – sixteen, seventeen."

"I'm twenty." She laughed.

"It good to look young. You not like now, but you like it when older."

"Perhaps," he said, somewhat disconcerted.

"Anyway, you want short-time?"

"Of course."

"I expensive. Fifteen dollars one hour."

"That's OK."

"You got money?"

"I'm on leave, I've got plenty."

"OK then, we go."

She went over and chatted for a moment with the older woman behind the small bar. Then she came, swinging her hips, back to the table. "Come, you follow behind me."

They left through the far exit and he followed her plump behind in the red silk along Bugis Street, then into a side alley. They came to a door already open. An old woman was crouched at the entrance. Polly spoke to her in Cantonese as she allowed them to pass, up a flight of stairs to the first floor. Polly's room was small with a strong odour of joss-sticks. Through the open window-shutters Steve could see the lights of the street and hear the high-pitched calls of vendors.

Polly slipped out of her dress. Underneath, she was wearing nothing but a pair of emerald-green silk knickers. She bent down and stepped out of them. Steve undressed quickly enough, throwing his shirt and trousers over the bamboo chair next to the mattress. Unlike the episode fourteen months before he had no anxieties and was soon aroused, caressing her pale brown thighs and buttocks. She felt for his prick and smiled.

"Good boy," she said, pleased that he'd responded so quickly. "You strong now. Come into me." Her fingers guided him. Once inside, warm and snug, he started to thrust, but slowly, savouring the voluptuousness of her body. She quickened her pelvic movements, rotating her hips. With his hands beneath the resilient mounds of her buttocks, he came quickly and loudly. "Good," she was murmuring. "Good, you come good. It good, no?"

"Very good."

He gave her fifteen dollars. They dressed and walked back together to the New World. He had another beer with Polly, then as it was gone midnight decided to find a hotel in Chinatown. He kissed Polly on the cheek and strolled out of the New World. The streets were still busy and there were many small hotels around. He chose one that appeared to be typically Chinese, all bamboo and rattan furniture in the foyer, a black iron-framed lift, unenclosed so you could watch people going up and down.

The unsmiling clerk, or perhaps owner, gave him a key to a room on the second floor. It cost him ten dollars. Upstairs, he found that it was a large room lit by a bedside lamp, with a mattress on the floor, a slow whirring fan, a rattan chair and a bedside locker. There was a wash-basin in the corner, a shower and a toilet – a hole in the floor, but clean. The Persian blind was down over the barred window. The room smelled faintly of cinnamon and joss-sticks.

He'd undressed and settled down on the mattress, smoking a last cigarette, the lamp still on when there was a knock at the door. Then it opened and a slender Chinese girl in her late twenties, dressed traditionally, came in. She didn't say anything, but smiled shyly and began to undress.

"I didn't ask for a girl," Steve said.

She answered him in Cantonese, clearly not understanding a word he'd said. Naked, she lay down beside him. She was slim and delicate with tiny breasts and a small smudge of black pubic hair. Suddenly it occurred to Steve that this was all part of the service. He was in a traditional hotel after all; one that automatically sent a girl up to the room of an unaccompanied male. He wondered whether there would be an additional charge the following morning.

After Polly earlier in the evening he didn't think he wanted a woman, certainly he didn't *need* one, but caressing her slim passive body, he got erect, slipped between her thighs and penetrated her. She was small, tight – at least at first – and lay there almost inert, expecting him to fuck her, but scarcely encouraging him. Somehow her passivity turned him on and hands on her small breasts he began to thrust. He tried to kiss her on the mouth, but she turned her face away. He watched her open slanted eyes, wondering what she was

Medal for Malaya

actually thinking. Taking longer than usual, he only came when she, sensing this, raised her knees and dug the heels of her small feet into his buttocks. It was the kind of response he needed. He came sharply, his hands under her shoulders. He was sweating, rivulets running down his chest while her body gleamed with sweat – his.

Afterwards he must have dropped off to sleep for when he awoke the light was streaming into the room through the slats of the blind. And the girl was gone. Suspiciously, he grabbed his trousers and felt for the roll of money wrapped up in a handkerchief in his front pocket. It was still there, safe and untouched. He showered, got dressed and went downstairs. The same Chinese clerk took the key and smiled as Steve checked out. There was no additional charge so he gave him a two-dollar tip. "For the girl," he said, hoping he'd pass it on.

Steve stayed at the Leave Centre for a couple of days, then on the Friday went to the other amusement park, the Happy World, in Geylang. There he was surprised to bump into Salmah, the small Malay girl he'd gone out with one Sunday before being posted up-country. More surprisingly she remembered him.

Ten months had changed her. It appeared that she'd been fairly successful on her own terms, but then she was young, no more than Steve's age. She seemed a little harder, more mercenary perhaps, but just as pretty and vivacious. Steve spent much of his remaining leave in her company and as he had money, she was happy enough to go along with that.

One evening they were at a bar called The Seventh Heaven. Salmah was talking rapidly in a mixture of English and Malay. Steve could only half-understand her. They were drinking liqueurs. She was on brandy-and-benedictine; he was on kummel.

"I very hungry," Salmah said at one point. "Buy me nasi goreng." Steve ordered a couple which they ate at the bar. There were some British civilians at the far end. Several of them tried to get off with Salmah. Steve knew they had every chance; they had more money than he did. It made his responses prickly. A slanging match developed with the most aggressive of them who seemed to regard Steve as a callow uncouth youth.

"I think you'd better leave this bar before we eject you," he said. "It isn't your sort of place and we don't tolerate loutish young soldiers here." Incensed by their snobbery, Steve was prepared to take the three of them on. And he said so.

"Just phone the MPs," another said. "They'll settle his hash."

At that point Steve decided to get the hell out. With a final parting shot – "Fuck off, bastards!" – he left, dragging Salmah by the hand. She was giggling as if it were all great fun. Outside the lights appeared to be dancing all over the city. Feeling a tremendous surge of confidence, Steve took Salmah – and Singapore – into his arms in one sweeping gesture. And Salmah hailed a trishaw.

"To the Cathay," she said.

Steve bought expensive seats in the cinema. The film was *Valley of the Kings*. After the humidity, the air-conditioning was a relief. The sweat evaporated, but Steve also realised he was drunk. He tried to concentrate on the flashing technicolour of the screen, horses galloping across the desert, clashing music, the kinetic poetry of battle and fancy dress. Looking around he noticed that there were a number of army families in the cinema and officers in mufti. Salmah was still giggling and people were turning round to stare. Steve was feeling dizzy – the world seemed to be turning upside down. He had to get to the gangway. Making his way there he tripped and disturbed some people. They mumbled in complaint. Back again he felt better. The screen had stabilised and he could focus upon it.

"She's a you-know-what," a woman behind them said. "Stands out a mile. It's a disgrace. Someone ought to fetch the manager."

"She's my Singapore wife," Steve said.

"Some of us would like to watch the film. Sit still and keep quiet."

Steve laughed out loud. A matronly European woman made a peculiar snorting noise. Around them people were moving, looking for vacant seats.

"They're all fucking snobs," Steve said loudly enough for some to hear.

"They should call the Military Police," he heard someone say. He was beginning to see the film clearly, the drunken feeling subsiding. Salmah's hand was in his trouser-pocket, then she unzipped his fly.

Medal for Malaya

The matronly lady heard something, turned round and saw Salmah touching him up. "I'm going to find the manager," she said. "To get the two of you removed."

A few moments later Steve caught sight of a civilian policeman at the end of the gangway. Someone was pointing in their direction. They stumbled to their feet, reached the aisle, then trotted towards the far exit, pushing past some people who tried to block their way. Suddenly they were outside, the air warm, heavy with the smells of the city. They caught a taxi back to Salmah's place.

Steve spent three days at her apartment, a modern one near the airport in Geylang. One evening, with music on her record-player blaring forth, a crate of beer that Steve had bought on the floor beside it, one of Salmah's old boyfriends, a lance-corporal in the REME called. His expression turned sulky and morose when he saw Steve.

"Have a beer," Steve said. "Help yourself."

"No thanks! What are you doing here anyway?"

"Salmah invited me," he said. "I'm on leave. I'll be gone in a few days."

"Where?"

"Up-country. 18th Infantry Brigade, Kuala Lipis."

"I love that girl," the soldier said. "I'm her boyfriend."

"You not my boyfriend," Salmah said. "This my room. You go now."

"Stay and have a drink if you like," Steve said.

"You're drunk already."

"Yes, I'm a hedonist."

"You don't give a fuck about her."

"Look," Steve said. "If Salmah wants you to stay, I'll go."

"You stay," Salmah said, pointing to Steve. She was sitting on the double-bed, half-drunk. Steve felt sorry for the lance-jack, if he was genuinely fond of her for it was clear that money was her first priority. Steve would only remain there as long as his cash didn't run out.

Suddenly Salmah pulled her dress up round her waist, displaying her slim brown thighs, boyish hips and the smudge of black pubic-hair. Semi-naked, there was something strangely vulnerable about her, perhaps because she was so slight, but Steve knew she could be

171

hard as nails. She began pointing at her cunt, playing with her clitoris. "Let's all jig-jig," she began to chant. "Let's jig-jig. Come and fuck me!"

"Go on," Steve said to the lance-jack. "That sounds like an invitation to stay, if not an order."

"You go away," Salmah said to the lance-jack. "Go away, you never have money." She stretched out, knees raised, legs apart. "Come on then," she said, teasing him. "Come and have a good look." The lance-corporal didn't move. He appeared to be on the verge of tears. "You want to look?" Salmah said, turning to Steve.

"Sure." He did just that, looking hard at the neat black inverted triangle of hair and rosy-brown labia. "Beautiful," he said.

"Stevey come," she said. "I want jig-jig now. Go away," she said to the REME soldier. "Less you want to watch."

"You drunken bastard," he said to Steve. "She's a fucking whore."

"That's right. That's her profession."

"Fuck, fuck, fuck," Salmah was chanting, her face contorted. It was too much for the Royal Engineer. He grabbed Steve's shoulders. Steve pulled away quickly just in time to duck his clumsy swing. He was looking as self-righteous as a born-again Christian.

"You disgust me," he said.

"This time you better fuck off, before I lose my patience."

"Don't worry, I'm going." He opened the door, left, slamming it behind him. Salmah was waiting on the bed, grinning. He joined her there and they made love quickly in the manner she liked.

The following afternoon Salmah decided to wash all her clothes. She piled them in the bath, a colourful collection of sarongs, tunics, dresses, bras and knickers. Steve helped her rinse them out, then wring them, splashing around in soap suds, the bathroom an inch deep in water; then they hung them out on the roof that overlooked the sea and airport. Once they were drying in the hot sun, Salmah went to the market in Geylang. Steve gave her ten dollars for food and beer.

Not long after she'd left, a plumpish Chinese girl from the flat below knocked on the door. She was complaining about water dripping down into her room through the ceiling. Steve went back into the bathroom and discovered that Salmah had left the tap running. Once again the bathroom was several inches deep in water. He started baling out, sweeping the water towards the drain on the adjacent roof. The Chinese girl, Ming, helped him dry the tiled-floor of the bathroom so when they'd finished cleaning up, Steve offered her a beer.

They were drinking beer when Salmah returned from the market. She looked surprised to see Ming there. Suddenly her surprise turned to anger. "You pimp!" she shouted at Steve, but flew at Ming. Both girls began to wrestle and scream abuse at each other. Steve wondered where Salmah had picked up the word "pimp" and whether she knew its actual meaning. Eventually he was able to calm things down, explaining the reason for Ming's presence there.

"You give her beer?"

"She helped me clear up the mess."

"You fuck her? You give her money?"

"Of course not."

As only one beer had been involved and no money, Salmah's professional face was evidently saved. The two girls separated on amicable terms as if nothing out of the ordinary had occurred.

Later that day Steve left Geylang as his money was running low, had a few beers in the city, then jumped on a bus to Changi. Once at the Leave Centre he went for a midnight swim and afterwards crashed out almost the moment his head hit the pillow.

Not long afterwards he was awoken to find his sheet on fire and one of the other soldiers trying to put it out. He couldn't recall smoking a last cigarette in bed, but assumed that he must have been. He was unhurt, but the sheet was ruined and Steve had to explain to the sergeant in charge of the Leave Centre what had happened. He warned Steve that he'd be charged for damaging army property and ordered him to remain in camp for the last two days of his leave.

Angered by what he regarded as an injustice, Steve borrowed five dollars, walked into Changi village, sold some personal items and borrowed a further ten dollars from his acquaintance, the silk merchant. With twenty in his pocket he returned to Salmah's apartment. He retained enough for bus-fares and cigarettes, then gave the rest to Salmah and stayed with her a final day. When he got back to the Leave Centre in the early afternoon he was put under arrest and escorted to GHQ Tanglin. An hour later he was interviewed by a major there.

"I realise you are on leave and for that reason I'm not charging you with being AWOL," the Major said. "I should just like to know where you spent the night."

"With my girlfriend," Steve said. "She's a Malay."

"Did you take any prophylactic measures before – or afterwards?"

"No Sir."

"None at all?"

"She's my girlfriend," Steve repeated. "We'd like to get married," he added on an impulse, thinking about Rick Walker's experience and Ben Hood's up in Kuala Lipis.

"You realise that she must be a professional woman?"

"At the moment she is, I suppose."

"Well, whatever your feelings for her, we simply couldn't allow any marriage to take place."

"Why not, Sir?"

"Because you're a twenty-year old National Serviceman about to be demobbed. We're under an obligation to ensure your safe return to the UK. Shotgun marriages to indigenous women are quite unacceptable."

"I see."

"We're acting for your own good though you might not think so now. So I'm afraid you leave me only one course of action. You'll be escorted to Singapore station tonight and put aboard the express to Kuala Lumpur and back to your unit. You'll only lose a day of your leave as punishment, if you like, but that's lenient under the circumstances."

"Thank you, Sir."

Steve was escorted back to the guard-room and later taken to Keppel Station and bundled onto the Golden Blowpipe. He wasn't to be charged; the Army merely wanted him safely back at 18th Infantry Brigade as soon as possible. His Regimental Police escort watched him depart. He had strict instructions to catch his connection at Gemas and they had, he was informed, already telephoned his unit to let them know he was on his way back.

Sitting in the compartment he watched the scenery as they crossed the Island, the city of Johore coming into view as the train rattled over the causeway. Not long after that darkness descended. He'd lost a day's leave, but that didn't worry him. He was just glad that he had avoided being charged.

Chapter 15

There was plenty for Steve and Jock Robinson to organise during the last couple of weeks in the Brigade. Their battledress uniforms, which had been in store, had to be retrieved and Steve took his down to the Chinese tailor in town. He narrowed the trousers and waisted the jacket in order to accentuate the shoulders. He also did something to the texture so that the nap was smoother and the colour faded. And he sewed on the green-and-purple medal ribbon.

Steve did a last convoy-patrol to Kuala Lumpur when he had to go for his final check-up at the hospital in Kinrara. They set out at dawn and, high-up in the armoured truck, behind his double-bren, he was well aware that it would be the last time he did this journey. Below them flowed the reddish-brown Lipis River as the convoy raced through the small villages towards the rice paddy and the mauve hills ahead. There was the usual stop at Raub for a bowl of curry, hot buttered-toast and black coffee, then the winding ascent through the jungle-rounded hills to the top of the pass; speeding on down through Kuala Kuba Bahru, passed the chunks of snake-infested limestone of Batu caves, into the outskirts of Kuala Lumpur to the Transit Camp.

He had a quiet drink that evening, then early Saturday morning took a truck through the city, out along the Kelang Road to Kinrara. At the hospital Steve was pronounced free from infection and knew that nothing could now delay his demobilisation.

That night he didn't seek out Rukhsana, Meena or Molly Chan. He hadn't got much money and didn't want to take any unnecessary risks. He visited the Lucky World and the Rainbow Cabaret, enjoyed the dancing and music, but returned to camp. On Sunday evening, just outside the Lucky World, he bumped into Molly Chan who was looking extremely attractive in a yellow cheong-sam.

"You want to come home with me?" she asked.

"Not tonight," he said. "I haven't got much money."

"Don't lie," she said. "Ten dollars, fifteen dollars, you must have some."

"Honestly. It's my last weekend here. In a couple of weeks I'm going back to England. I'll be out of the Army in a month or two. Next year I may be a student like you."

"Ha! You finish with Army. No more dirty work for imperialists then," she said smiling.

"That's right."

"OK Johnny," she said. "I make your last night in Kuala Lumpur a good memory to take home, yes? You come with me now. No money, a fuck on the house as you people say."

Surprised, for the proposition was uncharacteristic, so unexpected, Steve laughed. Impossible to turn such an offer down and, indeed, Molly did make the hour memorable, laughing and joking, a trace of mockery still, but a gift from the heart that amazed and touched him. It made him feel even more ambivalent about returning to Europe and the North. He liked Malaya. He liked its people.

Apart from Steve Revill and Jock Robertson, there were two other signalmen being demobilised: Lennox and Cameron, both Scottish. All four of them were interviewed by the CO before their departure. He was friendly in manner and even congratulated Steve on making a good job of being acting pay-sergeant, but the comment he wrote in his pay-book was more in character.

"Not suited to military life," was the laconic phrase he had written there; his terse way of describing Steve as a rotten soldier. Ironic, too, for Steve now felt eminently suited to military life. He'd seen combat at first hand, developed a more sanguine attitude towards the vicissitudes of army life, had lost some of his sensitivity and most of his intellectual pretensions. He'd never be quite the same again. The Army had marked him in a way for life, he supposed.

After their interview, kitbags packed, documents and pay finalised, farewells made, they were taken by jeep down to the station. As their train wasn't leaving until two o'clock, they had over an hour to wait so they went for a walk round the town, leaving the kitbags in the care

177

of an Indian porter. They strolled through the familiar Chinese market, had a last look at the Jelai meandering sluggishly round the town, the jungle on its far banks viridian in the sunlight, then wandered up to Tong Kok's.

It was cool inside after the sweaty heat of the streets. They ordered beers and sat drinking in the backroom. Two of the girls, Endal and Aissa, came over to their table. Steve bought them beer and rice. Afterwards they begged for cigarettes.

"A last jig-jig with Malay girl," Aissa suggested after Steve had told them they were on their way home. He was half-tempted, but the train was leaving in half-an-hour. At the tip of Malaya was the causeway, Singapore Island, the troopship, a month's cruise and Blighty. He gave both girls a kiss and they said they'd accompany the four soldiers to the station. The Chinese proprietor at Tong Kok's had witnessed such scenes a score of times and disapproved. He could understand the girls, ever-ready to make a few dollars – easy money, but some of them struck up friendships with these uncouth boy soldiers who in their jungle-green uniforms and navy-blue berets all looked much alike to him, and that he failed to understand. It was weakness and sentimentality.

At the station they bumped into Pierce, the off-duty cook. He was drunk and very miserable. He had another twelve months to serve in Kuala Lipis and he wanted out now. He was envious of their leaving. He swore vehemently at the town, at the girls and at the four soldiers.

"You lucky bastards!" he kept saying. He was almost in tears from frustration, his black hair falling over his sweaty forehead, his striped blue-and-white Catering Corps shirt grubby.

"Go and take Aissa to the houseboats," Steve said. "Screw the afternoon away. You're better off here. It's a good place."

"Fuck off, Revill!"

Their last view of Pierce, as the train drew away from the station, was of him taking a running kick at a stray duck pecking in the dust, the duck flapping away in a cloud of feathers, squawking madly. They crossed the suspension bridge over the confluence of the two rivers, Kuala Lipis behind them, and began rolling through the jungle to Mentakab.

Medal for Malaya

At eight o'clock that evening they were at ill-fated Gemas, half-way to Singapore. There they would have to wait until midnight for the train from Kuala Lumpur. With time to kill they wandered into the small town. Around the market-square there were stalls selling food. These were crowded with Malays and Indians from the rubber plantation. At one open-air cafe they ordered curry and beer. By the time they left sweat was glistening on their faces. Back on the southbound platform they still had a couple of hours to wait for their connection.

Lennox and Cameron got talking to a civilian, resplendent in white shirt, shorts, socks. He turned out to be Scottish, a rubber planter. At some point he thanked them profusely for protecting, albeit indirectly, his Malayan interests. As a token of his gratitude – and because three of them were Scottish too – he presented them with a bottle of brandy. For the next hour or so they took intermittent swigs from the bottle. To amuse the others, and out of some obscure belligerence, Steve slammed a round of ammo up the breach of his rifle and aimed at the station clock. The portly station-master, a Sikh, came running across to remonstrate. About the same time the troop-train from Kuala Lumpur drew in.

Smiling foolishly, drunkenly, Steve flicked back the bolt, ejecting the cartridge, picked it up and returned it to his bandolier, but the Sikh was already in conversation with a young officer who had stepped onto the platform. They grabbed their kitbags, heaved them onto their shoulders and hurried towards the train.

"You're drunk," the officer said, intercepting them. "Drunk while on duty – which is an offence. And messing about with rifles, that's serious."

"Piss off!" Steve said. "You can't order us around anymore, we're off to be demobbed. Screw the Army!"

"Come on, Steve, for fuck's sake," Jock Robertson said. "Get into the train or we'll be in trouble."

"On that train," the officer said. "That's an order, soldier."

Once aboard they found an empty compartment and settled down. Steve must have passed out almost immediately for he remembered nothing until waking up a few hours later with the train stationary in

Johore Bahru. Stirring groggily, hungover, he began to recall in a disjointed way incidents from the night before. "Oh Christ!" he muttered. "What a bloody idiot!"

There was an unpleasant odour in the compartment and Steve realised that he had thrown up on the floor. He got water from the toilet and did his best to swab it away. His head heavy, he returned to the lavatory, stripped to the waist and cleaned himself up. He shaved, brushed his teeth, rinsed his mouth and combed his hair. As he was engaged in these ablutions, the train began to cross the causeway to the low-lying shore of the Island. He began to feel better. Jock Lennox had some aspirin and Steve swallowed three tablets with a pint of water. The headache and the feeling of dehydration began to recede.

At eight-thirty all the soldiers from the train paraded on Singapore station to hand in rifles and ammo. While they were standing there a truck-load of MPs arrived and the young officer Steve had sworn at the previous night was soon engrossed in conversation with an officer in the MPs. He was pointing in their direction. Within minutes half-a-dozen MPs approached.

"These are the four," the young officer said.

"Attention!" an MP sergeant barked. "One pace forward, quick march. Halt! You're under close arrest, the four of you."

With their kitbags slung across their shoulders, they were marched between the MPs to the truck. Guarded by four of them, their red-peaked caps vaguely sinister, they were driven out of the station into the garish light of the city, through the familiar streets already packed with people, to Fort Canning, the Military Police HQ. Steve thought they'd be charged with disobeying an order, or conduct to the prejudice of good order and military discipline. He had no idea what their punishment would be, but didn't suppose for a moment that it would put their departure in jeopardy.

The four of them were put into separate cells and it was an hour before Steve's was unlocked and he was escorted along a corridor, up a flight of stairs and into an office. Waiting there was a colonel in the Military Police.

"Well, Signalman," he said after the opening formalities. "What have you got to say for yourself?"

"You mean about last night, at Gemas, Sir?"

"You tell me."

"We'd been celebrating, Sir. This planter we met gave us a bottle of brandy. In gratitude, he said. We got a bit drunk, Sir. I was very drunk and I'd just like to apologise if I was disrespectful to that officer on the platform. I didn't mean anything by it, Sir. It's just that I was drunk."

"That's not my concern," the Colonel said. "I'm not a scrap interested in whether you were drunk or not – half the troops on that train had been celebrating." He hesitated and Steve waited, puzzled, for him to continue. After a pause, the Colonel said: "I just want you to make a clean breast of the whole thing. In other words, come clean and confess."

"I don't know what you mean, Sir. I've explained what happened."

"You know very well what I mean."

"I'm sorry, Sir, but I don't know what you're on about."

"Come on, come on, soldier, don't play games with me, you'll only make matters worse for yourself."

"I'm not playing games," Steve said. "Anyway, confess to what? That's what I don't understand."

The questioning continued for ten minutes. At one point the Colonel offered him a cigarette, then snatched it away and began shouting. Steve figured that he must have picked up this trick from some B-movie. He hadn't the slightest idea what he wanted him to confess to, if not to being drunk, to insulting an officer or inserting a round of ammo into the breach of his rifle and aiming it at the station clock.

"All right, Signalman," he said. "I can see you have no intention of telling the truth. In fact you've been damned evasive. A civilian, Malayan, was beaten up last night at a station somewhere between Gemas and Johore. He's in hospital now, seriously injured, on the critical list as a matter of fact. And we know that you were responsible. If you admit it, we'll be able to manage a cover-up, an explanation for the civil authorities – whom, I might add, are after blood – get you on that ship and off the Island, but you must co-operate with us and tell the truth."

"I didn't beat anyone up," Steve said, in a panic now. "I was paralytic, I tell you. I remember nothing from the time I flaked out on the train until we arrived in Johore."

"If you remember nothing," he said. "You might well have done it then."

"I remember nothing because I was asleep. I'd have remembered something like that. I slept the whole way. I'd had far too much to drink."

"How do you account for the fact that a seat was missing from your compartment?"

"A seat?"

"One of those long wooden seats. There's little doubt that it was used to beat up the civilian. It was found on the line."

"I know nothing about that, Sir. I didn't know that there was a seat missing at all."

At that moment an MP sergeant came in. He whispered something to the Colonel, then stood aside. The Colonel's expression assumed a new gravity.

"Well, soldier, you're really in big trouble now," he said. "It seems that your victim has since died from his injuries. Unless you tell us what happened we shall have no alternative but to hand you over to the civil authorities. You'll find yourself on a manslaughter charge."

"But I didn't do it. I know nothing about it. I swear I don't."

"Manslaughter or murder," the Colonel said. "You can take your pick. And unless you confess to me you'll be tried in a civilian court before a civilian judge. You'll be found guilty for sure. They'll put you in Changi jail and you'll never get off the Island."

"But I didn't do it," he said. "I'm innocent." Hysteria was creeping into his tone of voice. He was almost shouting. On the verge of tears. Christ, they were going to miss the ship! His father would have to fly out for the trial. He'd be stuck in Singapore. In prison. Jesus, where was the justice? It seemed impossible that such a thing could happen to him, but it *was* happening. "Sir, I didn't do it," he muttered. "You must believe me – please."

"All we want is your signed statement, then you can leave it to us. We'll get you on that troopship and you'll be away. You'll just get a

Medal for Malaya

couple of weeks of jankers, or detention which you'll serve on board. That's all. You'll be on your way to Blighty at least. A free man."

It was a trick. If he admitted doing it he'd be whisked straight into the cells. Two weeks of jankers for manslaughter? That was absurd, risible. He was far from convinced of the Colonel's paternalism or the Army's benevolence. They must think him stupid to confess to something he hadn't done.

"I didn't do it, I'm telling you. I'd have known if I had and I know I didn't."

"All right, if that's the way you want to play it," he said. "Take him back, Sergeant. I'll see him again after lunch. You've got an hour to think about it, soldier, then – by God – I intend to extract the truth from you."

It felt to Steve like a bad dream from which he'd awake and there would be sweet relief. He knew nothing about any beating-up. He liked the Malays. Surely he could convince them of that. He had no racial prejudices. None whatsoever. Besides, he'd been incapable of punching his way out of a paper-bag at the time. Stupidly, ridiculously drunk on beer and brandy. Out like a light. For one weak moment he thought of telling them he was so drunk it was just possible he could have done it and had no memory of the fact. But could he have got out of the train at night and beaten some poor bastard senseless at some jungle outpost? No, never. It was ludicrous.

At lunch-time, oddly enough when they considered it, the four were reunited and taken under guard to the canteen. In whispers, although the MPs who were guarding them didn't seem a scrap interested in what they were saying, they compared notes. Jock Robertson thought it all had something to do with the young officer at Gemas. He believed that they'd concocted the whole incident in order to instil some respect into them. If so they'd succeeded profoundly. The others rejected the theory. Someone had died, that was for sure. The Army had seized upon them as scapegoats. They'd been conspicuous because they'd caught the train separately at Gemas.

"You know I didn't do it, don't you?" Steve asked.

"Of course you didn't. You were too fucking pissed," Cameron said. "They tried to get me to implicate you though."

The reassurance their reunion had given Steve was immediately replaced by an element of fear. So far these mates of his had held out; they'd corroborated his story – because it was the truth. But in the afternoon, as sailing time approached, one of them might weaken, might crack. All it needed was for one to admit just the faintest possibility that Steve could have done it. And that would be that. He felt that he could trust Robertson, he knew him, but he didn't know the other two. They'd be under increasing pressure. They might be tempted. One small lie and they could be away to the docks, the troopship.

After lunch each of them was returned to their separate cells, then briefly interviewed again. Though still apprehensive, Steve's resolve had strengthened. Not long afterwards the four of them were taken together to the Colonel's office. He offered them a last opportunity to confess. They each repeated their original stories.

"We're going to release you," the Colonel said finally, "and get you on that troopship." There were small quick smiles from the four of them. An almost audible sigh. "However, don't for a moment think I like it. I don't much like what you've done and I don't care much for any of you ...."

"We did nothing, Sir," Jock Robertson said testily.

"Though I've got to admit to a grudging admiration for your loyalty," he continued, ignoring the interruption. "I've just got to say, finally, that you're four of the most consummate liars it has ever been my misfortune to encounter."

"Don't call me a liar," Robertson said, almost shouting, his slight stutter gone. "I'm from Glasgow and I've never lied in my life. I'm not lying now and I think you should apologise for the accusation – Sir."

"Leave it, Robby, leave it," Lennox said. "For God's sake." Steve thought they'd surely be detained once more, but the Colonel remained calm, even seemed slightly amused.

"I'm not arguing with you, soldier," he said. "You'll be driven under escort to the docks and put aboard. The ship sails in half-an-hour or so. You can just thank your lucky stars that the civilian authorities haven't got hold of you. And I only hope your sense of fair play will give your consciences a hard time over the next few years.

You'll have plenty of time to think about things on board. Plenty of time for remorse."

"I've got nothing on my conscience," Robertson said, refusing to let things go. "Nothing to feel guilty about – absolutely nothing. And I'm not a liar."

"You're dismissed, soldier," the Colonel said abruptly. "And that's an end to the matter."

Ten minutes later, Jock Robertson still protesting about the slander, the rest of them silent, they were speeding through the streets towards Keppel harbour. As they clambered out of the truck, Steve blinked in the sunlight and saw in front of him the bulk of the troopship, very white against the turquoise of the water. It was, as the Colonel had said, on the point of departure, its rails lined with troops leaning over and casually watching the four latecomers.

A rope-ladder was thrown over the side. Their kitbags were hurled up on deck and they clambered up after them. The soldiers aboard cheered ironically. Minutes later the ship was steaming between emerald islands towards the Malacca Straits. The four of them stood for a long time in the stern watching first the docks, then Singapore itself recede below the horizon.

Their arrest, they discovered later, had been the main talking point on board all day, especially among those troops who'd been on the train. Naturally they tried to find out more about the incident. Someone, they gathered, had been attacked, but under what circumstances and how seriously they never found out. Someone told them that a group of MPs had actually been responsible, but the Gemas four were the obvious scapegoats.

The four of them were placed on fatigues from the start of the voyage. They assumed that this was a result of their arrest. Their daily work was to clean the troop-deck where they lived, including the ablution area. It took about two hours each morning. The corporal in charge was a fussy, officious individual. One morning, somewhere in the Indian Ocean, he started criticising their work. His manner was infuriating. Momentarily Steve lost his temper and grabbed him by the lapels.

"Listen." he said. "We're doing the job well enough – and we're doing it our way. Leave us to it and stop interfering."

The effect was immediate. The corporal fled. They turned round to each other and laughed at his ignominious departure, realising that he, and probably a number of the soldiers in the ship, thought they'd committed some violent and criminal act. They had a reputation. They were dangerous hardcases, not to be crossed. After the incident the corporal left them alone. He didn't even report them for the assault. And once they arrived in Colombo they were taken off fatigues.

They went ashore at Colombo, taking a rickshaw, visiting a Buddhist temple and having a hot vegetable curry in a bamboo and thatch restaurant. It didn't seem eighteen months to Steve since he'd last been there. Little had changed. The same bumboats were selling silk cloth, ivory elephants, pineapples and coconuts. Rusty scavenger birds scoured the wharfs and the dockside. The red British-built centre with its tall green palm-trees looked vaguely incongruous. The sun was extremely hot; the sea in the harbour a yellowish-green.

They were only docked for a few hours and once aboard again began the second leg across the Arabian Sea to Aden. It took a week; a week in which, not only the incident at the MP headquarters, but Singapore itself seemed to recede into the past.

Aden in early December was much cooler than it had been in June, but it was still drab, ash-grey, colourless in contrast to the places they'd left. After another four hours ashore, bartering with Yemeni Arabs, buying trinkets, they were back on board, heading towards the Red Sea and Suez Canal.

At Port Said more British troops from their draft came aboard, delighted to be on their way back to Blighty. Steve met a couple of friends from Catterick, but gradually the thought of returning home began to fill him with apprehension. Leaving Port Said, they were ordered to put on their English uniforms, for the weather was cool and getting colder, with harsh winds out of Africa whipping across the water. They steamed non-stop through the Mediterranean, passing Gibraltar, then northwards along the Portuguese coast. As they crossed the Bay of Biscay, the sea rough and the sky overcast, the weather turned wintry.

It was a week before Christmas when the troopship approached the low-lying Dorset coastline and headed for Southampton waters. It was a typically-English December day. The sea was blackish-grey and turbulent, low cloud hung ominously over the coast and there was a light drizzle in the south-westerly breeze.

Most of the troops were on deck watching the approach of the English coast. Most seemed to be in a triumphant mood. They knew that they would be back home for Christmas, probably demobbed before their draft date, January 2nd. Steve, however, suddenly felt a stab of nostalgia for Malaya. The English scenery seemed drab, even a shabby grey after the tropics. The closer the ship approached the more his sense of anti-climax increased. He suddenly felt that he would never settle happily back in Birmingham. And would be homesick for the exotic places he'd experienced over the last eighteen months.

They docked alongside a black wharf partly roofed-over with corrugated-iron. On the jetty there was an army band. It began to play a medley of military marches and familiar tunes. And in one corner was a gaggle of civilians. A few minutes later an announcement blared out over the tannoy system and the names of soldiers who had been granted permission to disembark in order to meet relatives was read out. To his embarrassment Steve's name was amongst them.

They felt like a privileged minority, but were jeered by the other troops as they descended. Approaching the civilians, Steve spotted his mother, father and brother, Jonathan. Their faces looked anxious and pallid. He went over to them nervously, shook hands with the father and kissed his mother. He put his arm round Jonathan's shoulders. It was acutely embarrassing in front of the troopship with soldiers shouting down and cheering ironically.

They exchanged the formalities of greeting in an oddly-formal manner. Steve found their accents, particularly Jonathan's, forced and posh. Eighteen months ago he himself must have sounded the same way. No wonder he'd got some stick in the barrack-room.

"Good God!" his father said. "Your accent's changed. You sound vaguely Scottish, or something."

"There were a lot of Scottish blokes at 18th Infantry Brigade," Steve said. "Anyway, you sound posh to me."

"Oh Steve," his mother said. "You *have* changed. You don't look the same boy."

"I don't suppose I am the same boy," Steve replied. "I've been on active service, in a combat zone, I've got a medal to prove it."

"You're very suntanned," his mother said. "But you don't look like my Steve at all." She appeared to be on the verge of tears.

"Well, I am. I'm pretty much the same, I think."

"When are you actually getting demobbed?" his father asked.

"Probably for Christmas. We're going first to that transit camp near Newton Abbot."

He asked Jonathan about some of their mutual friends and what he himself was doing at the moment. Jon said he was on his last year at school. The following October he was going to University College, London, to study medicine. His father boasted about their car, his first, an Austin A40. His mother was proud that they were now on the telephone and had bought a television.

They didn't have long together before the troops ashore were shepherded back on board. Once his family had left, Steve felt a little better. The quayside meeting had been unexpected and surreal. In most ways he felt more comfortable with these soldiers who'd been his companions for the last two years. And he had a further presentiment that adjusting to home, to civilian life and to Birmingham would not be easy. His father had intimated, even in the brief time they'd been together, that he had ambitions for Steve now that he'd got National Service out of the way. University, a career in commerce or industry, he'd suggested. Certainly not something as precarious as a writer which was Steve's own ambition. Actually he hadn't really considered the future for ages – for two years in fact. He had a further perception that, yes, he had changed. And not for the better, not in his parents' eyes. He wasn't even sure he could handle university, let alone a career in commerce, or whatever. His mind was rusty. Emotionally he felt numb.

A couple of hours later, in an organised manner, they scrambled down the gang-plank and were herded through Customs. The Royal Signals contingent was soon on a train speeding through the west country towards Devon. They spent five days at Newton Abbot, handing in kit, getting medical examinations, finalising their pay, being, as it were de-briefed.

They were informed that they were to be demobbed in time for Christmas. Steve telephoned his parents to let them know. He was beginning to get excited about returning to Birmingham and civvy street, but simultaneously regarded home itself with some trepidation. He guessed he would find it difficult trying to fit into his parents' routine and wondered whether his presence would be unsettling, increasing the tension in the house. He would have liked a few months without employment so that he could write his stories and poems about Malaya, but knew his father would never countenance that. Employment and work were almost sacred in his father's view. Still it *was* Christmas. He would be able to have long conversations over a beer or two with Jonathan. He'd be able to renew acquaintance with some of his old friends and the girls he'd known. Perhaps when Jonathan went to London in the October, he would accompany him and they could share a flat together. Moreover, in April, he would be twenty-one and free to do whatever he chose.

OTHER BOOKS FROM SHOESTRING PRESS

MORRIS PAPERS: Poems Arnold Rattenbury. Includes 5 colour illustrations of Morris's wallpaper designs. "The intellectual quality is apparent in his quirky wit and the skilful craftsmanship with which, for example, he uses rhyme, always its master, never its servant." *Poetry Nation Review.*   ISBN 1 899549 03 X   £4.95

INSIDE OUTSIDE: NEW AND SELECTED POEMS Barry Cole. "A fine poet ... the real thing." *Stand.*   ISBN 1 899549 11 0   £6.95

COLLECTED POEMS Ian Fletcher. With Introduction by Peter Porter. Fletcher's work is that of "a virtuoso", as Porter remarks, a poet in love with "the voluptuousness of language" who is also a master technician.   ISBN 1 899549 22 6   £8.95

STONELAND HARVEST: NEW AND SELECTED POEMS Dimitris Tsaloumas. This generous selection brings together poems from all periods of Tsaloumas's life and makes available for the first time to a UK readership the work of this major Greek-Australian poet. ISBN 1 8995549 35 8   £8.00

ODES Andreas Kalvos. Translated into English by George Dandoulakis. The first English version of the work of a poet who is in some respects the equal of his contemporary, Greece's national poet, Solomos.   ISBN 1 899549 21 8   £9.95

LANDSCAPES FROM THE ORIGIN AND THE WANDERING OF YK Lydia Stephanou. Translated into English by Philip Ramp. This famous book-length poem by one of Greece's leading poets was first published in Greece in 1965. A second edition appeared in 1990.   ISBN 1 899549 20 X   £8.95

POEMS Manolis Anagnostakis. Translated into English by Philip Ramp. A wide-ranging selection from a poet who is generally regarded as one of Greece's most important living poets and who in 1985 won the Greek State Prize for Poetry.
ISBN 1 899549 19 6   £8.95

SELECTED POEMS Tassos Denegris. Translated into English by Philip Ramp. A generous selection of the work of a Greek poet with an international reputation. Denegris's poetry has been translated into most major European languages and he has read across the world. ISBN 1 899549 45 9   £6.95

THE FIRST DEATH Dimitris Lyacos. Translated into English by Shorsha Sullivan. With six masks by Friedrich Unegg. Praised by the Italian critic Bruno Rosada for "the casting of emotion into an analytical structure and its distillation into a means of communication", Lyacos's work has already made a significant impact across Europe, where it has been performed in a number of major cities.   ISBN 1 899549 42 0   £6.95

A COLD SPELL Angela Leighton. "Outstanding among the excellent", Anne Stevenson, *Other Poetry.*   ISBN 1 899549 40 4   £6.95

BEYOND THE BITTER WIND: Poems 1982–2000, Christopher Southgate.
ISBN 1 899549 47 1   £8.00

SEVERN BRIDGE: NEW & SELECTED POEMS, Barbara Hardy.
ISBN 1 899549 54 4   £7.50

WISING UP, DRESSING DOWN: POEMS, Edward Mackinnon.
ISBN 1 899549 66 8   £6.95

CRAEFT: POEMS FROM THE ANGLO-SAXON Translated and with Introduction and notes by Graham Holderness. Poetry Book Society Recommendation.
ISBN 1 899549 67 6   £7.50

TOUCHING DOWN IN UTOPIA: POEMS, Hubert Moore
ISBN 1 899549 68 4   £6.95

WAITING FOR THE INVASION: POEMS, Derrick Buttress
ISBN 1 899549 69 2   £6.95

HALF WAY TO MADRID: POEMS, Nadine Brummer
ISBN 1 899549 70 6   £7.50

GIFTS OF EGYPT: POEMS, Michael Standen   ISBN 1 899549 71 4   £7.95

THE ISLANDERS: POEMS, Andrew Sant   ISBN 1 899549 72 2   £7.50

COLLECTED POEMS, Spyros L. Vrettos
ISBN 1 899549 46 3   £8.00

FIRST DOG Nikos Kavvadias. Translated into English by Simon Darragh
ISBN 1 899549 73 0   £7.95

TESTIMONIES: NEW AND SELECTED POEMS Philip Callow. With Introduction by Stanley Middleton. A generous selection which brings together work from all periods of the career of this acclaimed novelist, poet and biographer.   ISBN 1 899549 44 7   £8.95

PASSAGE FROM HOME: A MEMOIR Philip Callow. Angela Carter described Callow's writing as possessing "a clean lift as if the words had not been used before, never without its own nervous energy."   ISBN 1 899549 65 X   £6.95

Shoestring Press also publish Philip Callow's novel, BLACK RAINBOW.
ISBN 1 899549 33 1   £6.99

For full catalogue write to:
Shoestring Press
19 Devonshire Avenue
Beeston, Nottingham, NG9 1BS UK
or visit us on www.shoestringpress.co.uk